A BLOOD RED DIARY

A Jameson & Argenti Thriller, Book 3

JOHN MATTHEWS

The Write Direction Publishing

Published in the U.K. in 2020 by The Write Direction Publishing, St. Albans, U.K.

Print edition — A Blood Red Diary
ISBN: 978-1-78875-022-6

WELCOME TO THE JAMESON & ARGENTI SERIES

Thank you for purchasing ***A Blood Red Diary*** — I hope you enjoy it.

This is the third in a series of thrillers featuring pathologist **Finley Jameson**, one of the first in a new breed of forensic examiners, and **Joseph Argenti**, a tough-nosed detective, who are leading criminal investigators in New York City during the 1890s.

The series currently comprises the following books:

1. ***Murder in Manhattan***
2. ***Diary of the Dead***
3. ***A Blood Red Diary***

If you enjoy this book, I would like to keep in touch. This is not always easy, as there are many authors and books out there. The best way is for you to be on our Readers Group email list. We can then send you updates on the next book, plus occasional special offers.

Details of how to join the Readers Group and receive a FREE ebook thriller can be found at the end of this book.

John Matthews

CHAPTER ONE

New York. May, 1895.

Michael Tierney side-stepped the punch aimed at him and cut in with his own right-hander, catching his opponent hard on one cheek. A return punch came quickly to his forehead, but it lacked strength, glanced off one side.

'Come on, yer can do better than that!' Tierney taunted, smiling. But he could see the uncertainty in his sparring partner's eyes: the worry that if he hurt the lauded and feared Michael Tierney, the city's leading mobster, he might not turn up for the next sparring session. His legs and arms broken, or perhaps 'retired off' like many of his gang rivals: weighted down with cement blocks at the bottom of the East River or chopped up and fed to Tierney's hogs at his upstate farm.

'Okay. Sorry,' Tierney's sparring partner said, as if it had been a momentary distraction rather than fear holding him back. He moved in with a more solid body punch and a keen jab to Tierney's face.

'That's more like it,' Tierney gloated, answering with a couple of sharp jabs of his own. He liked to get a good workout in these sessions, and he'd had to get rid of his last sparring partner because he'd been too tentative and pussy-footed. Tierney had beaten him half to a pulp in one of their last sessions, but still nothing fiery had come in return.

Two yards to one side of the ring was a large ornate window with a view over half of Manhattan, and the other side a fully-equipped gym. But Tierney found he'd quickly get bored in the gym, so the sparring sessions had become his main regular workout. Beyond was his four-bedroom penthouse. He'd taken up the whole of the top floor of his recently finished twenty-two storey building on Fulton Street, the tallest in Manhattan; the floors below had all been sold or leased for office space.

By his corner-post was a nineteen-year-old girl with flowing red-hair in a white sheer camisole top and emerald-green satin shorts to match her eyes. Iona, the most perfect example of Irish beauty he could find to remind him of the old country, he'd plucked her from one of his clubs early on, before she was too sullied from getting groped and humped by older men. She'd towel him off when he was finished, soap-lather him and wash him down in the shower, followed often by an oil massage and some lovemaking if the mood took him.

The door to one side opened and his right-hand man, Liam Monahan, stepped in.

'What is it?' Tierney asked; a sharp tone, only a half-glance towards Monahan as the sparring continued. Tierney had made it clear that he didn't like his boxing sessions interrupted.

Monahan simply nodded, as if in acknowledgement that he wouldn't have interrupted unless it was important. 'I thought you'd want to know straightaway: Teddy Roosevelt has just been named the new Police Commissioner. He's holding a full press conference tomorrow.'

'I see.' A heavy jab and a quick feint, the return blow glancing off one cheek. 'An' why should this news particularly concern me?'

'Because part of Roosevelt's announced stance is to combat police corruption. Word has it he wants to clean up Mulberry Street.'

That information hit Tierney stronger, made him more hesitant for a second, a return blow catching him heavily in the face — his sparring partner equally hesitant that he might have overstepped the mark; a faint glimmer of fear showed in his eyes.

'He does now, does he?' Tierney smiled it off, recovered quickly, taking advantage of his sparring partner's hesitancy by landing a heavy return blow square to his face that made him stagger back a few feet. 'I think we might both find that's jus' political soap-boxing to advance his career. The proof of the pudding might be somethin' else.'

'Let's hope so.'

'In any case, I'm a respectable businessman now. Tha's all behind me.' Tierney leered as he took a step back from sparring and swept one gloved-hand out at the penthouse and the city view. Then with a perfunctory nod, he leaned back in and returned to trading jabs, as if to make clear their conversation was finished. But Monahan stayed there, his expression still heavy with concern. Tierney glanced at him sharply. 'Somethin' else?'

'Yes, there was.' Monahan paused for a second, as if waiting for the best time between jabs to deliver the news. 'It appears our old friend Maccione has returned to the City. Just a week or ten days ago.'

Tierney's face clouded and he took a step back, holding one glove up. A clear indication the sparring session was over. He went to the corner and Iona moved in to towel the sweat off his body, but he just grabbed the towel off her brusquely and started towelling himself. 'Why wasn't I told straightaway?'

'We just picked up on it now. Looks like he was lying low at first, keeping out of sight.'

'And we all know why that is, don' we?' After Maccione's suspected bombing of his Pearl Street brewery, Maccione had hi-tailed it to Atlantic City to stay with local casino empire builder Abe Weimann. Tierney had issued a warning through a go-between that while Maccione remained in Atlantic City, he might be inclined to leave him be, but if he turned up again in Manhattan, his days would be numbered.

Although that hadn't been entirely true. A month ago, thinking that enough time had passed that Maccione might have dropped his guard and become more complacent, he'd hired a gunman in Atlantic City, Erik Gevorgyan, a recent Armenian immigrant — so no ties or allegiances to either Irish or Italian gangs — to get rid of Maccione. No answer yet from Gevorgyan. So either he'd failed or was waiting on the best time to take out Maccione.

Monahan grimaced. 'But looks like we were right about someone here meanwhile taking care of Maccione's import business and protection of Italian shops on the east-side. Because he was seen meeting up with them at Brugnera's Pizzeria just the other day.'

'And who might that have been?'

'Ed Corcoran.'

Tierney nodded thoughtfully. Corcoran had taken over the operations of George Sheehan, his main past adversary. Corcoran had also laid low, kept out of his hair so far, but with his meeting now with Maccione, that looked about to change.

* * *

'And what advantages do you think Mr Roosevelt will bring to the New York police department?'

'Whatever advantages and virtues of Mr Roosevelt I could offer would only go so far,' Mayor Watkins answered the New York Post reporter in the front row. He gestured to one side. 'I think Mr Roosevelt could best answer that himself.'

'Indeed. Thank you, Mayor Watkins.' Roosevelt cleared his throat and briefly surveyed the crowd of almost two hundred in the hall: newspaper reporters and photographers taking up the first few rows, Tammany and City Hall officials the next two, and half of the Mulberry Street police force filling the rows behind. As much of the hierarchy and high-ranking detectives and lieutenants that could be spared without the station ceasing to function. At the back of the hall, a few Broadway showgirls had sneaked in. Thirty-seven years old, Roosevelt was stocky and vibrant with sharp blue eyes, and they were keen to catch a glimpse of this handsome fast-rising politician. 'I would hope first of all to bring more clarity and positive function to the current operations. Clearer guidelines and chains of command.'

A New York Times reporter raised his pencil. 'Are you talking about the graft and corruption mentioned when your appointment was announced yesterday?'

Strained smile from Roosevelt. 'Those were terms used by a fellow reporter of yours. It might be that some officers are simply unaware of how they should be acting. What might be considered *incorrect* behaviour. That's why I mentioned more clarity and clearer guidelines. So that those same officers are left in no doubt whatsoever how they should be acting under *my* command.'

Five rows back, Finley Jameson leaned in towards Argenti. 'You can tell he's a politician.'

'What? In not answering a question directly.'

'No. I meant in answering questions subtly, diplomatically. Not simply using the same brash terms posed to him by the reporter.'

Joseph Argenti nodded. Five years now he'd been working with Finley Jameson, he could have guessed that he'd favour Roosevelt's mode of speech. Not just his obvious erudition, but ensuring the conversation was handled on his own terms. Within seconds, Roosevelt was in command of the direction of the conversation, rather than the reporter.

That difference in speech, manner and background — Jameson had been from a highbrow English family, one of the leading forensic experts in the Jack the Ripper case, whereas Argenti was a rough-edged, street-worn Italian cop from Hell's Kitchen — had put a barrier between them at first. But over the years they'd warmed to each other's differences and eccentricities, and a solid working bond had been forged. In fact, those differences had probably helped their partnership: they would each look at crimes from different angles, and where the expertise of one left off, the other would fill the gap and take over.

'Are you admitting though that things haven't been going right at Mulberry Street?' the NY Times reporter pressed, eager for a strong quote for tomorrow's headlines.

'That could be deduced simply from my presence here before you all now.' Roosevelt smiled. 'But, again, that would be more your choice of words than mine. I would prefer to simply say that there is decided room for improvement rather than things having specifically gone wrong.'

There was silence for a moment, the row of reporters pondering where to head next. A New York herald reporter was first to lift his hand.

'And do you think responsibility for that 'lack of improvement' might rest with past Commissioner Latham? That whether *corruption* or not, part of that would lie at his door?'

This time Theodore Roosevelt's smile was wryer, as if in appreciation of that more considered question. He'd have to be more cautious. 'I'm sure as head of the New York Police department, Commissioner Latham did his level best. But as he's not here today to defend or counter that comment one way or the other, it would probably be remiss of me to offer any comment on the subject.'

A gentle murmur rose around the hall, some in approval of Roosevelt's diplomatic handling, others no doubt thinking that his avoidance of direct condemnation of Latham had been a mis-step. Jameson commented to Argenti, 'Do you think Latham has already taken up his position with the Philadelphia police force?'

'He's actually joined Pinkerton's. Assistant head of the agency for the entire eastern seaboard.' What Argenti didn't want to add with people close each side was that with the whiff of corruption in the air, Latham would have found it difficult to join another police force.

'So you're saying there might have been corruption,' the Herald reporter rode the point, 'But you don't wish to comment on it too openly. At least where Commissioner Latham's responsibility is involved.'

Roosevelt took a fresh breath. Obviously, this hot potato was proving more difficult to lay to rest than he'd first envisioned. 'Put it this way. I'm sure there was much going on under Commissioner Latham's watch of which, in retrospect, he would not be that proud. In addition, much going on of which he was simply unaware. I'm sure there was also much happening of which he was justly proud.' Roosevelt's gaze searched the audience, picking out Argenti and a few others. 'Officers who, in turn, I'd feel immensely proud to be working with.'

Only a moment that Roosevelt's eyes had rested on him, as if to say, '*I'm depending on you,*' but Argenti had immediately felt uncomfortable. Obviously, Mayor Watkins had gone through a list of officers at Mulberry street who he felt could be relied upon and would stand behind Roosevelt's anti-corruption fight.

It was a stance he'd wholeheartedly upheld himself, until two years ago when he'd crossed a certain line with Enzio Maccione, a rising Italian east-side mobster. But it was a line crossed that nobody else knew about, not Mayor Watson, not his partner Jameson, not even his own wife, Sophia. It had just been between himself and his own conscience.

And for the past two years while Maccione had been away in Atlantic City, he'd hoped it would stay that way, his secret safe. But then just the other week he'd heard that Maccione was back in Manhattan, and a note had been received through Carlo Brugnera requesting a meeting.

Roosevelt finished on a rousing note. 'And if you are one of those officers whose actions I would be proud of, then you have my full support. But if you are partaking in actions of which I would not approve, then your days are numbered. Because rest assured, whatever might have gone unseen or unnoticed under Commissioner Latham's watch, I have no intention of that being the case on *my* watch.'

As Roosevelt said *my*, he tapped his own chest and a few powder flashes went off from the front rows, the main photos to accompany tomorrow's front-page story. Even from a few rows back, Argenti felt the heat of those flashes hit his cheeks. Although maybe it was as much a rising anxiety flush with Roosevelt's final words. He was sure Roosevelt's eyes had moved fleetingly his way again as he'd said *proud of*, as much as he fancied he'd seen that gaze shift to Bill Griffin and a couple of others on *not approve of*.

But how much longer might he remain in Roosevelt's favour before his secret came out?

CHAPTER TWO

Glenda Lorton walked on the northern part of Mercer Street, where it started to become more respectable: less flophouses and tramps huddled in doorways, more women in fine dress like herself. Although every now and then she'd still pass a tramp who'd reach a palm out for money, eyes imploring. Some of them had learned that there were richer pickings on this northern stretch of Mercer Street.

She'd shake her head in apology, 'No', as she passed them, a slight wince as she did so, as if she felt sorry for their plight but couldn't help them. She had her own problems, especially right now.

She looked determined in where she was heading, but any tramp's eyes that had lingered on her as she'd approached would have noticed that her gait was stilted, awkward, as if she was in pain from her movement, and that she in fact winced every few yards with that pain.

Only nineteen, Glenda looked a few years older than her age; a fully-fledged and bold woman with long auburn tresses and warm brown eyes, rather than just a girl. She would have been considered strikingly beautiful, but the regular wincing detracted from that, and the left side of her jaw seemed strangely frozen and slack, as if it couldn't fully join in with the rest of her facial expressions.

As she reached Spring Street, she took the slip of paper from her burgundy embroidered jacket and checked the address written there. Then she continued with her stilted gait, wincing with the pain that each step seemed to bring.

* * *

'Oh, my goodness... my goodness!' Ellie Cullen hissed in her breath as she studied the extent of the bruises on Glenda Lorton's body. Only three on her breasts, but almost a dozen on her mid-section and stomach, a few on her back, and two even on her thighs. 'And who did this to you?'

'Kenny Harvey, manager at the Mirabelle Club.'

Ellie nodded knowingly. One of Michael Tierney's clubs, she'd heard word that the new manager there, Kenny Harvey, was rough with the girls. But none as bad as this — at least that she'd heard about or had come to her notice; Glenda had practically fallen through the doors of the Beth Jacobs refuge, and she'd heard the alarmed voices by reception from where she was on the main floor even before Glenda had asked for her by name, '*I'd like to see Ellie Cullen.*'

Ellie shook her head. 'This is something you should go to the police about, press charges. Men like Kenny Harvey have got to be put a stop to.'

'No... *no*. I wouldn't want to do that. Would just make matters worse for me.' She looked around tentatively. 'Just if perhaps I could stay here for a while, where he couldn't find me.'

'You're not safe at home?'

'No. That's where he found me and did this to me.' She gestured down her body, her expression forlorn, pitiful. 'I didn't show up at the club last night because I had a cold, so he came by my place on Mercer Street this morning and beat up on me.'

'And are you sure about not going to the police about this. What if Harvey beats up another girl from the Mirabelle in the same way?'

'I know.' Glenda cast her eyes down in shame and penance. 'But I don' want no more trouble. Just want to lie low for a while, out of sight.'

Ellie grimaced in understanding. Four years now she'd been helping run the Beth Jacobs refuge, a haven for abused women, waifs and strays and past street and club girls like herself. She'd spent enough time living in fear of or hiding away from Tierney and his henchmen that she understood more than most. But it was her duty to ask, otherwise Tierney's reign of terror and abuse of these girls — whether directly or through his army of 'dues-collectors', pimps and club managers — would continue unfettered. Ellie took a fresh breath.

'So, you're seeking official sanctuary at the Beth Jacobs?'

'Yes, if... if that were at all possible.'

'I'm sure that can be arranged.' Ellie's smile was tinged with concern. 'But first thing, we gotta get these injuries seen to. Now I can bathe and salve them, but you'll need to see a doctor in case there are internal injuries.'

Glenda's face clouded. 'But won't he feel duty-bound to inform the police? I'll just be putting myself in hot water again with Harvey and Tierney.'

Ellie was touched by Glenda's fear, almost afraid of her own shadow. She herself had been little different a few years ago. 'Don't worry, a good friend of mine, Finley Jameson, is a skilled physician. He can be trusted to be discreet.'

* * *

'Does it hurt when I press here?' Jameson enquired as he probed Glenda Horton's lower rib cage.

'Yes. That's quite sharp.'

'And here?'

'Tha's not so bad. Still hurts plenty, though.'

Jameson grimaced. 'Much of that will be from the surface bruising. But, as I mentioned to you, what we're seeking to detect here is any sharper pain from your ribs beneath. To see if they've sustained any injury.'

Glenda nodded numbly. 'That one's not so bad beneath. Only sharp above.'

'Now I'm going to the other side,' Jameson said, looking up briefly as his assistant Lawrence walked in with two enamel bowls full of water with white flannels floating in each. Steam rose from the bowl in his right hand. 'We'll commence treatment on your bruises as soon as I've finished examining your ribs. The hot water's too hot now in any case, would scald you.'

Ellie looked on with concern. She'd found a white towelling robe for Glenda to wear. Underneath, she was just wearing lace bloomers, her breasts and stomach bare, and Ellie now held the robe in strategic positions to preserve Glenda's modesty as Finley probed and examined.

Jameson looked up after a moment. 'Now I'll have to examine the upper ribs, which could be more awkward. I'll do the left side first.'

Ellie nodded and slid the robe to one side to expose Glenda's left breast.

'I'll have to manipulate your breast to one side and press quite hard, I'm afraid,' Jameson said. Glenda squealed with the first pressure, so he asked, 'Is the pain just on the surface or deeper beneath?'

'Some deeper down as well.'

'And this upper side of the same rib?'

'Not so bad.'

Jameson tested the remaining ribs. 'And now the right side.'

As Ellie slid Glenda's robe the other side to expose her right breast, Jameson noticed a faint wry smile rise above Ellie's consternation. Despite almost five years now of their association and how close they'd become, he was seeing more now of this girl's body than he'd ever seen of Ellie's. Or perhaps Ellie thinking to herself that girls like Glenda showed their naked bodies to a dozen strangers a day without giving it a second thought, so now performing this attempt to cover Glenda's modesty struck her as amusing; or maybe it was just his own and Lawrence's obvious discomfort at examining a half-naked woman that Ellie found amusing.

After all, their main experience came in at point of autopsy. So the many naked women they'd seen would already be dead and on a slab; not live, vibrant and breathing.

Jameson turned to Lawrence as he finished examining. 'It appears there's a fracture on rib seven on the left-hand side, two inches from the sternal divide.' Lawrence had flipped open a pad and started making notes. Jameson paused a second for him to catch up. 'Another suspected fracture on rib four on the right side, but this time only hairline.'

Lawrence looked up sharply. 'And its position?'

Jameson smiled primly. Whenever he himself was remiss on any detail, he could trust Lawrence — a veritable memory-man from his savant-autism — to pick him up on it. 'About three inches in from the sternal divide.'

Glenda's expression was quizzical. 'What will that mean to me in practical terms?'

'It means you'll have to be heavily bandaged and strapped for a while. A tight corset might also help' He took a fresh breath. 'But I don't think even the more serious fracture on your left-side is heavy enough for the bone to separate or knit back out of line. So the long-term prognosis is fair to good.'

'So, I'm going to be okay?'

Jameson's countenance became sterner. 'If that might be an appropriate term for being beaten within an inch of your life, yes.' He sighed. 'The first thing will be treatment to reduce the bruising, then calamine lotion applied before the bandage strapping.'

As Lawrence bathed the bruises with hot and cold water, Glenda wincing at intervals, Jameson looked on forlornly, the full horror of the girl's injuries hitting him stronger from a few paces away. 'I trust you've shared with Ellie who did this to you?'

'Yes, I have. But I don' want no trouble mind.'

Ellie, still performing her peekaboo robe routine as Lawrence worked, smiled primly with a small '*I'll* explain' sideways nod, and when Lawrence had finally finished—Glenda meanwhile shown to a bed and brought a cup of coffee by one of the Beth Jacobs helpers, Meghan —Jameson got that explanation in Ellie's adjoining office.

'It was Kenny Harvey, the manager at the Mirabelle Club where Glenda worked.' Ellie said as she sat behind her desk with a strained breath. Met with Jameson's nonplussed expression — he didn't know the name — she elaborated. 'He's one of Tierney's club managers. Got a reputation of being handy with his fists with the girls.'

Jameson nodded. 'And I'm assuming, from what Glenda said about 'not wanting trouble' that the police have not been notified.'

'No. She's too nervous and frightened to do that.'

'Even though men like this Kenny Harvey must be put a stop to.'

'Tried that already. Even pushed that other girls might be harmed if she didn't speak up. But she wouldn't budge.' With

Jameson's downcast expression, his head shaking lightly, she added. 'You can see how anxious she is. Afraid of her own shadow.'

'Yes, I can.' Jameson eased a heavy breath. 'And with good reason from the looks of her. But it just seems wrong that this Harvey fellow should get away with such a beating without being brought to account in some way.'

'I know.' Ellie held a hand out helplessly. 'But what do we do?'

That sense of helplessness sat heavy on Jameson's shoulders too. Over three years now Ellie had been fighting against that tide of gang and pimp-controlled street and club girls, but sometimes it seemed their hands were tied by a wall of silence. The same wall that Jameson often faced in pursuing investigations with Joseph Argenti. People and witnesses would be reluctant to speak openly, especially where gang leaders were concerned. So the girls would turn up at the Beth Jacobs, or often with their throats cut in a ditch or alleyway if they fell out of grace with their pimps or managers — but the gang leaders remained untouched. Protected by that wall of silence.

'There is one thing I could try,' Jameson said, gripping the silver head of his cane. He'd held it at his side as he'd sat across from Ellie's desk, but now his firmer grip mirrored his tougher resolve. 'I could have a word with Joseph, see if we could arrange a raid on the Mirabelle, ruffle this fellow Harvey's feathers.'

A shadow of concern fell across Ellie's face. 'But surely that will simply trace back to Glenda? Will make matters worse for her.'

'Don't worry, I'll get Joseph to delay a couple of days so that it's not connected to Glenda, Perhaps claim that the raid stems from a complaint from some customers.' Jameson wrapped the head of his cane with his knuckles. 'Seems wrong to just leave things be. Something's needed to fire a broadside across Kenny Harvey's bows, shake him up a bit.'

* * *

Michael Tierney enjoyed his Pearl Street brewery the most when it was full pelt, and it was coming up to that time of day now: 9-9.30 a.m.

At 8 a.m. sharp, the yard horses would be brushed down and fed and the wagons loaded with barrels. His yard manager, Simon, would check all the consignments were fully loaded and correct, and by 9-9.10 a.m., the first wagons would head out of the yard, bound for various destinations in Manhattan, upstate New York, New Jersey and Boston.

The crack of the horse whips, the clatter of the wheels on cobbles and the whirlwind of dust and straw kicked up from the yard, Tierney found the most exhilarating time of the day; a sense that the weeks and months of brewing were finally reaching their climax, on their way to customers who would savour and appreciate those efforts.

The brewery was probably also the most honest of all his endeavours, though in part also served as a cover for many of his other activities. If anyone ever asked how he earned his money, he'd simply hold a hand out, 'Why, look at my fine brewery. One of the best purveyors of stouts and malt ales in Manhattan.'

So the brewery held a special place in Tierney's heart. He was particularly proud of the fact that they only lost five weeks production after the bomb attack on it. A quick flash image hit him as he looked back at the building from the yard... *hearing the clicking of the timer by the Mash-Tun, then running and throwing the strapped dynamite sticks through the barrel loading hatch as far into the courtyard away from the building as possible*, landing not far from where he stood now.

The explosion had caved in half of the exterior wall, though thankfully by then he'd run far enough away inside to be only on the edge of the deluge of falling bricks and cement dust; otherwise, the explosion would have taken his life, along with a number of other workers. His only long-term residual injury had been his hearing affected on his left-hand side, and sometimes he'd have to lean into people and ask them to repeat, '*What was that yer just said?*' An affliction he often played up when a comment was made he took exception to.

He had little doubt it had been Maccione planting the dynamite, though he had no firm proof. But as the Italians themselves said, '*Revenge is a dish best served cold*', which is why he'd waited almost two years before sending a trigger-man to kill Maccione.

As the last wagon trundled out of the yard, Tierney walked back towards the brewery, taking a half-flight of steps up towards its mezzanine level, leaning for a moment on the railing which afforded a view of the brewery floor below. One advantage he'd made of Maccione's bombing: rather than have the front re-built as before with two separate floors, he'd had the front pulled out four yards with a gallery looking onto an open area below, and added two more Mash-Tuns to one side; the builders had still been working on the new additions when the brewery was in full operation again.

From where Tierney stood now, he could view most of the brewery floor, and a large window behind let in more light than before.

'How's it going, Tilly?' he called out, spotting his brewery manager below.

Approaching sixty, Tilly tipped his cloth cap from his ring of grey hair. 'And a good morning to you too, Mr Tierney. Going fine, I'd say. Reckon the next month's batch is gonna be even better than last month's, and that was award winning.'

Tierney smiled. They'd finally won a blue-ribbon award for one of their stouts, and much of that was no doubt down to Tilly, fresh over from the Guinness factory floor in Dublin just over a year ago. 'Good on yer, Tilly. Hopefully, the first of many such awards to follow.'

Tierney found he always slipped into a stronger Irish brogue with Tilly, maybe to make him feel more at home. But then he'd speak in more polished, reverent tones when talking with Tammany Hall politicians or architects for his new Fulton Street monolith. Perhaps he was splitting into two or more people, or just trying to be a man for all seasons? Anything to bury his rough Pittsburgh mining background. He even found himself favouring high- collared shirts and jackets for those City Hall and planning meetings to hide the canary tattoo on his neck.

'Post's arrived,' Monahan announced as he walked into the general office at the end of the mezzanine. Monahan gestured to his desk. 'Eight or nine personally marked for you, the rest just general mail.'

Tierney nodded. Practically the same routine every morning. Monahan would collect the mail, would give Tierney any mail personally addressed, then sort through the rest, checking any suspect packages as he went before slotting into wooden pigeon holes on the back wall for various shop-floor managers or their accountant. Or passing to Tierney if they were personal or required his attention.

Monahan was halfway through pigeon-holing, so was a moment slow in picking up on Tierney's consternation as he came to a small package among his personal mail. 'Do you want me to see to that, check it out?'

A small brown cardboard box, five inches by two, Tierney tentatively lifted it up, shook it by his right ear, smiling after a second. 'No, it's okay. Too small to be a stick of dynamite, let alone room for a timer.'

Tierney started opening the box, the last trace of his hesitant smile sinking as he fully viewed what was inside: a human finger, cut off at the hand-knuckle joint.

Monahan came over quickly as he caught Tierney expression, stood by his shoulder looking down at the open box. '*Jeezus*. And who might that belong to?'

Tierney's eyes were drawn to the ring on the finger: a gold swirl spreading out from a central diamond, with a cross on each side of the ring band. A quick flashback to when he'd last seen the ring, though perhaps he wouldn't have noticed it if Gevorgyan hadn't kept fingering it anxiously as he'd given him the final instructions about Maccione.

'What is that symbol on the ring, by the way?' Tierney had asked.

'It's an Armenian eternity shield with a Khachkar Cross. It's for protection.'

There was a small card below the finger, and Tierney picked it up, wondering if it might be a personal note. But it was just a card for an Atlantic City seafood restaurant with the sketch of a fish prominent on its front.

'It belongs to Erik Gevorgyan, the trigger-man I hired to get rid of Maccione,' Tierney muttered to Monahan, a crooked leer rising: so much for the ring's *protection*. The message was also clear: not only was Gevorgyan now with the fishes, Maccione knew he'd sent Gevorgyan to kill him. The gloves were off.

CHAPTER THREE

Joseph Argenti walked into the saloon bar and restaurant of Brown's Hotel just off The Bowery. It was the same Saloon room where he'd met Michael Tierney two years ago, when he suspected Tierney was putting pressure on his wife and Anton Faggiani's provisions store.

Along one side was a row of curtained booths where the girls ambling through the Saloon would give male customers nude table dances for only fifty cents. But it was perfect also for private meetings. Argenti noticed in his side vision Enzio Maccione at a far table, but didn't look at him directly. Maccione nodded towards the fourth curtained booth along and moved towards it. Argenti held up a hand in acknowledgement in his general direction, approached the bar and ordered a lime and soda, then a moment later took it across the room and entered the same curtained booth.

'Good to see you, Joseph.' Maccione stood and embraced him heartily, patting him on the back. 'It's been a while.'

Argenti smiled softly, as if that sentiment was reciprocated, if not so enthusiastically. As he took a seat, he noticed that Maccione had a glass of red wine on the small table between them. 'It certainly has. What kept you away for so long?'

Maccione shrugged. 'Some business with Abe Weimann in Atlantic City with his casinos. But I also thought it a good idea if I kept clear of Manhattan for a while.' Maccione gestured across the table. 'For perhaps *both* our benefits.'

Argenti nodded. *Never a truer word*; but probably not in the way Maccione intended. 'So why the return now?'

'Believe me, I would have stayed away longer, business was going well with Abe in Atlantic City.' Maccione looked down, shadows crossing his face for a second before he looked up again. 'But I suddenly realized I wasn't safe there either from Tierney. He sent a trigger-man to Atlantic City to kill me.'

'When was this?'

'Just two weeks ago.'

Argenti nodded slowly. 'Seems a long time for him to wait to strike back at you.'

'I think he was waiting for the best time and opportunity.' Maccione sipped at his wine, held a hand out. 'Hoping that with the time elapsed, my guard would be down.'

'But obviously it wasn't.' Argenti grimaced. 'He wasn't successful.'

'Obviously.'

Argenti's brow furrowed. 'And how could you be sure he was sent by Tierney?'

'I could answer that it was a matter of simple deduction — who else would send such a man to kill me?' As Maccione lowered his proffered palm, he looked across the table levelly. 'But in this case, the man told me himself.'

Argenti met Maccione's level stare for a moment before glancing away, a faint shudder running through him. He doubted that the information was offered readily. *What methods of coercion or torture might Maccione have employed?* He didn't want to know, which then also made redundant the other question on his lips: what happened to this trigger man? The less he knew, the better. He couldn't later claim any innocence in their relationship if incriminating information was shared which he didn't in turn share at Mulberry Street.

'I shouldn't be here,' he said, waving one arm; a discarding gesture. 'I've only come today out of respect of our past association. But it was mainly to say that we shouldn't meet any more.' He eased a strained breath. 'Especially now with Roosevelt taking over at Mulberry Street.'

'Ah, the anti-corruption saviour.' Maccione raised his glass. 'You should get on well. A police Commissioner singing from the same song sheet for once.'

'All the more reason, if Roosevelt is looking to me and other officers for support, not to let him down. Fall from his favour.' Argenti exhaled softly. 'I have to be careful now more than ever.'

'Yes, I understand that, Joseph. But I have never come to you with anything that might equal corruption.' Maccione gestured. 'In fact, quite the opposite. That information I brought to you about Tierney manipulating incoming goods through bribery at some customs warehouses would definitely be considered an anti-corruption move.'

'Indeed.' Argenti looked across coldly. 'And look how that ended. A good friend of mine Paolo's life lost standing up to Tierney's gang, his young widow and three kids left to fend for themselves.' *His step heavy as he took the three flights of stairs to tell Pia Calvi that her husband was dead. He could feel the weight on his shoulders again now.* Argenti prodded his own chest. 'And all because I intervened on your behalf.'

Maccione closed his eyes in supplication for a moment. 'If that information came to you another way, it might have ended the same way, Joseph. So it's wrong for you to blame me or, more importantly, *yourself* for how that ended. It was

Tierney who took that action, nobody else. Also, harsh but just retribution was taken against your friend's killer.'

'I hardly need reminding.' Now it was Argenti's turn to close his eyes momentarily. *Tommy Falway found with a stiletto wound piercing his heart.*

Maccione looked at him searchingly as he took another sip of wine, shaking his head as he put the glass back down. 'What are you saying now, Joseph? That any information about corrupt dealings of Tierney's, you're going to shy away from because of the risks involved? Surely that's the opposite of what Roosevelt will be calling for.'

'Of course that's not what I'm saying,' Argenti blustered; but then he had to pause for a second and consider what he did actually want. 'I just have to be careful, that's all.'

'I could have guessed that alone from this cloak and dagger meeting now in a curtained booth.' Maccione smiled primly. 'But I both understand and share with you that same caution, Joseph. After all, in my profession, a man seeing a policeman regularly would usually be seen as an informer, not to be trusted. So I have to be careful with our meetings too.'

Argenti nodded sagely. 'Is that what you're suggesting as a possible cover for our meetings, should they come to light? That I say you're an informer.'

Maccione shrugged. 'Certainly, one way of handling it, among others. After all, I will indeed be giving you information about Tierney's corrupt dealings, if and when they come to light.'

'I don't know.' Argenti sank deeper into thought, sipping at his lime and soda. He'd come here with the firm intent of telling Maccione they shouldn't continue their meetings, and already he could feel his resolve slipping. Perhaps sensing his uncertainty, Maccione leaned forward.

'You and I both know Tierney of old. He's become bolder in trying to have me killed, and Ed Corcoran says that he's started to lean more on local shopkeepers on the East side. In no time, Tierney might feel bold enough to start pressing again against Faggiani and your wife Sophia's provision store — especially given the bad blood between you. And perhaps the best way to stem that would be to put pressure on Tierney in other areas — with focusing on his corruption probably the most ideal way right now, especially with Roosevelt's arrival.'

Argenti nodded again. Maccione argued a strong case. Maccione was the antithesis of Tierney: urbane, charming, always immaculately dressed in cream or light tan suits and sporting a royal blue cravat — whereas Tierney was a rough and brutal street thug with few redeeming graces. But he knew that in the final clinches Maccione was an equally brutal killer — *the image of Maccione in that dark alley sliding a stiletto up Tom Brogan's jaw and into his brain still brought a shiver to his spine*; and, as before, he was hit with the uncomfortable feeling that in trying to rid the City of Tierney, he'd simply be aiding the rise of another monster; one of a different ilk, but a monster all the same.

'I need a few days to think about this,' Argenti said at length.

'That's fine. Take longer, if need be.' Maccione eased a pained smile. 'After all, having waited two years for any final push against Tierney, a few more days won't matter.'

CHAPTER FOUR

Lucy Bowen had a fascination with clocks. She'd stand and admire the workings of a clock for long periods at a time; the more elaborate, the longer she'd stand admiring it.

This particular clock on Kenmere Street, she'd observed probably more than any other; not just because it was quite elaborate, but because it was suspended above the shopfront only five feet above her head and she regularly passed this clock-smith on her way from the Beth Jacobs centre just around the corner.

She'd be on her way to a local bakers, milliners or grocers and would find herself distracted once again by the clock, staring up at it in wonder. She checked her pocket-watch to see if her timing had been right, whether her own watch was fast or slow.

'Only twenty or thirty seconds now, I reckon,' she muttered to herself.

She drew her breath in anticipation as a loud clicking came from the clock, followed by a sharp bang; a chime and then another bang. Lucy watched in fascination as the model blacksmith below the clock face rotated another notch before bringing his hammer down on the iron rail beneath. Seven p.m. She knew that as it hit the seventh chime and bang, the blacksmith would be facing the front again.

She'd been particularly fascinated with how the blacksmith turning could be adjusted for every hour, so on her third observance of the clock, she'd gone into the shop and asked.

'It makes a ratchet-turn adjustment for every hour,' the shop owner informed her.

'How ingenious. What gave you such an idea?'

'It's in fact based on a clock not far from where I used to live in England. A little village called Abinger Hammer. That clock had a static blacksmith who always faced the front, but we wanted to make it more interesting by having it turn. So we took inspiration from some of the clocks in our showroom — mainly from Austria and Switzerland.'

She'd spent an hours inside perusing all manner of clocks, from Tall-Case, Grandfather, Vienna, Cuckoo, Pendulum, Symphonian to more elaborate Rococo, Lenzkirch and Eisenlohr designs.

She'd been back inside the showroom a few times, but had stopped at the point that it had become obvious to the shop owner and floor managers that she wasn't actually going to buy a clock. She might not have a hundred-percent social graces and awareness, bust she was savvy enough to know when she was pushing her luck, outstaying her welcome.

Since then, she'd sought out more clocksmiths and showrooms further afield on Broadway and as far west as 34th Street; but being just around the corner from the Beth Jacobs, this was the only clock-smith's she'd pass regularly.

She'd often therefore time it, so that she was passing just as it was approaching the hour, so that she could watch the clock's mechanism in action.

And if she caught the eye of the shop owner or managers

looking at her outside as she observed, she'd lean in close to the window and give a smile and a small wave — but wouldn't go inside.

As the last blacksmith's strike came on seven, she noticed a flicker of movement the other side of the window and a light on at the back; they must be working late doing stock-taking. And as she caught sight of one of the managers looking her way, she did the same now — traded a small wave and smile with him.

If it had been half-an-hour later and the light inside had been off, the stock-keeping finished, Lucy might have noticed in the window's reflection the man across the street looking her way.

* * *

At just below average height at five-foot-five, the man was a study in grey: mid-grey suit, derby hat a shade darker and matching cape — nothing that would make him stand out among the throng of men in similar dress in this part of lower Manhattan.

A grey evening too, he thought, inhaling the faint mist that had risen after an earlier rain and the first shades of dusk began to settle.

As an extra precaution against anyone noticing him, he'd pulled his Derby hat down sharply, and would appear as if he was waiting on someone, looking from side to side along the street rather than at the girl by the clock-smith's.

To support that image of impatience, he wrapped a rolled-up copy of the *New York Times* against one thigh. Though the rolled-up newspaper served a dual purpose; concealed inside was a razor-sharp six-inch blade. No clumsy delays in drawing the blade from inside his jacket. His victims would merely think they were being prodded with a rolled-up newspaper before feeling the blade plunging through from beneath.

The girl was on the move again from in front of the clock-smith's. He'd wait a moment more, wrapping his newspaper impatiently and looking each way, then with a final glance at his own pocket-watch would discreetly follow.

* * *

'How's Glenda settling in?' Ellie asked Meghan as they ambled through the main hall at the Beth Jacobs.

Used in the daytime for general recreation and activity, girls as young as fourteen to women over sixty were at different tables sewing, reading, playing dominoes or cards — though strictly no gambling. Now at 7.40 p.m., trestle tables had been put end-to-end in preparation for supper being served at 8 p.m.

'She's fine. Settling in well, I think.'

'The bruising's gone down?'

'Mostly, yes. Some marks still visible with the heavier bruising. But the main things is, she's able to move easier now.'

Ellie smiled towards Glenda at the far end of the room, a last game of dominoes with two other girls in their late teens before the table was laid for dining — an easy smile returning, as if in support of Meghan's prognosis.

In five or ten minutes, all the girls would have to step lively to help with the table-laying for dinner. The Beth Jacobs was run on a communal basis, and in the process women would learn general domestic chores of cooking, cleaning, baking, sewing and generally fending for themselves. Lunch-time and dinner were therefore main events in the day, not only when everyone was together, but also a culmination of the day's work and activities. The fruits of their labour.

'But with no shortage of food here,' Beth Jacobs had announced at one of her opening dinner speeches, which she would periodically repeat, especially for the benefit of new arrivals. 'No wondering where the next meal might be coming from. No recrimination for calls of 'More' here.' Which would raise some applause and cheers. Dickens's *Oliver Twist* was one of the popular books of the time.

Ellie paused, her brow knitting as she scanned the hall. 'Lucy not here yet? I don't see her.'

Meghan joined her in looking for a second. 'No. I don't think she's returned yet.'

'Where's she gone?'

'Said she was meeting a friend at Montfort for a quick tea before dinner. Said she'd be back by seven, seven-fifteen at the latest.'

Ellie nodded. 'I'm sure she'll turn up soon.'

But as it got closer to dinner, the tables being set and the water-pitchers put out, Ellie started to get more concerned. They liked to give leeway to the girls about going out, otherwise it would simply seem like a prison or sanatorium — the other harsh options to the streets for many of them — but Lucy was a stickler for time. It wasn't like Lucy to be late like this. Ellie noticed that it was getting dark outside, reminded that Lucy was uncomfortable staying out in the dark.

'Maybe she got carried away admiring that clock around the corner,' Megan commented, seeing Ellie's increasing consternation.

'Maybe.' A couple of other girls from the refuge had seen Lucy staring at the clock, seemingly transfixed by it. But then Ellie knew a private reason for Lucy's fascination with clocks which they weren't aware of. And, in turn, her fear of darkness — the two of them oddly linked. She gave one last look towards the dying light outside before turning to her office to grab her jacket and hat. 'But I think best I check. It's not like Lucy to be late like this.'

* * *

He watched the two girls from the back of the Montfort tearoom. Lucy's 'friend' he guessed was two or three years older than her, in her early twenties, and wearing fine clothes, although a touch heavy on the rouge. *Another street girl similar to Lucy a year or so back?* Perhaps Lucy was trying to talk her into taking refuge at the Beth Jacobs as well. Or just swapping stories and comparing notes? *Street life versus refuge life*.

He had no idea of knowing, although briefly checking his pocket watch, they had been talking a while now; almost half-an-hour.

He'd ambled about across the road for a few minutes before deciding to go inside. He'd be too conspicuous staying outside for too long, and the café was quite busy. He could take a seat at the back without hardly being noticed, and Lucy's gaze hadn't shifted his way for even a second as he'd walked in. The other factor that had concerned him: whether she'd picked up that he was the same man standing across the road from the clock-smiths. Obviously, she'd been to absorbed with the clock outside to notice him.

He sipped at the last of the lemon tea the waiter had brought him, suddenly jolting as a hand reached towards the rolled-up *New York Times* on his table.

'That's mine,' he said, putting a protective hand over it. He still had his blade concealed inside it.

'Oh, I'm sorry,' responded a middle-aged man with thick ginger-beard and equally thick bifocals.

He gestured towards the side wall. 'The café's newspapers are all over there.'

The man looked to where he was pointing, though

seemed to take a second bringing into focus the rack of newspapers with wooden holding handles.

'I see. Yes, thank you.'

The man ambled away, and he was on his feet only a second after. The girls were leaving! Settling the bill with the waiter.

With the distraction, he'd been a second late in noticing. It was vital he left ahead of them, so that he could get in the right position for when Lucy approached.

He beckoned the waiter, but he was busy finishing with the girl's bill — they were getting to their feet, ready to leave. No time!

He slapped a dime on the table and pointed to it as he got to his feet. Four-cents left for the waiter, a generous tip. The waiter nodded his way in acknowledgement.

Rolled-up newspaper in his grip, he hustled past Lucy and her friend as they were halfway to the door. His heart was pounding hard. Despite his rapid pace, they were only ten yards behind as they exited, and he needed at least a fifty or sixty-yard lead on Lucy for his plan to work.

Had the waiter picked up on his rushed, agitated state and could later identify him? Or perhaps the man reaching for his New York Times. Even Lucy or her friend might have picked up on him rushing past them. And what if Lucy's friend stayed with her for a while, walked back with her towards the Beth Jacobs?

Then he'd have to choose another day; and already he'd delayed three previous times where he'd followed Lucy, watching her movements and habits so that he could pick the ideal time and place. A fourth or fifth time and someone might notice him: one of the floor managers at the clock-smiths or other shop-keepers en-route to the Beth Jacobs.

The street ahead was not too busy, one or two people

passing every ten yards or so; he should be able to find a suitable gap.

In his side glance-back vision, he noticed Lucy and her friend pause about eight yards from the Montfort entrance, their conversation more animated for a moment before they embraced and parted. His breath eased as his pace picked up again; one pressure gone, but would he reach his designated side-alley far enough ahead of Lucy? It was only seventy yards ahead, and Lucy's pace seemed brisker now that she'd parted from her friend.

He wasn't sure he'd make it, and he also needed a minute spare with nobody passing to slide his pocket-watch a few yards into the cobbles of the alleyway. The distraction to hopefully catch Lucy's eye.

* * *

'Have you seen Lucy?'

Ellie was frantic. She'd spotted a small oil-lamp light on towards the back of the clock-smith's, and had rapped on the window rapidly three times before the manager came to the front to see what she wanted.

'Lucy?' His brow knitted. 'I'm not sure I know a...'

'Young girl of eighteen, fine dress,' Ellie prompted sharply. 'Admires your clock out front here more than most.'

'Ah, yes. She was here earlier. She left a while ago.'

'How long ago?'

'About thirty-five or forty minutes.'

'Thank you,' Ellie said from a pace away, rushing to see if Lucy was still at the Montfort. She found it hard to openly run with her calf-length dress, but she managed a speedy walk, half-ran the two blocks to the Montfort tearoom.

A quick scan around as she entered. No Lucy. She approached the waiter at the counter, giving him a quick description. '...Was with another young lady friend, slightly older. Would have turned up about thirty-five minutes ago.'

It took a moment for the waiter's expression to lift in recognition. 'Yes. They both had tea and pastries. You've just missed them.'

'How long ago?' With Ellie's sharp, insistent voice, he flushed slightly.

'Only a few minutes.'

Ellie grimaced, 'Thanks,' and headed out, looking frantically each way. Surely she'd have passed Lucy on her way from the Beth Jacobs? Unless she'd headed the other way with her friend for a while.

She was still peering into the distance each way, deciding which way to head, when she heard the piercing scream from a hundred yards back the way she'd come, sinking into a guttural groan.

* * *

As Lucy approached the point where the alley turned off, he looked around desperately, flustered as his eyes scanned the surrounding sidewalk. He purposely caught her eye as she came close.

'What's wrong?' Lucy enquired.

'I appear to have dropped my pocket-watch, but can't see it anywhere.'

'What does it look like?'

Silver with a gold trim. Quite ornate.'

Lucy joined him in scanning the ground for his watch, as he knew she would.

'Ah, there it is,' she said after a moment, looking three yards into the alleyway.

'Where?' He feigned that he couldn't quite make it out, hoping she'd take the lead.

'There,' she said, taking a step into the alley.

He squinted as if he still couldn't bring it fully into focus, and she took another couple of steps towards it.

'Oh, yes,' he exclaimed finally, following a step behind as she bent down and picked it up.

'It is very ornate, as you say,' Lucy said, admiring it for a moment, seemingly transfixed.

'Why, thank you.' He was happy to let her admire it a moment longer, conscious of a couple of people passing the alley entrance.

Then, as soon as they were past — the next people were at least twenty yards away, so enough of a time-gap — he held his hand out for his watch, and in the same motion clamped one hand around her mouth and tumbled back with her against the wooden gate behind.

It gave way, as he knew it would — he'd checked it earlier, the back-yard of a disused milliners — the gate clicking shut again behind them before the next people passed the alley-way. Nobody had seen them.

She stared at him wide-eyed for only a second, then held one arm across her eyes so that she couldn't fully view him. She started mumbling something, so he lifted his hand an inch away and leaned closer to hear.

'Take my pocket-book, if that's what you want,' she said. 'There's not much in it, mind. Only a few dollars.'

'What makes you think I want your money?' He reached out and moved her arm away: her eyes darted for a second, trying to work out what he wanted, before closing them. 'And why are you shielding or closing your eyes.'

'I haven't seen you — so I can't identify you properly.'

'That's reassuring,' he said, smiling ironically as he let the newspaper fall and thrust with his blade.

But with the rustle of the newspaper falling, Lucy's eyes

had flickered open for a second, curious — and as she saw the glint of the blade, she let out a piercing scream.

* * *

Ellie moved swiftly towards where she'd heard the scream, but couldn't discern anything tell-tale at first. Nothing visible on the main thoroughfare, 31st Street — but had the scream come from one of the buildings flanking or a side alley?

Ellie thought she saw a man moving away more hastily and anxiously than most on the street, but then a small group of people seemed to get in the way in-between, partly obscuring her view. And when she got a clear view beyond them again, she couldn't pick out anyone moving anxiously away. They all seemed to be moving at the same pace — a landscape of grey and brown suits and Derbies, with little to distinguish between them.

As Ellie got close to the source of the scream, she could see that the group of people had in fact formed a ragged semi-circle facing a side-alley, with a few venturing deeper into the alley.

Ellie weaved her way through the semi-circle, seeing then for the first time the girl visible from the waist down through a half-open side-gate, her dress front covered in blood.

'Oh, God... *no*!' Ellie's hand went to her mouth, praying that it wasn't Lucy. But as she took in the lilac linen of the dress beyond the heavy swathe of blood and recognized it as the dress Lucy had been wearing earlier, her worst fears were realized.

An elderly man in a brown suit leaned over the body, but nobody else was venturing close.

'I'm a doctor,' he explained, looking up as Ellie came to his side.

'I know her,' Ellie said. 'She's one of my wards from the Beth Jacobs Refuge.'

The man nodded, grimacing tautly as if to indicate the prognosis wasn't looking good as Ellie crouched down and gently clasped Lucy's hand.

'Who did this to you, Lucy?' Lucy's eyes flickered and struggled to focus as she recognized Ellie's voice. 'Did you know him?'

'No... uh.' A guttural wheeze which brought up specks of blood. 'N... never seen him before.'

'But would you recognize him again?'

'I... I made sure not to look at him fully.'

Even without that factor, looking at Lucy's ravaged, blood-soaked body, Ellie realized the chances of Lucy surviving long enough to give a description to the police and a sketch-artist were slim.

Ellie pressed Lucy's hand more insistently, as much to urge her to hang on as anything else. 'Anything significant you can recall about him?'

Lucy's eyes drifted again for a moment before focusing back on Ellie. 'He had a nice pocket-watch,' Lucy said.

CHAPTER FIVE

Everything seemed in order in the Argenti household.

Dinner had finished half-an-hour ago. Chuck steaks with cheese cannelloni on the side, as if — as with many dishes Sophia would prepare of late — she was attempting to bridge their two cultures, old and new.

Joseph would usually spend a while after dinner talking to Sophia, sharing how their respective days had gone, but tonight he'd begged off, saying that he had some work files and notes to catch up on. Truth was, he wanted to get his thoughts clear on how to broach the thorny subject of Enzio Maccione's renewed contact.

'I should have finished with my notes by the time Marco and Pascal have gone to bed.'

Joseph checked his pocket-watch. Half-an-hour more to go. They'd played for the most part quietly — some new board game called 'Mail Express'. But then ten minutes ago, their voices had become more excited and animated, and he'd had to go into their bedroom and quieten them down again. 'I'm trying to finish some work.'

He'd had a file open at the same place for much of that time without being able to concentrate on it even before the excitable voices had come from their room. As he walked back towards the end-of-corridor-alcove which served as his at-home office, the gentle rhythm of Oriana's piano playing rose from downstairs, faint clatter of dishes and pans of Sophia finishing clearing up from dinner.

Everything seemed in order. Except that it wasn't. How would he broach the subject of Maccione? *And when might he share his deeper concerns about what Maccione represented?*

The rhythm of Oriana's piano playing suddenly became harsher. More abrupt, syncopated chords. Scott Joplin. Oriana had played some of Joplin's music for him a couple of weeks back, and she'd lapsed into them on occasions since. As if constant Beethoven, Bach and Mozart recitals became too boring and tiresome after a while, so she needed some relief with the contrast of 'new music'.

He'd smiled softly the last time she'd played Scott Joplin; on one hand encouraged that she could play such a range of music, but on the other anxious because it reminded him of the piano players in the taverns on the East side and tenderloin — street-girls dancing to it with prospective clients. That wasn't the future he envisaged for Oriana, playing at such clubs: he pictured her playing the classics at concert halls, or at the very least in higher-class tearooms.

But he hadn't wanted to voice his disapproval too openly; all he'd commented was that she shouldn't break-off from her recital practice for too long. 'You want to get the best possible marks.'

'Don't worry. I'm ahead of most of my group.'

'Most? But not *all*.'

She'd returned his gentle smile, sensing he was teasing; and, sure enough, five minutes after he'd left the room, he'd heard Oriana return to her classical music playing. Perhaps it was the fact also that he found the classical music more soothing, whereas Scott Joplin? Haunting images of Mariella working in the same clubs he checked up on and sometimes raided. And that was the last thing he wanted reminding of. Especially now.

He found his nerves tensing with the sharper cadences and rhythms, found it hard to concentrate on the file open before him — only a page on from when he'd started — but he didn't want to go down and mention anything to Oriana, make it something of a repetitive issue between them; and, as before, Oriana finished of her own accord and returned to her classical recital minutes later; she didn't need prompting.

Oriana was a good girl, he reminded himself. The streets wouldn't claim her, as had happened with his sister, Mariella. But perhaps what had happened with Mariella had made him more guarded and protective than he should be.

Now his worry was more if he could save himself from the streets. *Maccione?*

Ten minutes after Marco and Pascal had been settled down for the night, and having skirted around the issue with general niceties and how Sophia's day had been, finally he broached the subject of Maccione being in contact again.

'Over two years, and suddenly out of the blue he wants to talk again.'

Sophia nodded slowly. 'He in fact came by the store a couple of days ago.'

'Oh?' Joseph's brow creased. *He wasn't the only one keeping secrets*. 'You didn't tell me.'

'There hardly seemed any point.' She held a hand out. 'He came by mainly to see Anton over some fresh new lines he was importing that he thought might be of interest.'

'I see.' Joseph's expression eased, reminded that

Maccione's relationship with his wife and Anton Faggiani was very different. To them, he was just a food and provisions supplier; provisions which in fact filled most of their shelves. His darker dealings and turf-wars with Michael Tierney wouldn't necessarily be known to them.

'So, what was it he wanted to talk with you about after so long?' Sophia asked.

Even with the question, the opportunity, laid out before him so openly, still he found himself holding back, eager to soften what he shared. But how could he open up about everything with Sophia? Admit that he might have inadvertently brought about Paolo Calvi's death by trying to help Maccione with a Custom's-House wrangle with Tierney. *That he'd openly seen Maccione slide an ice-pick through Tom Brogan's neck up into his brain, and hadn't told anyone*. Not a soul in the police force, nor Jameson or his own family. And that he suspected Maccione was responsible for two more deaths of Tierney's henchmen, as well as the bomb-attack on Tierney's brewery. While much of that had been led by the good intent of ridding the City of the scourge of Michael Tierney — *was he, as he'd feared before, simply replacing one monster with another?*

'He was asking me if there had been any pressure from Michael Tierney on local stores?' The initial event that had brought Maccione into their lives: offering fresh supply lines along with protection to ease that pressure. 'I told him, not that I know of.' Joseph sipped at a strong black coffee, held a palm out. 'Have you encountered anything personally at Faggiani's?'

'No, nothing. Since that first day when Enzio came to Anton's aid in the store when he was attacked, we haven't been troubled. Haven't seen any more of Tierney's men.'

'What about when you haven't been there? Has Faggiani experienced anything personally?'

Sophia shook her head resolutely. 'No, I'm sure not. He'd have mentioned something.'

'That's good, then.' Joseph took a heavier slug of his coffee. 'I said as much to Maccione, but felt it was worth checking personally.'

'I see.' Sophia sank into thought for a second, then: 'But why didn't Enzio ask me something directly, if pressure on the store was his concern?'

Joseph in turn took a second to hit the right answer. 'Perhaps he thought the subject indelicate to raise with you directly. After all, his dealings with yourself and Anton were more shop-provisions related, rather than any renewed threats and problems from Tierney.'

Sophia nodded slowly, but her eyes lingered on him, sensing there was more. And he was just contemplating what more he could or *should* share when a heavy knock came at the front door. Usually he dreaded these late-night calls; invariably, it was bad news: an investigation that needed his urgent attention and would often keep him out half the night.

But on this occasion, he was glad of the interruption. Put off having to talk about Maccione too deeply. Halfway along the hallway, another heavy, more insistent knock.

'I'm coming.'

If he'd shouldered these dark concerns for two years, what difference would another few weeks or months make? Besides, the right words might then come easier.

* * *

'She was just nineteen, Finley. Nineteen.' Ellie shook her head. 'Her life cut short far too soon.'

'I knew that she was young, but not her exact age.' Finley grimaced tightly. 'And also that you were fond of her.'

'Fond? I suppose that's one way of putting it.' Ellie looked absently around at the crowded restaurant, her thoughts seemingly lost for a moment before focusing back on Finley. 'I was certainly very close to Lucy — you could say that she was one of my favourites.' Her expression became strained. 'Except we're not meant to have 'favourites' at the Beth Jacobs. They're all meant to be equally in need, in God's eyes and our own.'

'I'm so sorry.' Finley reached out and gently clasped Ellie's hand across the table. She met his eyes questioningly for a moment. Though they too had become 'close' over the past few years, their relationship hadn't become physical; such displays of open affection between them were rare. But Jameson felt in that moment that he couldn't leave her alone with her grief without some heartfelt consolation. Ellie nodded, closing her eyes for a second, as if she in turn understood and appreciated the gesture.

Jameson broke off and leaned back as their waiter approached with a silver tray with their lunches: lamb casserole and trimmings for Ellie, fillet steak for Jameson.

Jameson poured a glass for them each from the bottle the waiter set down. 'It's just a light sparkling rose, not too heavy for lunch,' and they ate in silence for a moment.

They'd gone to Henning's on 3rd Avenue. A middle-class workaday restaurant, not too ostentatious or elaborate, but not slumming it either like the slop-houses of the Bowery or taverns on the East side.

Ellie probably knew or at least guessed that this was the lowest-standard restaurant he'd grace. He'd taken her on a couple of occasions before to his favourite, *Delmonico's*, and she'd seemed overwhelmed by its grandeur. That would have been the wrong setting now; the food and surroundings a distraction and at odds with the matter being discussed: the brutal slaying of a young girl.

Jameson had wanted somewhere plain and serviceable,

where the food and ambience would be no more than a backdrop. Their conversation would be the main fare.

'Do you think it might be the Ripper again?' Ellie asked at length.

'Probably not. Though I'll know more after a secondary examination with Dr Sorvensen at Bellevue later today.' He'd spent two hours late last night with Lawrence examining Lucy's body, and halfway through, having received an urgent message at home via Mulberry Street, Joseph Argenti had joined them. But he was loath to mention that the early signs looked disturbingly like the Ripper's handiwork. Ellie had enough on her shoulders with Lucy's death without the added spectre that it might be the Ripper returned. 'We've had a number of copy-cat killings before. Probably another one of those.'

'Yes, I suppose.' Ellie expression was strained. 'And some of those no less disturbing.'

Jameson nodded sombrely. Ellie had in fact been the target of one such copy-cat with Tom Brogan, Mike Tierney's old henchman.

'The last communication I had from Eugene Dove, aka the Ripper, was eighteen months ago from Biarritz in South-West France. It's doubtful he'd have returned. I don't think he had anything left here to settle or that might draw him back again.'

Ellie nodded slowly. 'Even though it's a girl close to me again?'

Jameson was thoughtful for a second as he took another mouthful of steak. The first Ripper attacks in New York had been girls from a small east-side street-girl commune, which Ellie had been a part of at the time. 'But, as we saw with Brogan, that connection to girls close to you has also been used by copycat killers — so doesn't really mean much.'

Another slow nod of acceptance from Ellie after a

moment. But Jameson wondered whether he was fooling himself as much as Ellie; and if later it was indeed proven as the Ripper's handiwork, the shock might hit her all the harder if meanwhile he misled and assuaged her that it wasn't the Ripper.

Ellie looked towards the clock on the far wall for a moment; not particularly ornate, but large and functional, like the restaurant.

'I think I mentioned to you before about Lucy's fascination with clocks,' she said.

'Yes, you did. And you mentioned it again last night as one of your concerns as to why Lucy might have been late returning — held up admiring a particular clock around the corner from the Beth Jacobs.'

Ellie nodded. 'That and my concern that it was starting to get dark.' Heavier shadows crossed Ellie's face. 'But I don't think I told you how that fascination came about.'

'No. I don't believe you did.' Jameson took another sip of wine as he watched those shadows wrestling, Ellie seeking clarity; or perhaps having second thoughts about elaborating on the subject.

'It goes back to when Lucy was younger, only eleven or twelve,' Ellie said with a resigned breath. 'Her real father had abandoned her and her mother when she was only five years old, and there were a few lean, difficult years following before her mother met a new partner, a respectable businessman who ran a nearby tannery.' She cocked her head to one side, shrugging. 'He seemed kind and gracious at first, and of course her mother was glad of the money and help after those lean years. But when Lucy was only eleven, he started coming to her room at night. At first, it was just playing and fumbling under her nightdress, but pretty soon it became heavier, until finally he was having his full way with her.' Ellie skewed her mouth, as if she'd sucked on a sour lemon. 'Doing so regularly from then on, two or three nights a week.'

Jameson closed his eyes for a second as he shook his head, said nothing. Feared spoiling Ellie's flow and, besides, the right words were difficult instantly to find and might have come across as empty consolation.

Ellie took a sip of her own wine as she focused back, as if she was alongside Lucy in that moment, picturing the scene. 'And what would get her through those dreadful nights was focusing on a small snowflake-scene clock she had on her bedside table. You know, one of those you shake up and snow falls. This one depicted a small Austrian village, and Lucy told me that she used to stare at that clock while it was going on and feel herself transported there — imagining herself playing in the snow in that small village rather than in her bed being raped by her own stepfather.'

Heavy silence settled, the clatter of the surrounding restaurant seeming to be cut off from them for a moment. 'The poor girl.' Jameson grimaced as he took another swallow of wine. 'Did she not mention anything to her mother? Try and put a stop to it?'

'She tried to broach the subject after a while, but her mother didn't want to know — said she was making the stories up, fantasizing. Lucy thought her mother was afraid of confronting him, losing his money and support. Back to hard times again.' Ellie pulled a face. 'And when she did finally force the issue with her mom, that's when things blew up and her stepfather threw her out of the house — she was left to fend for herself on the streets. She was only fourteen.' Ellie shook her head, traced one finger absently on the tablecloth.

'And that's when Lucy became a street-girl, turned to prostitution?'

Ellie looked back sharply. 'What option was there? What option in fact for any of these girls?'

'I know... I know.' Jameson nodded, sank his head for a second in contrition. He'd merely been confirming, not questioning. But it was a reminder of the days when he'd first met Ellie and she'd regarded him as somewhat cut off and out of touch with the realities of street-girls, which she'd also been at the time. Cut off by his cosseted, upper-class background. She'd had a few sharp words for him then, pressed home the harsh lack-of-choice for street-girls, which he'd subsequently become keenly aware of with her work with the Beth Jacobs the past few years.

'But in a strange way that vigil of Lucy's with her side clock helped,' Ellie said. 'Got her through the dark days of working the streets. She kept it up, you see. Told me that she took her small clock with her and used to look at it while with clients, lose herself from what she was going through.'

Jameson nodded grimly. 'I suppose people in such a situation will cling to whatever they can, if they feel it might help.' He recalled when he'd first met Lawrence at Bedlam, Lawrence would fixate on objects, stare at them for a long while. Perhaps he too was sinking into whatever memories those objects gave him to escape his dire surroundings.

'And it also then led to Lucy's fear of darkness. She'd keep a small oil lamp by her bedside to be able to see her clock — but one night her stepfather reached out to put it out. She screamed for him to keep it on, that she was afraid of the dark.' Ellie shook her head, her expression clouding. 'But it was more a fear of not being able to see her clock in that darkness, escape the horrors of what was happening to her. And now her fixation has led to the only thing she recalls about her killer — his stopwatch.'

Ellie's attempted tragi-comic smile misfired, her mouth curling down sharply. But Jameson sensed something else in her mood; not just Lucy's tragic background, but Ellie left with the feeling that she'd let Lucy down. In the end, the Beth Jacobs hadn't been enough to protect Lucy.

'I'm so, so sorry.' But this time as Jameson reached out and clasped Ellie's hand across the table, consoling, Ellie's gaze lingering on it was different. Not just the rarity of such gestures between them, but that she'd like him to keep his hand there. She'd sink into that consolation, that closeness, in the same way that Lucy would escape with her clocks.

CHAPTER SIX

No doubt you'll have concluded your autopsy by now, so you'll know with all due certainty that it is my handiwork. Nobody has quite the same precision with their cuts, do they? Some attempting to copy come close, but you and I both know that in no time you'll have uncovered them as imposters. And if there was any remaining doubt in your mind, now you have this letter.

What made you think that after my attacks on those first girls, my business here in New York was finished? Ah, what precious virtues they try and cling to as well. Thinking that if they hide away in a refuge, they'll be safe from me.

They're fooling themselves not just about their safety, but what they've become. They think that being in a temperance led refuge, makes them suddenly ladies. But they're still the same harlots they've always been.

As you know, my return last time was somewhat forced, not of my choosing. How dare someone else be lauded as a more ingenuous killer than me. The matter needed to be put right, but it distracted me for a while from my own aims and purpose. Two years it has taken me to get those finally clear again. But I think you always knew I'd return, didn't you? After all, I'd spelled out only one fallen angel. What about all the others?

* * *

The murmur of voices rang around the small auditorium — one of the larger Temperance Halls on 29th Street, just two blocks from the Beth Jacobs refuge — like the low drone of a swarm of bees.

Jameson felt he could judge the mood among the audience from reading the rhythm of that drone: a heavier more unsettled drone with the starker, more worrying comments and questions. After an introduction from Mayor Watkins and Commissioner Roosevelt on the stage alongside Jameson and Joseph Argenti, there was a bit of roundabout circling from the reporters in the front row before the key question was posed.

New York Times: 'Do you think it might be the Ripper returned?'

'No, I don't,' Jameson said flatly; no reserve of doubt.

'So who do you think it is?'

'A very good copy, no more. We've had a number of those before.'

The Post: 'Like the one from when Tom Brogan was involved?'

'In Brogan's case, the slashes and cuts were far deeper and more brutal — almost an exaggerated example of the Ripper's handiwork.'

'But the letter arriving afterwards was accurate, in the same handwriting?'

'Yes, it was. As now. But the incisions weren't as precise as in this murder now.'

The front-row reporters were lost in thought for a moment. Jameson noticed that they were asking questions in rapid rotation today, as if they realized that quick-fire questioning might catch him on the hop. The competitive spirit of being the first to get a more telling, breakthrough response didn't seem to matter, because they'd all be noting it at the same time for tomorrow's headlines. The *New York Times* reporter was first to lift his pen again.

'But if the letter now looks like the Ripper's writing, and, in your own words — this murder now is more alike in the precision of its cuts — what makes you so sure it's not the Ripper returned?'

This time it was Jameson falling silent for a second, feeling Watkin's and Roosevelt's eyes on him keenly from alongside. Joseph Argenti kept his eyes ahead on the auditorium audience, as if less concerned what Jameson might say. But Watkins and Roosevelt had impressed upon him beforehand that if there was even the slightest of doubt that it was the Ripper returned, it was better to maintain that claim than the reverse.

'The last thing we want is to cause public alarm,' Watkins had concluded, giving his moustache a last preen and bringing his shoulders back as they prepared to go out and face the auditorium crowd.

'I concur,' Roosevelt had supported. 'No point in worrying the public until we're a hundred-percent sure.'

But Jameson's first thought was that Roosevelt probably didn't want anything which might divert headline attention from his anti-corruption stance.

Now, Jameson said, 'There are elements which don't perfectly fit which I can't go into too much detail about. Because, once declared and in the open, our killer might simply copy those too.'

Jameson noticed Argenti smiling meekly; recognition of his trademark obfuscation, adroitly sidestepping direct questions — *they knew each other so well now* — or the fact that his answer put that element out of the reporters' reach? They couldn't probe and test him on it.

But from the quizzical, brain-racked expressions among the front row, they were obviously desperately trying to work out what it might be, find an angle in.

The Herald: 'Are we talking now about the symbols left on organs in past murders? Were no symbols found on organs removed from the body this time?'

'That's part of it, but by no means all.'

'So, no symbols found?'

'No.' Jameson exhaled tiredly, making it clear he didn't like being forced into a corner. 'But no organs removed from the body, either — so not something that's likely to turn up later.'

A heavier drone for the hall, but more satisfied rather than unsettled. This might not be the Ripper after all. A brief lull in the questions, then:

New York Times: 'Might that be because there simply wasn't the time on this occasion? I understand that there was little time before the next passers-by of the alleyway where it happened.'

'That is so,' Jameson said curtly, glancing to his side. This was more Joseph Argenti's territory.

'Fifteen or twenty seconds, at most,' Argenti picked up. 'Probably not enough time to remove an organ completely.' Argenti in turn glanced back at Jameson in acknowledgment of the forensic cross-over, but Jameson simply nodded his concurrence.

Post: Yet no sightings of this suspected killer, no descriptions? Despite people being so close.'

'No *clear* descriptions,' Argenti stressed. 'but we have a sketch artist working with those who thought they did see somebody, however fleetingly.'

Jameson nodded. 'One of whom is in fact Ellie Cullen, one of the patron-carers at the Beth Jacobs.'

A heavier murmur again, but now more undecided; and in its wake, with a lull again in questioning from reporters, Commissioner Roosevelt interjected.

'I trust Detective Argenti and his esteemed colleague, Finley Jameson, have answered your questions satisfactorily today. Made it clear there is no cause for alarm. This doesn't appear to be the notorious Ripper returned. But still a brutal killer, on whom we will duly focus all police department resources to ensure his capture. So, gentlemen, if there are no further questions...'

'Just one!' The *Post* reporter held his pen aloft. 'If the killer this time didn't leave any markings on organs removed — then why does he make reference to spelling out fallen angels in his letter afterwards? Why not gloss over that issue, or simply avoid it completely?'

'As I've long-discovered, the logic of killers doesn't always add up.' Jameson smiled ingratiatingly. 'But I'll ask him myself when we've caught him. Which, as Commissioner Roosevelt has made clear, we have every intention of doing.'

Roosevelt and Watkins were already half on their feet, Roosevelt's tight, approving smile affirming to Jameson that he'd ended on the right note: *dispel any remaining doubt*. Even if it was at odds with the increasing doubt and concern gnawing at Jameson's stomach after the last autopsy.

CHAPTER SEVEN

Bill Griffin pressed the elevator button again as its doors opened and he was faced with a bare concrete floor spreading out thirty yards ahead of him. No response. He jabbed again sharper, once, *twice* — still nothing. The doors stayed open, the elevator refusing to move.

Beyond the concrete expanse, Griffin could see white tarpaulin sheets along two sides, but with an open area between them of twenty feet, as if it was a window framed by an Arab-tent arrangement — the lights of Manhattan visible through that gap, twinkling twenty-one storeys below.

Griffin was confused. The concierge had led the way to the elevators, turned a key and pushed the button himself for Michael Tierney's penthouse. The only way to gain entry to that top floor. But this wasn't Tierney's penthouse. Griffin had only visited once before, but that was a mixture of mahogany furniture and red velvet sofas and chairs with gold brocade.

This area was totally bare, *except*... at that moment the flame on a small oil-lamp was turned up, and what before had been some vague shadows, Griffin could now see was a desk with a man sitting with his back to the elevator, looking out at the Manhattan view ahead. A stocky man, who Griffin now recognized as Liam Monahan, straightened up from adjusting the oil lamp, took a seat to one side.

'Glad you could make it,' the voice rose from the man at the desk. *Tierney*. He didn't look around, simply gestured with one hand ahead.

Griffin moved closer. An office chair on casters, Griffin could now see. He took up the seat tentatively, a brief nervous look over one shoulder at the dazzling view behind. The chair was positioned too close to the sheer drop behind for Griffin's liking. No more than a couple of feet away. He could feel the breeze wafting up from the East River far below, licking at his hair.

The tarpaulin-tent arrangement was also in stark contrast to the bare concrete flooring; as if Tierney behind his desk was a Pascha looking over his domain of Manhattan spread before him.

'I thought I'd be meeting you at your penthouse,' Griffin said; a flat, quizzical tone, trying not to give away his anxiety.

'Sometimes I come down here t' get in touch with reality,' Tierney said. All that red velvet an' brocade — hardly seems real at times. Rich man's trappings. There t' please you and other visitors rather than myself. Whereas this 's gritty and real. The raw concrete that built this monolith. Yer can almost still smell the sweat and labour that went into it. An' the blood. Three deaths from accidents along the way.'

Griffin nodded sombrely. 'Yes, I read about those.'

Tierney shrugged. 'Well, four actually, if yer count Ballard, the city surveyor who fell t' his death.' Tierney smiled slyly. 'He went off the edge not far from you, as it happens. But I don' really count that. He wasn't a real labourer — just a city surveyor sticking his nose in, gettin' above himself.'

Griffin nodded. Suddenly his shirt collar felt tighter. He'd heard about city surveyor Trent Ballard falling to his death. Tierney and his builders on site at the time had claimed that Ballard lost his footing while taking some measurements close to the edge. But there were rumours on the street that Ballard had been pressing for some back-hand money from Tierney to approve the final stages of his building, to which Tierney had taken exception.

Gettin' above himself. Now Tierney had all but confirmed those rumours.

'I needed a storeroom for tools, supplies and fittin's for the building's finishing.' Tierney hooked a thumb towards a door in some boarding ten yards to their side. 'But that left more than half the floor spare. So I kept it as is as a reminder of th' blood and sweat that went into this building.'

'I see.' Griffin glanced towards Monahan, as if to gauge his reaction to this bare, windswept concrete floor, some of the side tarpaulins billowing in the breeze as Tierney spoke. But Monahan, a square block of a man, stared back impassively. No hint of emotion either way. The coldness of his gaze seemed more detached and remote behind wire-framed glasses; in turn out of keeping with his brawn and bulk. The glasses looked like they should belong more on a stamp collector or bookkeeper.

'Anyway, to business.' Tierney leaned forward. 'How are you copin' with this new push of Roosevelt's? This purge to rid Mulberry Street of corruption. Are yer feelin' any pressure yet?'

'I can't say I have.' Griffin smiled uncertainly. 'But then he has no reason to suspect me.'

'Has he not?' Tierney looked at Griffin incredulously. 'Despite yer being suspended a while back on suspicion of involvement wit' me?'

'That was only a brief suspension, of which I was fully

cleared.' Griffin held one hand out. 'And was over two years ago. There's been nothing since.'

Tierney nodded slowly. 'An' what about your visits to me last time and now?'

'I covered for that with a suspected safe-break investigation with the insurance adjusters on the twelfth floor. And I've covered with the same now with a follow-up on that.' Tierney continued to stare at him, and Griffin added, 'One of the insurance investigators there, Varick, is an ex-copper — owes me a few favours.'

Tierney was slow to break his contemplation of Griffin, stroked his chin. 'But that could all change soon. Word has it that Roosevelt's aimin' to put pressure on suspect officers with an amnesty programme. Offer 'em early retirement and escape from prosecution if they come clean on their dealin's.'

'I've heard rumours too — but haven't seen anything being put into practice.'

'That as may be.' An imperceptible nod from Tierney, and Monahan got up and moved towards Griffin's chair. 'But the problem I got with that is that if Roosevelt decides to put on pressure — you simply know too much about my dealin's for me to feel comfortable.'

As Tierney spoke, Monahan leant in close, staring into Griffin's eyes from only a foot away, then on the word 'comfortable', he braced hard against Griffin's shoulders, shoving the chair on its casters a full foot back.

Griffin's breath caught in his throat. The sheer drop behind was only a foot away, the wind whipping up from below feeling suddenly sharper and fresher against the back of his head.

'I... I wouldn't say anything,' Griffin stammered. Then, observing Tierney's wry smile, as if he held little store in such promises — had heard them countless times before — he added, 'And if you get rid of me, you'll have nobody left at Mulberry Street to watch your back.'

'There's always your sidekick, Tom Henderson.'

Monahan braced against him tighter, the chair shoved back another couple of inches. Griffin tensed his legs, trying to drag his feet, resist, but Monahan was too strong, the chair rolling too freely. If Monahan shoved hard, he'd fly over the edge in the chair without being able to stop it.

'Henderson's too new and fresh — doesn't have any sway or influence at Mulberry Street.'

'Ah, but that newness also has an advantage. He also doesn't know about my business to cause any harm by talkin' out o' turn.

Another sharp shove, two more inches back. 'It would be too obvious, too clumsy,' Griffin spluttered. 'Two people falling off the edge of your building in a similar way.'

Tierney's smile broadened. 'All that would prove is that policemen are as clumsy with their footin' as surveyors. Support the theory of 'em being flat-footed.'

Another short shove, and Griffin's breath went, fearing for a second he'd gone over the edge. But Monahan had him braced tight, only inches from the edge. 'Besides,' he stuttered, 'Roosevelt's more occupied now with this possible Ripper-return killer to pay much attention to his anti-corruption purge.'

Tierney held one hand up. 'Finally, you hit a golden nugget that's got my attention. Are you sayin' that's keeping Roosevelt's mind occupied right now?'

'Very much so. They held a big conference about it earlier today.'

'And how did that go?'

'Could have gone either way. We'll know more from tomorrow's newspaper reports.'

Griffin didn't want to say outright that they'd been

emphatic about it not being the Ripper. Right now his only interest was buying some time, even if it was only one day.

But then it struck him that Tierney might have had someone present at the conference, already knew how it had gone; or perhaps Henderson had told him. A barge horn sounded far below them on the East River, the wind whipping up sharper at the back of his neck.

Tierney's eyes stayed fixed on him, his expression cold. Then as Tierney raised one hand, a sly smile touching his lips, Griffin closed his eyes, expecting the worst.

* * *

'Good to see you, James. How are you?'

'Very well, thank you, Mr Argenti. Are you keeping well as well?'

'Yes, fine, under the circumstances. Given my profession.' Joseph Argenti sat back in the corner armchair in the small parlour Oriana used for her music practice. Joseph took out a packet of Admirals from his jacket pocket and lit a small cheroot. One of his treats of the last year, no more than ten a day, with one before dinner and one after. James Denton, his daughter Oriana's 'friend' of now the past two years. They studied at the same music academy, where in fact they'd met, and young James would come by two nights a week to practice with Oriana. They sat alongside at the piano, now half-turned towards him. 'And how was the 'End of season Ball' last month?'

'Very good, thank you. A grand affair. It was good of you to allow me to accompany Oriana. We very much enjoyed it.'

Joseph noticed James exchange a brief look with Oriana. Perhaps concerned that he shouldn't be speaking for her, or that this exchange now was unfamiliar ground; normally,

Joseph would just peek his head in to greet him, then head to the kitchen to talk with Sophia.

At the breakfast table that morning, he'd felt Sophia's eyes on him, perhaps sensing that he hadn't opened up fully about Maccione, and the right words still weren't there yet. And now he had the pressure of a renewed Ripper investigation.

Joseph blew out a soft plume of smoke. 'My pleasure. After all, you have been seeing each other for a while now. It was about time.'

James nodded mutely in thanks, but Joseph reflected that it had been far from the truth. Oriana had been pressing for weeks for James to be able to take her to the Ball, and Joseph had been reluctant to agree, still clinging to the image of Oriana as his little girl. And it had been Sophia who'd pressed the issue.

'She's eighteen now. On the edge of being a fully-grown women. You can't keep her tied to the home and protected forever.'

'I know... but I see so much out there. Harmful influences and dangers that you're just not aware of.'

'That's the nature of your work, Joseph.' Sophia held a hand out desperately. 'But this is just a music academy ball. Not some east-side street-girls club.'

She'd picked up the flinch in his face then, realizing that she'd subconsciously connected his fears over Oriana with Mariella, his sister lost to the streets and clubs years ago.

'I'm sorry.' Sophia came in close and touched his arm, and he'd in turn apologized.

'You're right. It's wrong of me to restrict her like this. James is a nice boy. I'm sure she'll be safe.'

Safe. He'd reminded himself that in fact after Oriana's horrendously close attack on her way to the nearby music academy, Joseph had asked James if he could accompany her each time back home to ensure her safety. If he could trust James with that, then he could certainly trust him with accompanying Oriana to a music ball.

'Yes, a grand affair,' Oriana agreed. 'Although perhaps they could have had less military two-step given our ages.'

Joseph grimaced. His knowledge of dances for Oriana's age-group was limited. 'Well, at least you both enjoyed yourselves — despite the orchestra's choices.'

'*Orchestra*?' Oriana raised a gentle eyebrow. 'No more than a pianist and a string section of three.'

'I see.' Joseph tempered his smile. Another area of limited knowledge. 'End of Season Ball' had a somewhat grand ring to it, so perhaps he'd envisaged something bigger. His own experience with going to 'Balls' was virtually nil. Even when he'd first joined the police force, his family was still dirt-poor. He'd hardly had the money for a pair of shiny dress shoes, so hadn't even bothered to go to the first Mulberry Street Christmas gala.

Behind them in the kitchen, the soft clink of plates being set down had replaced the clatter of pans. Dinner would be served soon. Safe ground, because Sophia wouldn't raise the subject of Maccione with the children at the table.

But a heavier sound superimposed: a sharp rapping at the front door.

'Excuse me.' Joseph nodded politely to James and Oriana and went to answer it.

John Whelan, his main assistant at Mulberry Street stood there, a quick glance and nod of acknowledgement past his shoulder as if in apology to Sophia, who'd drifted from the kitchen and now stood a few paces behind Joseph in the corridor.

'There's been another one,' Whelan said.

'What? Another girl murdered?'

'No, just disappeared. There's been no body found yet, nor sign of a murder.'

'So, just a disappearance?' Joseph' brow knitted, the message clear: there were scores of disappearances every week — why should this one warrant him being disturbed at night just before dinner?

'The girl disappeared — she's also from the Beth Jacobs refuge.' Whelan held a palm out. 'So I thought you'd want to know straightaway.'

CHAPTER EIGHT

'How long has she been gone now?' Argenti asked, while John Whelan at his side opened his notepad.

'Almost forty hours. She left at five-thirty on Tuesday, and has been away two nights now.' Ellie Cullen looked towards Beth Jacobs at the end of the table, a prim and attractive woman, now in her mid-fifties, as if for confirmation. Beth Jacobs nodded numbly. 'But we got worried late yesterday when she hadn't returned — especially after what happened with poor Lucy — so we contacted the police.'

'It's unusual for Joan to be gone so long, you see,' Beth Jacobs supported.

Opposite Argenti and John Whelan, Finley Jameson sat with Lawrence at his side; although Lawrence wasn't making any notes, just looked attentively from one to the other. With Lawrence's eidetic memory, Jameson knew he'd have no need to make notes. Argenti had asked them along because of any possible connections with the renewed-Ripper investigation. But so far neither of them had said anything, Jameson simply nodding at intervals. This was Argenti's phase of the investigation.

But with the following pause and nobody asking what he thought was an obvious question, Jameson interjected. 'You say 'unusual'. Did she not stay out overnight at any other time?'

Ellie held a hand out, made a balancing motion. 'Only to see her Aunt Maisie in upstate New York. A place called Corning.'

Argenti picked up the thread. 'And how long would she stay away when she saw her aunt in Corning?'

'Two nights, three at most. It takes her the best part of a day to get there.'

Jameson looked at Ellie, then at Argenti, shrugging at the obvious before commenting, 'Well, surely that might be it. She's gone to see her Aunt Maisie.'

Ellie grimaced. 'Except for a couple of things. She'd go to see her Aunt every three months, like clockwork, and she'd leave sharp at nine in the morning. Right now we're a month shy of the three-month mark, and she didn't leave until late.'

'But she might have gone because of an emergency,' Argenti commented. 'A message perhaps that her aunt had fallen ill.'

Ellie shook her head. 'She'd have said something, told someone. She did every other time she was going to see Maisie.'

'Maybe this time there simply wasn't the time,' Argenti said.

Beth Jacobs cut in. 'We've sent a Western Union message to her aunt, just in case. No answer as yet.'

They fell silent for a moment, contemplating the options with Joan Bourke's disappearance.

'Anyone else you can think of she might visit?' Argenti asked at length.

'Only one. Annie... Annie Jenkins,' Beth Jacobs said, a quick glance towards Ellie, as if wondering why she hadn't mentioned Annie first. 'Joan would meet Annie every other Friday at Bloomingdales, and she'd be out two or three hours.'

'But not overnight?' Argenti pressed.

'No, never.'

'I don't think she'd have been seeing Annie,' Ellie commented. 'Aside from the fact that she disappeared on a Tuesday rather than a Friday.'

'Oh, why's that?' Argenti asked.

Ellie looked awkwardly at Argenti, then at Beth Jacobs, before answering. 'Because Joan didn't meet Annie any of the other times, either. Annie didn't exist.'

In the silence that followed, eyes on her expectantly, Ellie went on to explain that she'd been coming out of Bloomingdale's one day, and had seen Joan there. 'I lifted one hand to wave to her, but she seemed lost in her own world. She bought a small bouquet of flowers inside Bloomingdales, then placed them by a lamppost in front of the store. Then she went to a tearoom directly across the street, and took a seat by the window looking at the lamppost and flower display. I watched her for a while from further along the street, but I never saw Annie Jenkins or anyone else appear. She stayed on her own throughout.'

'Perhaps Annie simply didn't show up that day,' Jameson ventured.

'No. Curious as to what was going on, I followed Joan on a couple of other occasions to Bloomingdales, and she did the same: bought a small bunch of flowers, laid it by the lamppost, and took a seat in the tearoom, looking on.'

'Very strange,' Jameson said. 'Did you confront Joan, ask what was going on?'

'No. I didn't want to embarrass her. But I did a bit of digging myself in the background — finally discovered an obituary notice and small entry in the New York Post about a girl of only nineteen, Annie Jenkins — hit and killed by a tram right in front of Bloomingdales two years ago. Joan was going every other week to lay tribute to her.'

Stilted silence for a moment, then Beth Jacobs commented, 'You didn't tell me?'

'Sorry.' Pained smile from Ellie. 'Same reason. I didn't want her to be confronted and feel embarrassed. Also, any official paperwork you had to fill out on the matter might have got taken the wrong way by some. The view taken that Joan might be unstable or mad.'

'That as may be,' Beth Jacobs said sternly. 'But at least some due extra protection might have been offered which could have avoided her disappearance now.'

'Yes. But we all know what that 'extra protection' can sometimes mean. Shut away and forgotten in hell-holes like Blackwell's Island.'

'I wouldn't have allowed that to happen,' Beth Jacobs defended.

'It might have been out of your hands, once it was down officially on paper. You know what it's like when —'

Jameson held up a calming hand, cut in. 'I can see reasons for concern on both sides. And, yes, sometimes the authorities can be too hasty with decisions where imbalances of the mind are concerned.' *The chill of his family home after his father's death and the discovery that his father had committed his mother to Bedlam when initially he'd been told as a child that she'd run off and deserted them.* Jameson had immediately gone to see her, but she was in her fading months. It was where in fact he'd first met Lawrence, who he'd discovered was far from mad. He'd simply been viewed as such because of his Itard's syndrome*. Jameson had become Lawrence's ward, with the thought, *If I can't save my mother, I can at least save Lawrence*. From then, Lawrence became a symbol of hope to counter his failure with his mother, getting to her too late.

He'd noticed Lawrence flinch at the mention of Blackwell's Island. When his ward had been challenged by the plot hatched between Bill Griffin and Tierney, they'd got Lawrence committed there for over two months before Jameson had been able to save Lawrence yet again from the horrors of a mental asylum.

Jameson knew all too well that they were so often used by society to hide away its failures.

Argenti took a fresh breath. 'So if there's no Annie — then the only possibility left is that of Aunt Maisie. Apart from our continuing search, we'll just have to wait on an answer from Western Union — or send someone out to visit her in Corning.'

Jameson nodded sombrely. 'Unless Aunt Maisie has also since died, so she now too has become imaginary. Joan's continued visits are simply to pay graveside tribute.'

CHAPTER NINE

It seemed that half of New York was looking for the 'Girl in the blue bonnet.'

'Well, turquoise to be precise,' commented the sketch artist brought into the Beth Jacobs refuge to colour in Joan Bourke's photo 'Or perhaps aquamarine blue.'

The photo was a sepia-toned black and white taken of Joan a year ago at the refuge, to which the sketch artist then painted in the blue bonnet, his efforts guided by Nancy Drayton, who was the last person to see Joan wearing the bonnet when she left the Beth Jacobs centre.

'Yeah, that's it,' Nancy had pointed excitedly, 'a lighter blue, but with a shine to it.'

It was Nancy who'd first come forward and mentioned that Joan had gone off in a hurry after receiving a note at the centre. 'My goodness, she said. Today's the anniversary of Annie's death. I've been going every other week on a Friday — but today's the actual anniversary. I've got to go!'

Jameson was halfway through checking back on the obituary notice for Annie Jenkins when Lawrence, who recalled the date, confirmed, 'That indeed correlates with the date Annie Jenkins died.'

Argenti asked Nancy, 'Did Joan mention who she'd got the note from?'

'No. But I was curious, like. So when she went out, I followed after a second and sneaked a peek. Saw her meeting up with a man a couple of hundred yards away, wearing her best blue bonnet she'd bought at Bloomingdale's a month back.'

'Did you get a good look at the man?' Argenti pressed.

'Not really. They were walking away from me, you see. I was only able to pick out Joan by her blue bonnet.'

'You didn't mention anything to me before?' Ellie Cullen interjected.

Nancy shrugged awkwardly. 'I didn't want to get Joan into no trouble. Thought she might simply be meeting up with a fancy man she didn't want anyone to know about.' Nancy nodded towards Argenti and Jameson. 'It wasn't until I saw the police involved that it struck me it was more serious, that she might be in some bother.'

Ellie grimaced. One of the drawbacks of a place like Beth Jacobs. Having worked the streets, many of the girls had got used to covering for each other.

Argenti returned to the main subject. 'Could you give us any sort of description?'

'Not that tall, but square-built. Mid or late-twenties, brown hair — almost seemed to merge in with the brown of his derby hat and suit.'

Argenti had nodded thoughtfully. Not nearly enough for a sketch artist to flesh anything out from. But the blue bonnet, especially as it was something Nancy described as being able to 'pick out at a distance', could pay dividends. So they'd brought in the sketch artist within the hour, who'd added not only colour with the bonnet, but soft-colour flesh tones to Joan's face as well.

The first rotary four-colour press had been invented four years ago, but the Post was the only New York newspaper to so far have one installed. So they were the only New York paper to run the photo of Joan Bourke wearing the blue bonnet on their front page, alongside a report on the Beresford and Marlborough top-drawer society wedding at St George's church.

Most of the other newspapers had carried the photo on page 3 in black and white, with the accompanying description of light blue for the hat. The Herald had added 'vivid' light blue, while the Times felt that its readers were sufficiently well-healed to understand 'turquoise'.

Nothing came in for most of the first day, apart from past sightings of a 'girl wearing a blue bonnet' in or near Bloomingdale's on the Tuesday. But none of those had mentioned seeing a man with her except for the manager of a pipe, humidor and tobacco shop across the road from Bloomingdale's.

'I didn't think she was with anyone at first, the manager commented to Argenti and Jameson when they went to visit him. 'But then I noticed a man ten yards the other side of her also observing her keenly as she put a bouquet by the lamppost.'

'Did you get a good look at the man?' Argenti asked.

'A bit.' The manager wavered one palm. 'He became quickly conscious of me looking his way, so turned away. But before he did, I noticed that his hair was quite unruly and unkempt. And he seemed to have part of it covering a scar one side of his forehead.'

'Left or right side?' Jameson asked.

'Right.' The manager touched his own forehead. 'The

wind lifted that forelock tuft for a bit, you see. And his hand went too to hold his Derby in place.'

The manager confirmed the hair-colour as brown and eyes dark-brown, and Argenti suggested a sketch artist come by later and try and draw a likeness from his description. 'About four-thirty to five, before you close.'

The manager agreed with a tight smile, some residual concern at how long he might be held up, and they left.

But then within half-an-hour of their return to Mulberry Street, they had a more up-to-date sighting. A New York Post reporter phoned to say they'd just received a possible sighting of Joan in her blue bonnet, 'On a number thirty-eight tram, heading north.'

Both telephones and electric rather than horse-drawn trams had exploded in number over the past four of five years. At first, there had been only a handful of tram lines and at most a hundred telephones in New York. Now there were almost sixty tram lines, and over five-thousand telephones.

'Where does the number thirty-eight line north-bound go?' Jameson asked, and Argenti was halfway through consulting a tram-line map when Lawrence commented:

'It goes up Sixth Avenue, culminating at Grand Central station.'

Jameson looked keenly at Argenti. 'Do you think he might be intending to take her out of town?'

'Possibility.' Argenti glanced at the clock, then lifted his jacket from his chair-back as he stood. 'But we might have a chance of catching them still there.'

* * *

'I didn't see anyone like that here — but I think I recall a girl with a blue bonnet at the fourth or fifth kiosk over there.'

Argenti and Jameson surveyed behind them in the ticket foyer, following the ticket-clerk's gaze.

'Third and fourth kiosk windows in from the end,' Lawrence prompted. He'd either picked out the small numbers above the kiosk windows before them, or perhaps even remembered their positions from previous visits.

They'd gone at breakneck speed in Jameson's Hansom with Lawrence at the reins, not trusting the possible delays of public Hansoms. The first two clerks approached hadn't seen the girl either, nor had any suggestions. Now this possibility.

As they started their way across, the clerk they'd just turned from called out, 'Sam or Mack — girl with the blue bonnet? Thought I saw a girl like that standing in one of your queues twenty or thirty minutes back.'

Sam at kiosk four lifted one hand and smiled tautly as they approached. 'That'd be me. And what might be your interest in her, gentlemen?'

Argenti showed his badge. 'We fear she might be in danger.'

Sam's face had already started to drop as Jameson slid across that morning's *Post* front-page with Joan Bourke's re-touched colour photo. 'Oh, right. Can't say with certainty it was her. But the blue bonnet was for sure the same.'

'Could it have been her?' Jameson pressed. Then as the clerk studied the photo more intently, still undecided: 'Was her hair colour and appearance the same, for instance?'

'Yes, she had dark brown hair. She wasn't as blonde, for sure. And she was young too.'

'Was she with a man?' Argenti asked.

'Yes, she was. He was standing just behind her — but she bought the tickets for the both of them. Which I thought was a little odd: usually it's the men who buy the tickets.'

'Did you get a good look at him? Did he have a scar high on his forehead, did you notice?'

'Can't say I did. Like I say, he was standing just behind in her shadow, and he had his Derby pulled sharp down. Like he didn't really want to be noticed in any case.'

'And his age?' Jameson enquired.

'Eight or ten years older than her, maybe.' The clerk shrugged. 'He wasn't a young sapper like her, if that's what you mean.'

Argenti nodded thoughtfully. 'And where were they heading?'

The clerk briefly checked a register to one side. 'Syracuse or Corning, if I recall correctly.'

'Which platforms are those on?'

'Fourteen and eighteen.' The clerk pointed. 'Times and platforms are on the board over there.'

Corning? 'Maybe she's going to see her aunt,' Argenti commented to Jameson, a small jolt running through him as he noticed that the Corning train was due to leave in only three minutes. 'Though we might not have the time to find out.'

He'd already started into a run, Jameson as quickly following as the train times registered.

'At least four minutes more to check the Syracuse train,' Jameson commented halfway through their run, already his breath falling short. 'If she's not on the Corning train.'

They took stock for a moment on platform fourteen, catching their breath as they looked the length of the train. A few people leaning out of the windows talking, waving or blowing kisses goodbye to friends and relatives on the platform — but no sign of a girl in a blue bonnet.

'Nothing else for it, 'Jameson said, starting his way along. 'We'll have to check the length of the train.'

They made their way rapidly along, peering into every carriage as they went.

But halfway along, Argenti anxiously checked his pocket-watch. Only fifty seconds left before the train departed. They weren't going to be able to check its whole length.

Clouds of steam billowed out as the engine built up steam, drifting along the platform. And as the heaviest billows cleared, suddenly they could see a girl in a blue bonnet leaning out thirty yards ahead, peering back through the steam as if she was trying to discern someone along the platform. Then she pulled back in equally as sharply, urged by the man at her side.

'I think that might be her!' Argenti exclaimed, pointing.

They started running quicker alongside the train — but the girl also appeared to be going deeper along, then suddenly ducked down inside a compartment.

The guard's whistle went, it's shriek echoing along the platform. No time to decide!

Argenti held a hand up towards the guard and swung open the closest carriage door, and they leapt aboard as the train started moving.

* * *

Argenti and Jameson made their way urgently along the train, with Lawrence shadowing a couple of paces behind, checking every open carriage and closed compartment.

They looked perplexed as they reached the end of the last carriage and could see no sign of a young woman wearing a blue bonnet.

'Where could she have possibly gone?' Argenti aired. He looked keenly at Jameson. 'You saw her, didn't you? She was in clear view, leaning out of the carriage window.'

'Yes, I did.' Jameson looked back along the carriage as he considered the problem. 'Perhaps she doubled-back past us without us noticing. Or she's concealed in a toilet or wash-room we passed.'

They headed back the way they'd come, looking intently from side to side as they went. Stopping by the toilet at the end of the next carriage, Argenti wrapped hard on its door.

'Could you come out, please. We need to check on you.'

No answer. And Argenti was about to knock again when the latch slid back and a portly, middle-aged woman emerged.

'What's the meaning of...'

Argenti held up his badge, which quickly quelled her protests. 'I'm sorry to disturb you. But we needed to make sure you weren't the person we're seeking.'

The initial flushing in her face gave way to a gentle smile at the possible excitement. Then as quickly dropped.

'We're not in any danger, I hope?'

'No, I'm sure not,' Jameson answered, tipping his top hat courteously from a couple of paces away, hastening after Argenti who was quickly in full stride again.

Halfway along the fourth carriage, only a carriage short of where they first got on the train and started their search, Argenti suddenly stopped.

'Something I need to check back on.'

He walked back to the compartment two along that they'd just passed, Jameson and Lawrence hanging just behind, curious. And as Argenti looked towards the far corner of the compartment, he saw what in quick passing he thought he'd seen a moment ago: a bright blue bonnet tucked in half-out-of-sight beside the young woman sat there. His eyes lifted to her face: not Joan Bourke, but a reasonable resemblance.

'Is that your bonnet at your side?' he asked her.

She looked at it for a moment, as if contemplating her answer. 'Yes, it is.' Then — with Argenti's steady stare on her — more challengingly: 'And what of it?'

Argenti ignored the return question. 'And were you

wearing that same hat as you put your head out of the train window a moment before the train left?'

'Yes, I did,' she answered after another brief contemplative pause; though this time with the intensity of Argenti's stare, she thought better of another, *And what of it?*

'Then why did you duck back in so sharply, then remove the hat once inside the train?' he pressed.

'I.... It... it almost blew off when I looked out.'

Argenti continued to stare at her. He didn't believe her for a moment. There hadn't been an ounce of breeze inside the station.

Jameson's attention was meanwhile drawn to the man at her side. Early thirties, he was studiously reading his newspaper and trying to ignore the confrontation.

'And are you with this lady?' Jameson asked him.

'Yes, I am.' But the man only half-folded down his newspaper as he answered; and, as the ticket-clerk had described, he had his Derby pulled down sharply and hardly looked up.

'Look at me when I address you!' The action was so quick, it caught the man by surprise. Jameson flipped the man's Derby up with the tip of his walking stick, so that it lifted clear of his forehead and exposed a few inches of hair.

The man was on his feet, reaching for Jameson's lapels. But Jameson quickly side-stepped, raising the silver Anubis-head of his walking stick in a threatening, coshing motion.

Argenti got between them, showing his badge. 'A good idea if we maintain some calm, don't you think?' His glare was aimed more at the man than Jameson. Hair quite neat, not unruly, Argenti noted; and no forehead scar. 'But I will need some answers from the two of you. First of all, why you displayed your blue bonnet so openly, then were quick to hide it away?' Argenti's gaze shifted to the man. 'And why you seemed so keen to keep your face hidden?'

The couple looked awkwardly at each other, then the man shrugged. 'Not a law against it, is there?'

Jameson sighed tiredly, quickly losing patience again. He thrust the front page of the New York Post in their faces. 'There is when the blue bonnet your girlfriend is wearing is identical to that of a missing girl — with half of New York's finest desperately searching for her.'

The girl's face dropped, and she looked at her partner anxiously again for a moment.

'I had no idea,' she said.

'No idea *what*?' Jameson asked with an even more impatient edge.

'No idea that's what the man intended.'

Argenti looked at her sharply. 'Which man?'

'The man who gave us the money to board this train today, with me wearing this blue bonnet.'

* * *

In the following minutes, they gained the full details: a man had approached them on the southern end of Central Park, and asked if they would, as a couple, catch the number 38 tram to Grand Central Station, then board the train to Corning. They were given the fair for the journey, plus another $30 for the task.

'That's half as much again as I earn in a whole week,' the man explained.

'Plus he assured us there would be no risk,' the girl supported. 'All I had to do was wear the bonnet where I'd be visible from the street on the tram, then poke my head out the train window just before departure — but pull sharply back in again if it looked like I'd been noticed by anyone.' She smiled wanly at Argenti, as if in apology for her actions. 'I had no idea you were a policeman.'

Jameson interjected, 'And you had no idea that something might be amiss when he offered such a high payment for your troubles?'

'No, we didn't. I'm sorry.' But the girl looked more at Argenti as she said it, before looking down in contrition.

'But you obviously both got a good look at this man,' Argenti said.

'Yes, we did,' the girl answered.

'And tell me — did he happen to have a scar on the right-hand side of his forehead?' Argenti touched his own forehead to indicate.

'Yes, he did, now you come to mention it.'

* * *

Argenti and Jameson found an empty compartment three along to confer, with Lawrence standing by its entrance, as if guarding against someone else coming in and interrupting.

'Well, it certainly looks as if it has been a ruse,' Jameson commented.

'And that the man with the scar on his forehead is at the centre of it.' Argenti's expression was taut. 'But at least we've now got a couple of other sightings of him — enough hopefully to get an accurate sketch-artist's impression.'

Argenti had arranged a time for the couple to come into Mulberry Street and left them with a stern warning that if they didn't show up, there'd be a warrant out for their arrest. 'And we'll have further questions for you then too. You're going to have to work for the thirty dollars this man gave you.'

Jameson commented now, 'You have no reserve of doubt about their account?'

Argenti considered for a moment. 'No. I think they're

telling the truth. Too much of a wild story to make up — and they're both saying the same thing.'

Jameson nodded after a second. 'I wonder too if he might have set up other couples with similar ruses. And, if so, how many?'

'We're not going to know until we get back to Mulberry Street to check.' Argenti glanced out at the farm fields hurtling by their window. 'Probably an hour or more to the next stop. Then almost another two hours to get back.'

'Not necessarily.' Jameson turned to the door at their side and slid its window down, looking out, his gaze shifting between the fields rolling by and the approaching terrain.

'You're not thinking of jumping out, are you?' Argenti leered crookedly.

'Forty-six to forty-seven miles an hour,' Lawrence said matter-of-factly. 'Risk of serious injury, or even death.'

'No, I'm not,' Jameson said flatly. 'I know some might consider me mad, but...' His gaze was drawn back to the fields and woodland rolling furiously by. 'Just trying to judge the best place for the train to stop.'

'Stop? But why on earth would the train...' Argenti's voice trailed off as he saw Jameson's gaze drift to the emergency cord. 'Now I can't recall the exact statute — but it's my duty as a police officer to inform you that it's illegal to pull an emergency cord unless it's a real emergency.'

But Jameson could pick up the smile in Argenti's voice and teasing the corner of his mouth. 'This is a *real* emergency,' Jameson said. 'We're in the middle of a murder investigation, and we can't afford to lose two vital hours during which a young girl might be butchered.'

Argenti nodded solemnly. 'Can't argue with that.'

Although something appeared to be holding Jameson back. One hand hovered by the emergency cord, his gaze increasingly frantic between the ground rolling past and the view ahead.

'What is it?' Argenti pressed.

Jameson didn't answer, simply held one hand up like a conductor waiting for the right moment to bring in the horn section, his gaze fixed steadfastly ahead out of the train window.

And finally he brought the hand down and pulled the cord in the same instant.

A suspended second, and then the screech of the brakes, steel on steel, was deafening. They found themselves thrown forward at first with a jerk, then it was as if they were fighting against gravity as the train rapidly slowed and finally ground to a halt.

'Ah, slight miscalculation,' Jameson commented, looking out. 'I didn't realize the train would stop so swiftly — so it's a slightly longer walk to the town ahead than I anticipated.'

CHAPTER TEN

Ah, what a caper. What joy to watch you and half of New York's finest run around in pursuit of the 'Girl in a blue bonnet'.

You probably thought you were being clever, using the newspapers, some of them now with their new colour presses, to try and find this girl. After all, I've also shamelessly used the newspapers too for these messages to you, so why not?

The vital component you overlooked was that I too would read those same newspapers and take advantage of it. How many girls in blue bonnets can you effectively pursue — eight, ten? And when you've finally tracked them down, which one is the right one?

None, as you've now discovered. As soon as I saw the newspaper pictures, I made sure she didn't wear that blue bonnet again. That is, even if she's still alive. I needed to take my time with this one, ensure I had the time to remove and mark an organ, a matter on which I was remiss with the last girl.

Ah, but now you have another conundrum. Is the attached from the girl in the blue bonnet, or someone else? Unless or until you find her body, you won't know.

* * *

'He's making a fool of us!' Teddy Roosevelt banged one fist on his desk-top for emphasis.

'Yes. That would appear to be the intention,' Finley Jameson commented.

'*Intention*?' Roosevelt looked at Jameson sharply. 'Looks very much to me like he's been successful in that. Six girls tracked down in Manhattan and upstate New York, and all to no avail.'

Bill Griffin tamely raised a hand. 'Seven, sir. We had another sighting come in late in the day while Inspector Argenti and Mr Jameson were on their way back to Manhattan.'

Roosevelt shook his head and looked sternly at the men assembled the other side of his desk — Jameson and Argenti, Bill Griffin and two other leading department Inspectors, Joshua Cummings and Isaac Leven. 'Can you imagine what this fiasco has cost in resources? Good manpower that could have been allocated elsewhere.'

The group stayed silent, some shifting uncomfortably. They'd obviously rather be anywhere else than here at this moment.

Roosevelt looked more directly at Jameson and Argenti. 'And what about this organ sent to the New York Times at the same time as this letter. Does that tell us anything?'

Jameson answered. 'It's a human spleen, from a girl who I would hazard has not long finished puberty. So it could be from Joan Bourke.' He held a hand out. 'Or indeed, as the letter suggests, any other girl of a similar age.'

Roosevelt half-cupped his chin, stroking his moustache thoughtfully with one finger for a second. 'And the letter mentions marking the organ. What has been found on that front?'

'Certainly a clear marking there,' Jameson said. 'And it

appears to be a Hebrew letter or symbol, as discovered in previous cases.'

Roosevelt raised an eyebrow. 'Conversant in Hebrew?'

'No, sir. But a local Rabbi we used in our last investigation, Sabato Morais, left us a copy of the Hebrew alphabet.'

Argenti interjected. 'It appears to be the letter or symbol *Aleph* in Hebrew. But I've arranged a meeting with Rabbi Morais tomorrow to make sure of our identification of the letter.'

'I see. So some positive progress in the case, aside from this multiple 'blue-bonnet girl' fiasco.'

'Yes, sir.' Argenti nodded eagerly. The first positive note since they'd entered Roosevelt's office. 'And there has in fact been a benefit from this fiasco.'

'What is that?'

'In setting in motion these various 'girls in a blue bonnet', he's been close enough to a number of them for us to get a description — detailed enough for us to get a sketch artist to work on.'

Roosevelt glanced down at his desk for a moment. 'Yes, I saw your note about that. How is that progressing?'

'He's worked up quite a strong sketch portrait from three people so far, and they all describe quite a distinctive scar on the right-hand side of his forehead. Then one more to see later today for any adjustments and refinements to that sketch.'

Roosevelt held his palms out on his desktop. 'Then it's ready to go to the newspapers?'

'Yes.' Argenti was suddenly struck with an afterthought. He looked at Bill Griffin two seats away. 'On which front — that late appearance of a blue-bonnet girl. Did you get a description from her too?'

'No, we didn't.' Griffin gave a strained smile. 'By that time, we'd already had a few wild-goose chases, so there was no point in chasing another.'

'You didn't pursue that lead?'

'No, we didn't.' Flat, impatient tone. 'Little point.'

'Ah, except we now see where you were wrong,' Argenti said with an ingratiating smile. 'Because we see in fact that she could have given a description to further aid our sketch artist. Or she might have noticed something about him that the others already spoken to didn't pick up on.'

Tired, laboured breath from Griffin, his face flushed. 'I don't see why I should—'

'Gentlemen!' Roosevelt held a hand up, cut him short. 'We're in the middle of a murder investigation, so must remain calm and focused. Yes, Inspector Griffin, wasted police time is a factor — as I've already made perfectly clear. But Inspector Argenti also has a point, that sometimes that extra hour put in — going that extra mile — can yield results. So there are good and valid arguments on *both* sides.'

Roosevelt's political prowess coming to the fore again, Argenti considered, noticing Jameson next to him gently smile and nod his accord.

'But right now,' Roosevelt continued with a fresh breath, 'we have work to do — to catch this century's most notorious killer. No mean feat, I might add, given that we're also potentially facing the biggest internal corruption upheaval this police department has ever seen.'

Argenti felt Roosevelt's gaze sweep across all of them intently, searching. Had that gaze rested on Griffin longer than the others? *Or had it also lingered on himself a second longer?* Had news of his association with Maccione filtered back on the grapevine to Roosevelt — perhaps even through Griffin, eager to divert suspicion away from his own suspected involvement with Tierney. Argenti focused back. Roosevelt was addressing him directly.

'When will this sketch appear in the newspapers?'

'We aim to get it to them before tonight's presses roll. So hopefully it will be in tomorrow's editions.'

Roosevelt nodded. 'Then all we have to hope is that he doesn't do the same thing and we find ourselves chasing an army of young men with prominent forehead scars.'

It took a moment for the assembled group to realize that Roosevelt was jesting. Though they waited for the prompt of his own gentle smile before following suit with their own smiles.

CHAPTER ELEVEN

Most eyes in the crowd were on the trapeze artists swinging high up towards the roof-rafters at Madison Square Gardens.

Then, as they swooped down, their trajectory would pass the other acts on display on the three stages beneath them — a troop of acrobats in harem trousers, a lion-tamer whipping three lions back into their cages, and two fire-eaters trying to outdo each other with how far they could project flames from their mouths — the trapeze artists holding one arm out as they swung, as if to say, '*Look what else we've brought you*,' the edges of those flames below seeming almost to touch them at the lowest point of their arc.

The *Barnum and Bailey* Circus had drawn a crowd of almost eight-thousand to Madison Square Gardens for the early evening performance.

Bill Griffin was caught up in the spectacle, as equally Michael Tierney next to him appeared to be.

'*Jeez*. What next?' Tierney muttered, his eyes drawn to the mock chariot race starting up on the circuit surrounding the three central rings. 'So much for yer bright idea of us meetin' up here.'

'I thought with the number of people here and the distractions on show, nobody should notice us.'

Tierney's eyes reflected the flaming torches around the arena and the brighter bursts of the flame-throwers for a moment.

'You were right 'bout that.'

Besides, I could hardly police-log another investigation at your Fulton Street building — it would have looked suspicious.' Griffin shrugged. 'And meeting at any of your clubs and bars would have been risky as well.'

What Griffin held back from saying was that he was keen to avoid a repeat of his last encounter with Tierney — held inches away from a sheer drop. Tierney wouldn't risk trying to harm or kill him among such a large crowd. But as an extra insurance, he'd also come along with Tom Henderson. Two of them killed would be a ludicrous risk and, besides, then Tierney would be left with nobody to do his bidding at Mulberry Street.

The only thing to unsettle Griffin was that Monahan had taken a seat behind them. Tom Henderson was the other side of him to Tierney, and he'd expected Monahan to take the seat on the far side of Tierney — the four of them in a row.

Tierney's leer at the spectacle subsided. 'Let's get to what we're here fer. What news?'

Griffin handed across that morning's *New York Post*, prodding at its cover. 'They spent much of yesterday getting a sketch-artist to do a mock-up.'

Tierney studied the artist's impression for a moment, then reached a hand up by his right shoulder without looking back. A copy of the *New York Times* was slipped into his hand by Monahan.

Tierney spent a moment longer comparing the two. 'Same picture by th' looks of it — only the *Post* has it in colour.'

'Yes. They made sure they got the sketch to all the majors late last night. I think all but one ran with it.'

'An' what's the news inside at Mulberry Street? Do they think this is the Ripper back again?'

'They know it's not the last man they had pegged for it — Eugene Dove, that's for sure. Too young, different facially, no forehead scar with Dove. But whether this man is working with Dove or is just a fresh killer, they haven't yet made up their minds.'

'And what do *you* think?'

'It's primarily Argenti and Jameson's investigation, has been from the start. I and other departments only get roped in on it when the load spills over — such as with this blue-bonnet girl fiasco.'

Tierney peered sharper at Griffin. 'Are yer sayin' you might not be that much use to me?'

As if on cue, Griffin felt Monahan's large hands grip his shoulders lightly from behind. A lump rose in his throat. At his last confrontation with Tierney, the only thing to save him at the last moment from a twenty-story sheer drop had been his promise of getting inside information from Mulberry Street the minute it happened. He looked straight ahead, his stomach plummeting. The lights from the flaming torches around the central stages only shone back so far; the back six or seven rows, where they were sat, were in pitch blackness.

He'd heard stories about Monahan silently snapping men's necks or running knives through their gullets in crowded cafes or horse-racing crowds, and hardly anyone around had noticed. Not a single reliable witness! It suddenly hit him with a sinking sensation that he wasn't safe after all. Among a crowd of this size, and in virtual darkness, Monahan could kill him easily and slip away unnoticed. As for Henderson, perhaps he'd been in on it, Tierney assuring him that as long as he stayed silent, he'd take over as his main contact man at Mulberry Street.

'Of... of course not,' Griffin stammered. 'I just thought that your main concern was with Roosevelt's internal corruption enquiry, that's all.'

Tierney nodded slowly, and Monahan's massaging of his shoulders became gradually heavier, one hand sliding up to rub his neck. Griffin's heart pounded heavily, not helped by the heavy thuds vibrating up towards them as a succession of eight elephants were led out and started parading around the circuit where moments beforehand the chariots had been racing.

Tierney watched the elephants for a moment in appreciation. 'Quite a spectacle. I doubt that anyone would be bothering to look at anythin' else at this moment, eh?'

'I suppose not.' Griffin swallowed, the pressure against his shoulders and neck getting heavier.

A suspended moment, which to Griffin seemed to last forever, then Tierney looked back at him keenly. 'I need t' know *everything* that goes on at Mulberry Street.' Tierney's gaze intensified. 'Every little thing tha' might grab our dear Mr Roosevelt's fancy. Is that clear?'

'Yes, that's clear,' Griffin said, his voice strained, barely audible above the noise from the arena. Although it was a moment more, after an imperceptible nod from Tierney — his gaze fixing ahead again at the spectacle of elephants, jugglers, trapeze artists and fire-eaters — before Monahan's grip from behind slackened and his hands finally slid away.

'Because yer see, this time I have somethin' valuable for you to pass back to Mulberry Street.' Tierney kept his gaze straight ahead a moment longer before looking back directly at Griffin. 'That man sketched in the newspapers. I think I know who it is.'

CHAPTER TWELVE

Joseph Argenti walked into Brown's restaurant at just after 9.18 am and ordered a breakfast of pancakes with maple syrup, which he washed down with a large mug of strong black coffee.

When he was finished twenty-three minutes later, he paid at the cash-desk, got a timed receipt, and left. Then only eight minutes later, having ambled meanwhile looking aimlessly in some shop windows in the nearby northern stretch of the Bowery, he returned and went straight into one of its curtained booths on the far side. Usually used for show-girls and prostitutes to do nude table dances for customers, at this early hour only two girls could be seen working the half-full restaurant. Most of the curtained booths were unoccupied.

Argenti waited only six minutes, at times tapping his fingers impatiently on the table, before the curtain slid back and Enzio Maccione walked in, carrying two glasses. He passed one to Argenti.

'I got you just a lemon. But you can have a shot of Campari in yours as well, if you like.'

'No, that's okay, thanks.' Joseph looked across. Maccione's drink had an amber hue to it, and a slice of lemon in as well. Too early usually to be drinking, but perhaps with Joseph's urgent call for a meeting, Maccione suspected he'd be broaching a tough issue.

The other thing to strike him was Maccione's dress. Usually dapper and stylish, with tan suits, silver or royal blue cravats and embroidered waistcoats — today Maccione's dress was drab and non-descript: dark trousers and brown jacket, with a dark fawn wool shirt. Maccione could have been one of many of the area's factory or sweat-shop workers — which was perhaps what he'd intended with Joseph stressing that their meeting should go unnoticed.

A brown Derby hat pulled down sharply completed the picture — he only recognized Maccione when Maccione looked at him directly. Though perhaps he'd have guessed from the Campari and lemon, he thought with a wry smile; the only remaining hint of style to give Maccione away, and certainly not something any local Bowery worker would drink. Yet it also reminded Argenti uncomfortably of another Derby pulled down to conceal a forehead scar. The main issue he'd come to discuss with Maccione today. He slid across yesterday's *Post* front page.

'I understand you know this man.' A flat statement rather than a question.

Maccione nodded slowly, solemnly. 'Yes, I do.'

'Then why didn't you tell me? Warn me.'

'I tried to.' Maccione gestured helplessly. 'I sent a message as soon as I saw the newspapers — but you didn't respond.'

'Oh, I see.' *So that's what that note had been about*. One of Maccione's young Italian street-runners had called at his door with a note two nights back requesting an urgent meeting. Argenti gestured back equally as helplessly. 'Why didn't you put something in the note about that? I thought it was simply you following up on your favourite subject: your ongoing battle with Michael Tierney.'

Maccione nodded slowly, sipped at his Campari and lemon. 'I thought given the delicate nature of the information, it was best not to put anything in the note. Who did in fact tell you that I might know this man?'

'It came from no less than Commissioner Roosevelt.' Joseph grimaced tautly. 'And he added that he understood that I had some sort of association with this 'Enzio Maccione — who I hear is a rising gangster in this city'.'

'Glad to see my reputation precedes me.' Maccione smiled crookedly. 'But I think that both you and I know that very few would describe me in such illustrious terms, and one of those is in fact Michael Tierney.'

'Yes, that struck me also.' Joseph sighed. 'Because I don't think Roosevelt would have drawn such a conclusion on his own. I think the information had been fed to him.'

Argenti took the first sip of his lemon. Maccione looked at him keenly.

'And do you have an idea who that might be?'

'My suspicion is Bill Griffin. There were allegations a couple of years ago that he was associated with Tierney, but he was finally cleared of those charges. Since then, he's been particularly sensitive and careful about any continuing contact with Tierney.'

Maccione smiled gently. 'As you are being with me.' His expression became more sober. 'And with good reason.'

'Especially now with fresh claims about our possible association.' Joseph eased a tired breath. 'Just what I've been trying to avoid all along.'

They were silent for a moment.

'But at least that then gives us possible motive,' Maccione said. 'With Roosevelt's anti-corruption stance, they're keen to feed that, give him names.' Maccione gestured. 'Because at the same time it diverts attention away from their own association with Tierney.'

· 'I thought much the same.' Joseph nodded eagerly. 'But it still doesn't answer or explain how and why you know this man, Frank Campbell.' Joseph prodded the *Post* picture. 'And his connection now with these fresh murders.'

'As I said, I know him. I can't deny that.' Maccione softly shook his head. 'But how and why he might be involved in these murders is beyond me also.'

'There's no doubt that he was seen with a number of these blue-bonnet girls the other day — we have no less than three direct eye-witnesses.'

'But not directly with any of the girls murdered?'

No,' Joseph said cautiously. Jameson had raised exactly the same point the day before when they'd discussed the matter in depth: '*The sketch is certainly not Eugene Dove or even a close resemblance. Yet the letters proclaim that it's the Ripper returned. Even if it's some sort of copycat killer, you'd have thought they wouldn't make a crucial error like that.*' Argenti had agreed, but that wasn't something he'd share with Maccione now. He wanted Maccione's account afresh, without any prompts or guidance. He took a fresh breath. 'Perhaps the best place to start is how you know this man? How you first met?'

Maccione nodded gently, seemed to sink in on himself for a moment. 'We were introduced first of all by George Sheehan. And like Sheehan, Frank Campbell as he's now known, originally had an Italian name, Francesco Campanelli, but had anglicized it to become more accepted.'

'Why was that? Did he have a boxing career as well?' Argenti knew the history of George Sheehan, originally Georgio Salvacci, who had changed his name so that it was more accepted by boxing promoters and audiences.

'No. It was because most of the early work was with Irish gangs in New York.' Maccione stroked his forehead. 'But our association and the reason George Sheehan introduced us was that Francesco came from the same town as my family in Sicily, Marsala. And he was also a skilled knifeman.'

'A knifeman?' Argenti raised a brow sharply. 'So he'd have certainly had the skills for killing these girls.'

'Yes, he would.' Maccione exhaled wearily. 'Except I've never known Francesco, Frank, to harm or kill a woman before. He kept strictly to men — and bad men at that.'

Argenti was thoughtful for a moment, assessing the information. 'And did you ever use Frank?'

Maccione smiled gently. 'Even if I had, I couldn't share that with you. Would possibly incriminate both Francesco and myself, if and when you catch up with him.' Maccione shrugged. 'Besides, you probably have enough on your shoulders without possibly holding back anything incriminating from me. If you didn't share it at Mulberry Street, it would reflect badly on you — so perhaps best you don't know.' A dry smile teased the corner of his mouth. 'Suffice to say, if you're ever asked, that since I'm a skilled knifeman myself, why would I ever need Frank Campbell's services?'

Argenti took a sip of lemon, nodded. 'I've already played down our association, for obvious reasons. Told Roosevelt straight that I knew nothing about your criminal activities — that I simply know you as an importer and supplier of provisions to many Italian stores in the city, of which my wife is a partner in one. Nothing beyond that.'

'And did he accept that?'

'It appears so.' Argenti grimaced. 'Don't forget, I have a clean sheet so far at Mulberry Street — unlike Griffin. So I don't think it was lost on Roosevelt when I said he might do better to question the source of that information. That it might be a diversionary tactic from other associations going on.'

'Playing them at their own game.' Maccione's smile broadened for a second before he became more serious. 'But I appreciate the risk you've taken in seeing me, Joseph. So, what now?'

'We obviously need to urgently find Frank Campbell, Francesco — if you might know where is?'

Maccione gestured. 'But won't me supplying you with that information go against your claim of us not having any association?'

'It could have come from a score of other sources in the course of my investigation. I'll cover with those.' Joseph looked across keenly. 'Don't worry, you won't appear as a 'snitch' — in my world or yours.'

Maccione contemplated for a moment, took a fresh breath. 'Thing is, as soon as I saw the newspapers, I went to see Francesco at the two places I'd normally find him. He wasn't at either. I fear that with his photo across half of Manhattan, he'll have gone deep into hiding.'

'Are you saying you won't be able to help?'

'No, I'll try, Joseph — in respect of our association that nobody knows anything about.' That faint tease again at the corner of his mouth. 'Just that it might be difficult.'

CHAPTER THIRTEEN

You disappoint me. I'd have thought you'd have found Joan Bourke's body by now. Half the police of Manhattan assigned trying to find this blue-bonnet girl, but then you can't seem to find her body even when it's put in the most obvious of places. In this case, an old stamping ground.

Did you not appreciate that much of this now is about making amends for past mistakes? Things that I might have got wrong last time put right now. But then it also gives you the same opportunity. Elements you might have got wrong in the investigation before, you have the chance of examining again now and remedying. How many of us get such second chances?

Now you have two organs to inspect and, when you've finally found that second body, two young girls' bodies as well. Except that with the first girl, Lucy Bowen, she was completely intact, no internal organs removed. So now you're faced with the same conundrum as last time. Will there be a third girl's body to match that other organ removed, or has it come simply from a waif or stray that you'll never find? Or indeed removed from one of the many cadavers of this city's hospitals and morgues?

* * *

It was dark inside the warehouse building, the last of the light seeping through a soot-and grime-stained window high up. A Constable stood with an oil lamp to one side of the body to illuminate the area.

Finley Jameson had spent the last few minutes crouching down examining the body with Lawrence close to his side. Joseph Argenti was with John Whelan on the opposite side of the body, looking on. Whelan had his notebook out, but had entered little so far.

'It certainly appears to be Joan Bourke,' Jameson announced as he studied the face closer.

'I thought as much.' Argent nodded forlornly. Although a heavy swathe of blood, now reddish-brown, ran from her breastbone to her hips, her face had only partial blood smears. Obviously, Jameson didn't want to clear those away to make identification a hundred-percent sure — that would be left until full autopsy at Bellevue — but there was sufficient with the fifty to sixty percent of the face visible to be reasonably sure it was Joan Bourke.

Jameson studied some bruising on Joan's neck and one shoulder before concentrating on the main stomach and abdomen wounds below.

'Four of five knife thrusts by the looks of it, probably from a long implement, six or seven inches. But difficult to tell the exact number of knife thrusts at this stage, due to the larger incision at their centre.'

'And does that larger incision indicate what organ might have been removed?' Argenti asked.

'Difficult to say...' Jameson leant in closer, lifting up one hand.

Lawrence reached into Jameson's leather medical bag to

one side, took out a large loop and passed it into his outstretched hand.

No words spoken between the two of them, their routine now so practiced that often only a small signal — combined with the point of procedure in an examination — was all that was required.

Jameson spent a moment more examining with the loop before straightening up. 'I'm afraid it's difficult to tell at this stage before a full examination. There are two or three possible organs such an incision would lead to.'

'And is one of those the kidney?' The organ that had arrived with the letter that morning at the *New York Times*.

'Yes, it is.' Jameson sighed, checked his stopwatch. 'Will the photographer be here soon? Because obviously we can't move her until he's done his bit.'

Argenti nodded. The new directive at Mulberry Street since Roosevelt had taken over. All crime scenes to be photographed.

'He shouldn't be long now. He was getting all his equipment together when we left — said he'd catch up with us.' With the pregnant pause following, Argenti was reminded of something he wanted to check meanwhile. 'I wondered if we could all go outside for a moment.'

Jameson, Lawrence and John Whelan took the prompt, but the Constable with the oil lamp paused uncertainly.

'You too — because I want in particular to look at light values and possible visibility for anyone passing here.'

They all walked towards the door where they'd entered five yards away.

Outside on the cobbles-stoned dockside, Argenti first of all tried to look in through the high window closest in line with the body. Only on tip-toe could he see in, but the lower panes were particularly grimy. He could hardly see anything inside — certainly not the body four yards back. Then he half-opened the door they'd come through and looked in. He could only pick out the first few yards, Joan Bourke's body was still in shadow beyond.

'What's troubling you?' Jameson enquired.

'I'm trying to work out why in the few days she's been missing, her body wasn't seen by anyone passing.'

'She could have been left here just yesterday. I won't know until I examine back at Bellevue, look at internal organ lividity.'

'But, still, even in that time...'

Jameson looked from the dilapidated warehouse across the cobbled dockside to the East River forty yards away.

'Not the busiest or most inhabited of areas. Except for rats and perhaps passing vagrants and tramps.'

'True.' Argenti joined him in surveying the area for a moment, a slight chill breeze drifting from the river.

It was a stretch of dockside they both knew well. Though the chill breeze from the river had been far more intense the night of their showdown with the Ripper, Eugene Dove. He'd emerged with a prostitute from the very same warehouse that night, then played a knife against gun jousting session with the girl in front of them, the two of them stood powerless thirty yards away under threat that Dove would kill the girl if they moved closer.

The girl that night had appeared to win the joust, Dove's body falling into the dockside water, a facial bullet wound clearly visible as his body floated back up. But they'd later discovered it had probably been a ruse, Dove's death faked.

Could that be what the letter that morning had referred to? *Elements you might have got wrong in the investigation before that you have the chance of examining again now...*

He'd spent much of the day brainstorming with Jameson what that might have referred to: Brogan's copy-killing, Jameson at one point a suspect, their close call at the opera

— they'd even visited the opera house and got a manager to open up a few back store rooms that might not have been inspected for a while — their missing Dove for a second time when he'd resurfaced to challenge another murderer... before Jameson finally hit on that first climactic confrontation with Dove.

'That's certainly the night we got most things wrong with Dove... partly because that's what he'd planned and intended all along.'

They'd got down to the dockside early evening, just as the sun was starting to dip below Manhattan's skyline and the warehouse buildings behind.

'One last thing I'd like to test,' Argenti said. He beckoned the Constable with the oil lamp. 'I wondered if you could stand just by the open door with your lamp.'

The Constable moved into position and Argenti looked into the warehouse again. As he noticed Jameson observing him curiously, he commented, 'I'm trying to replicate daylight as closely as possible. See what a passer-by might have seen in daylight.'

After a moment for his eyes to adjust to the light, he still couldn't discern more than a few yards inside. The brighter light only filtered in so far. Joan Bourke's body was just a vague shape beyond, still mostly obscured in shadow. Could have been just a bundle of rags, lost among the other rubbish, rags, rotting wood and crates strewn across the warehouse floor.

He looked around with the clatter and rattle of an approaching horse-drawn Hansom. It stopped ten yards short of them and a man in his late thirties with wild, unkempt hair, carrying a large leather holdall and tripod stepped down. Mulberry Street photographer, Eric Morrison, had arrived.

* * *

Argenti left Jameson and Lawrence alone for the first twenty minutes of Joan Bourke's autopsy, electing to smoke a cheroot cigar in the corridor outside the examination room. It wasn't so much that this was the bloodiest part of any examination, he'd become battle-hardened by countless autopsies over the years, but the fact that he felt redundant. This was Jameson's and Lawrence's area of expertise, and they'd probably work better without his eager eye observing their every move.

As he walked back in, Jameson looked his way, eased a tired breath. 'It is in fact Joan's kidney that's missing. So at least one part of the puzzle has been answered.'

Argenti nodded sombrely. 'But what about the main part of the puzzle? Does it look like the Ripper's... Dove's handiwork?'

'If it's not, then it's a handiwork so close that it's almost impossible for me to discern the difference. The same seven-inch slim blade, the same angle and style of stabbing motion. With the other copy-killers we've had since, that difference could be seen on closer examination.' Jameson sighed heavier. 'I can't say the same in this case.'

Argenti took in Joan Bourke's broken body in more detail, her torso now cleaned of blood, the knife wounds and the larger aperture where her kidney had been removed now clearer under the stark gaslight. The heat from the gas-lamps was insufferable in the small room, the mixed smell of body waste and formaldehyde heavy in the air. Argenti grimaced.

'The question is, how best to present that news to Roosevelt and Watkins, seeing as they're so keen to play down the Ripper possibly returning. Not unduly cause public alarm.'

'I'm not sure that a close-copy killer would be any less alarming to the public. And we've already steered away as much as we can from that likelihood.' Jameson dabbed at his brow with the back of one hand. 'Maybe in part because we're concerned that his return also reflects badly on us. We failed in stopping him before.'

'So you're saying we're equally guilty in playing along with Mayor Watkin's aim of 'public calming'?'

'Maybe subconsciously we are.' Jameson spent a moment studying and probing Joan Bourke's liver in a petri dish at his side. 'By the way, blood lividity in the body suggests it was where we found it in the warehouse for forty to forty-five hours, and that she was probably killed an hour or so before that and moved quite quickly.' Jameson took a fresh breath. 'I think now we should just pass on the information as we find it — leave the juggling of politics of how that information is presented to the public to Roosevelt and Watson. After all, I can't say with all certainty it's Dove, the Ripper returned. It could be just a very thorough facsimile.'

Argenti nodded, but his thoughts now were mainly on the blood-lividity timescale. 'So it appears she was killed some time two nights ago?'

'It would appear so. Certainly after dusk.'

Argenti considered: killed at dusk, or certainly within the last hours of daylight, then the body moved and deposited by the dockside under cover of darkness. His earlier thoughts about Joan's body being placed there sprung back.

'That little test I ran earlier, looking into the warehouse to judge if a passer-by might see the body easily. One thing puzzled me: why admonish us for not already finding the body — yet hide it away so?' Argenti gestured. 'It could have stayed there for another day or two before a vagrant sneaked in there for refuge on a cold night and stumbled across it.'

'Perhaps it was his intention to admonish us. After all, that has been his tone throughout — teasing, playing games with us.'

'Unless where we've found Joan Bourke now was somehow symbolic. Perhaps exactly the spot that he had Maureen

Blythe tied up that night before bringing her out for that little jousting show for us.'

Jameson looked at him sharply. 'Then that would make it far more likely that it is Dove again now, rather than a very precise copy-killer.'

'Except that the confrontation that night with Dove and his body found in the dockside waters was widely reported in the newspapers.'

'Yes, it was.' Jameson nodded keenly. 'But not the girl emerging from the warehouse behind, let alone a specific position in that warehouse. Only Dove would have been privy to that information. Indeed, outside of that, only you and I were aware that she emerged from part of the warehouse, then subsequently Commissioner Latham. It could make Watkins' and Roosevelt's political juggling with public furore over the Ripper's possible return far more acute.'

With Jameson's accompanying pained smile, Argenti wasn't sure if he was concerned by that added factor, or just thankful that the responsibility of how that would be handled with the public wouldn't be his. It would be left to Watkins and Roosevelt.

'But as you've rightly said before, Roosevelt is a very accomplished politician — so perhaps he'll simply take something like this in his stride.'

'Yes, I daresay he might.' Jameson's pained smile as quickly faded as he instructed Lawrence to finish up with any final examination and notes, then took off his leather morgue apron. 'But right now I have my own presentation problems to face. I have to go and tell Ellie that another of her girls has been found dead, and it's not going to be easy.'

* * *

Two days Frank Campbell had been in the same room without going out — without *daring* to go out — and it had felt as if the walls were closing in tighter with each passing hour. It felt smaller now than when he'd first arrived.

But maybe that was partly because he'd paced it numerous times since; part agitation, part exercise, to get a break from sitting on his rump — but always the same three paces each way. Hardly bigger than a prison cell.

Except that instead of a jailer bringing him regular slops, he had a fourteen-year-old street-boy bringing him meals from local pie and burger shops and stalls. A young member of the local 'Hudson's Dusters' gang, who if he wasn't bringing him food, no doubt would have been running betting slips or other errands for Don Mahler, head of the Dusters.

Frank had done some work for Mahler a year or so back, so Mahler had taken pity on his plight — after some explaining.

Mahler had looked down for a long moment after he'd finished his account, was slow in looking back up again.

'So, you're saying you didn't knife or kill any of these girls?'

'No. I was only involved in setting up the blue-bonnet girl chase for the police, and I didn't harm her either.'

Mahler had contemplated him steadily for a moment. An office rich with mahogany and sports trophies in cabinets, the smell of Mahler's chain-smoked cigars heavy in the air — a far cry from his fetid, cockroach-infested box of a room now.

'An' what story were you given for that?'

'He said that the police had old charges against her for prostitution and vagrancy, and she was held as a 'ward' at the Beth Jacobs instead. Once she got out of there, they wanted to lock her up again. He said that she simply wanted to work the streets again, might shift to Philadelphia or Chicago to do it.'

'You say *he*? Do you think the man who span you this story might have been the murderer of these girls?'

'I don't know. I only saw the second girl for a moment across the road from Bloomingdales — so I could have sight of the type of blue bonnet needed for the other girls. But she was just a girl who'd 'disappeared' then, not dead.' Campbell shrugged. 'So he might have just been another go-between, like me.'

'What did he look like?'

'Ten years older. Hair a shade lighter than mine, but cut shorter. Wiry build, maybe an inch taller than me.' Campbell grimaced. 'Thinking about it, maybe I should have doubted his story a bit more.'

Mahler nodded thoughtfully, pulled on his cigar. 'Perhaps why they came up with a story they knew would appeal to you — street girl in distress and giving the police the run around. Must admit, it would have appealed to me too. One hell of a run-around you gave to half the police in Manhattan over that girl.' Mahler smiled, waved his cigar to one side.

'I suppose.' Campbell returned the smile tentatively, unsure whether Mahler was just humouring him. Trying to make him feel like less of a mug for falling for it.

Mahler as quickly became serious again. 'But why me?'

'I wanted to keep as far away from the East Side as possible.'

'Okay.' Mahler nodded slowly. That seemed to make sense to him. 'I gotta couple of bolt-hole rooms in a building two blocks from the river. Nobody should find you there.' Mahler took a key from his cigar box and handed it across, so Campbell got the impression that Mahler had already pretty well decided in advance to help. 'Bobby, one of my boys, will show you where it is and bring you food and groceries.'

He got up and nodded from the half-open door, 'Thanks.'

Mahler shrugged it off, as if it was nothing or that

'Thanks' might be misplaced. 'It's the best I can do. Building should have been condemned years back, so don't expect no comforts.'

No comforts. Mahler hadn't been kidding. Yellow and green mildew patches showed on the walls, the air heavy with the smell of rotting damp and sewerage.

When he was pacing the room in daylight, he could dodge the cockroaches skittering across; but at night he'd squished a couple under his feet. The muted clank and rattle of passing trams and dray horses drifted up to his room from the streets, and in the distance the occasional hoot of barges and ships on the Hudson River.

He lit a cigar. He was smoking twice as much as normal, and most of those cigars. Maybe the anxiety, but he suspected it was as much to cut himself off from his surroundings. Closing his eyes, with the smell of cigar smoke redolent around him, he could imagine he was back in Mahler's mahogany-lined office. Or at the Waldorf with a couple of young showgirls each side of him.

Perhaps one with a blue bonnet...

His eyes snapped open again.

Faint rustling outside his door. He moved closer to it, leaning in to pick out sounds from the corridor. Faint rustling again, then nothing.

His heart was in his throat. Over an hour before Bobby was due to bring him lunch, and in any case Booby would knock. Two rapid sharp knocks, then another after a long pause. The signal. But there was nothing. Only a faint shuffling the other side. He put his ear closer to the door, could pick out shallow breathing too.

Then finally after a long, suspended moment, his own breathing held meanwhile, the shallow breathing the other side receded, as did the footsteps, moving away down the corridor. Silence again. No movement the other side of the door.

Campbell eased out his own breath and sat back down, took another heavy draw of his cigar. He sank back into his reverie too, imagining himself back at the Waldorf, the aroma of cigar smoke, polished mahogany and leather, a hint of French perfume from the girls at his side... and his cigar was halfway down as this time there was a heavy knocking at the door.

He shook his head as he got up. Perhaps it had been Bobby before, but he'd forgot something and gone back for it.

Then it struck him as his hand reached for the door bolt: three sharp knocks in quick succession. Why hadn't Bobby kept to the signal?

'Is that you Bobby?' he called out tentatively.

A heavy pause, then, 'No, it's me.'

Enzio Maccione! A voice he instantly recognized, but he was momentarily perplexed. What was Maccione doing here? How had Maccione found him?

'Are you going to let me in, then?' Maccione pressed.

'Yes, of course.' Frank Campbell slid back the bolt. A trusted old friend, Maccione posed no threat. Perhaps Maccione had some extra help to offer — some decent lodgings for a start — and Don Mahler had told him where he was. 'Did you come by my door a few moments ago?' Campbell asked as he opened the door.

'No, I didn't.' Maccione appeared equally perplexed, joining Campbell in looking behind him along the corridor.

The sound of another door opening, two doors down on the opposite side. An old lady with lank grey hair peered out, obviously curious about the fresh voices across the corridor from her.

They both looked at her for a moment, though Campbell

more cautiously so, keeping half in the shadow of the door-frame, his forehead scar concealed behind it. He'd done the same the couple of times she'd looked across when Bobby had been at the door, and Bobby had told him not to worry. *'Betty's just a busy-body, but she never goes out. So she won't have seen the newspapers. Besides, Betty can't read.'*

'No. But she can see pictures.'

'Even if she had, with her not bein' able to read the story at the side — she might think you're the new Mayor or a railway tycoon.'

He and Bobby had shared a laugh as they'd dived into the burgers Bobby had brought from a nearby stall. One of the few moments of light relief in the clawing tension of the past two days.

As Campbell shut the door behind them, Maccione commented, 'Perhaps it was her a few moments ago outside your door.'

'I don't think so.' Campbell related what Bobby had told him about Betty hardly every going out. 'So doubt she's seen the newspapers, either.'

'Shame the same couldn't be said for half of the rest of New York. No doubt why you're holed up here.' Maccione cast a glance around the decrepit room, took a fresh breath. 'Let's get to the problem faced now. There might in fact be some advice and help I can offer — but I couldn't even think of considering that if you've been involved in harming these girls.'

'No, I swear.' Campbell did a quick sign of the cross on his chest. 'I didn't touch them.' And under Maccione's intense stare, he shared the account he'd related to Don Mahler two days ago.

* * *

Betty Dalston squeezed the muslin pouch of tea as hard as she could in the boiling water she'd just poured in her cup. Tea was expensive, so she'd wrap a teaspoon of tea in a small muslin pouch first thing in the morning, then try and make it last all day.

The only problem was that her hands were frailer these days, the bones in her fingers aching the harder she pressed.

The man who'd called at the room across the hallway was still in her thoughts. Dapper and smart, not like the young scruff she'd seen at the door a couple of times before. She'd rarely seen his like before, especially in this building.

She'd stayed close by her door for a while afterwards, listening out. She thought she'd heard some raised voices at one point, then nothing afterwards. Silence again.

She'd moved away after a moment, nothing to hold her interest, and sat back down. Not long after she resumed her knitting again, looking at a grandfather clock periodically for when she should make her next tea. Living on her own now for twelve years since her husband died, if she didn't plan her day out carefully, the hours would drag. But even the knitting these days was telling on her fingers and wrist joints.

One last squeeze of the muslin pouch and she put it in a saucer to one side, ready to use again later.

But halfway back from the kitchen with her tea, she paused in thought. She couldn't recall now hearing the door closing with the man leaving. The doors were heavy, so she'd usually hear that from her room. *Perhaps he was still there?*

She took the first few sips of tea. But after a while, the grandfather clock like a metronome beat for her thoughts, her curiosity finally got the better of her. She shuffled back towards the door, one ear close to it, listening.

No faint sounds of mumbling, which she'd usually hear. Seemed like he *had* left. But then another sound suddenly reached her: the clank and grind of the tram making its way up Chapel Street, which she wouldn't normally hear her side of the building.

She tentatively opened her door, peered across the hallway. The man's door had been left half open — that explained it! Possibly his window too, judging by the sounds drifting up from Franklin Street three floors below.

She shuffled across — with her age, bulk and her aching leg joints, that was all she could manage — calling out as she approached the half-open door, 'Mister, it's Betty from across the way... you've left your door open.'

No response.

Even though it was open, she knocked on it — only polite — before calling out again, 'Your door is open. Are you okay?'

No response.

It was then that she noticed the bottom part of a body on the ground, one of its legs at an awkward angle.

She shuffled quickly towards it, repeating, 'Are you okay?'

But with still no response and the body remaining inert, she wasn't sure what to do. She couldn't see any sign of breathing, but if she crouched down to make sure, she might not get up again.

Then as she shifted angle around the body, she saw the small puncture mark on the far side of the man's neck, a four-inch line of coagulated blood trailing down from it.

A gasp caught in her throat, verging into a mumbled, 'Oh, no. Oh, my, my...*no*!'

She shuffled as quickly away. She doubted she'd make it down the three flights to the street. She'd knock on the Anderson's door five along; their son Ben who got groceries and ran errands for her might be kind enough to run and find the nearest policeman.

CHAPTER FOURTEEN

Joseph Argenti blinked to adjust his eyes back after the powder flash from the photographer.

'Is that the last of them?' he asked Eric Morrison.

'Just one more,' Morrison said, shifting his tripod and camera around to the far side of Frank Campbell's body laid prone on the ground.

A yard to his side, Finley Jameson and Lawrence also put one arm up to shield against the camera flash. With forensic photography only being utilized at Mulberry Street the past month with Roosevelt's arrival, Argenti was still adjusting to it. He'd got a potted history of its development on an earlier outing with Morrison: first employed by Alphonse Bertillon in Paris in 1890, it took a little while for the practice to become accepted with police forces elsewhere. 'London I believe only last year, then Stockholm and Berlin. Now New York.'

Jameson had insisted on a few moments privately inspecting the body before Morrison started with his camera and flash, concerned that the burning magnesium powder might contaminate the scene.

'How might that harm?' Argenti had asked.

'Well, for instance, if our victim was a non-smoker, the tell-tale smell of smoke or ash on his clothing might indicate that his killer was a smoker. The smell of a magnesium flash and its powder residue might obscure that.' Jameson straightened up and took a fresh breath. 'But from the level of smoke infusion in the victim's shirt, I would hazard that he was himself a heavy cigar smoker.'

Watching this exchange and the subsequent photography through the open door was Betty Dalston, young Ben Anderson who'd originally summoned a local police officer, and four others from along the corridor drawn by the police activity. Two Constables stood by the doorway to keep them back, and Argenti had informed both Ben Anderson and Betty Dalston that he'd need to speak to them in more detail once they'd finished their initial inspection of the body. Realizing it might take a little while, Betty had asked young Ben to get a chair from her room, and now sat observing a yard back from the doorway.

Argenti was assisted again by John Whelan, who started on some preliminary questions and note-taking with the group outside the door while Morrison finished up.

'I didn't see nothing,' young Ben said. 'I only ran to get the nearest policemen around the corner when Betty here tol' me what had happened.'

After asking which room Ben was from in the building, Whelan noted it and said he could go. He turned to Betty as Jameson crouched lower over the body.

'Quite a clean incision,' Jameson remarked, tracing one finger above the four-inch line of blood. 'Looks like our killer purposely missed the jugular, went straight up into the subdural cortex. That's why there's so little blood. Cause of death would have been internal bleeding rather than external.'

'And the advantages of that?'

'A far cleaner kill, less messy.' Jameson nodded towards the open door, and Argenti wondered whether that was in acknowledgement of Betty's exclaimed *'Quite smart and dapper, he was,'* before she'd gone into a closer huddle with John Whelan to take the rest of her statement. 'Also somewhat quicker with the shock to the brain and electric impulses cut.'

Lawrence at his side nodded. 'Only forty to fifty seconds from electrical impulses and motor functions being cut before death. Whereas with blood loss from a severed jugular, it can take up to two minutes.'

'Lawrence is perfectly correct, as usual.' Pained smile to indicate that some of that information was surplus to requirement. 'But fainting and unconsciousness can take place before that.' Jameson straightened up. 'Though of course we'll know more once we get the body back to Bellevue for a full examination. That's purely my first-sight prognosis.'

* * *

Argenti observed that Jameson was unusually quiet on the way to Bellevue. Something was on his mind — perhaps not relishing another autopsy so soon after Joan Bourke's — or it could be he was still emotionally drained after last night having to impart the news of her body being found to a tearful Ellie Cullen.

Argenti knew that Ellie felt very protective of her girls at the Beth Jacobs, so it might have felt like two failures: *hers* in not sufficiently protecting Lucy and now Joan, *theirs* in not putting a stop to the Ripper earlier, or his carbon-copy.

Lawrence was in the Hansom's upper-cab guiding its horse a steady ten yards behind the morgue wagon, while John

Whelan had headed straight back to Mulberry Street in the police Hansom to start typing up his notes.

After completing the brunt of his examination in the first half hour, Jameson got around to airing what was troubling him. Argenti sensed something was coming, because Jameson had commented to Lawrence, 'If you can leave us alone for a short while, Lawrence. You can finish up here later.' As soon as Lawrence had left the examination room, Jameson looked at Argenti sharply.

'We've seen something like this before, haven't we, Joseph?'

'I'm sorry. I'm not sure I follow you.'

'Don't play coy with me, Joseph. I'm your friend and partner — this isn't Latham or Roosevelt you're talking to now. That final night with Brogan and Ellie. The puncture wound and the severing of Brogan's subdural cortex with a thin stiletto knife was identical to this wound now.'

'You're saying it might be the same killer?'

'Yes, I am.' Jameson exhaled tiredly, wiping the blood from his hands with surgical spirit. 'And Whelan's and your questioning of that witness, Betty, in which she described that recent visitor's dress as particularly smart and dapper, with a silvery-blue cravat. How many men have that level of fine dress and are also skilled knifemen?'

'Well, you for a start — though your skill's mainly with surgery.' But as he met Jameson's steady stare, he looked down, knew his obfuscation sounded trite. The same concern had hit him as soon as he'd heard the description. *Enzio Maccione*! And now he was doing all he could to push that possibility away. 'I'm sorry, that was uncalled for.' He shook his head. 'But it couldn't possibly be Maccione — if he'd found where Frank Campbell was, he'd have told me.'

Jameson looked at Argenti incredulously. '*What*? You actually went to see Maccione about Campbell?'

'I didn't see a better way out. Roosevelt was already pressing me about a link between Maccione and Campbell, and in turn questioning about my own possible association with Maccione. I was walking a tightrope as it was.'

Jameson leered crookedly. 'And so you thought you'd risk crossing an even higher wire by meeting up with Maccione and talking about it, warning him.'

'*Warning* him?' Argenti shook his head, his voice strained. 'Of course not. I just wanted to find out if indeed he did have an association with Campbell and might know where he was.'

'Did anyone see you or know you were meeting Maccione?'

'No. I was very cautious.'

'And did Maccione know where Campbell was?'

'He said that he'd checked Campbell's usual couple of haunts, he wasn't there. But he'd try and find out where he was.'

'Obviously he *did* find where Campbell was, and went to see him without informing you.' Jameson drew a heavy breath and closed his eyes for a second, as if summoning strength. 'You can see how bad it looks, Joseph. You see Maccione over a suspected collusion with Campbell and the murders of both Lucy and Joan — then next thing Campbell is found dead, and it looks like Maccione was responsible.'

Joseph hung his head down for a second. 'I know. I *know*.' He looked up again more hopefully. 'But the substance of my conversation with Maccione shone a different light on things. He said that Campbell had never been known to harm girls, so Maccione didn't believe he could be involved with killing either Lucy or Joan. And you have to admit, Campbell wasn't seen by eye-witnesses directly either with Lucy or Joan — only with these blue-bonnet girl lookalikes.' It seemed odd, Joseph reflected ruefully, talking about Campbell with him laid inert on a slab only a yard away. 'So if Campbell didn't have anything to do with the girls' murders, and Maccione wasn't in any way implicated — why on earth would Maccione kill Campbell?'

'Yes, looked at that way it doesn't make sense.' A final thoughtful nod from Jameson. 'But the problem you face right now is that the description of the last person seen visiting Campbell sounds like Maccione. And the method of murder carries his trademark.' Jameson sighed heavily. 'Worse still, the dilemma that if you try to see him again to find out what happened — it might appear as if you've warned him off for now a second time. You'll have walked that tightrope too far, with no way back.'

CHAPTER FIFTEEN

Joseph Argenti hung his jacket up in the bedroom wardrobe and slid his leather holster and gun, a Remington .44, on the shelf above it, out of reach from the children.

He went back downstairs and stood uncertainly in the hallway for a moment. He'd already greeted Sophia as he'd come in, and now she was back in the kitchen, Marco and Pascal keeping her company, busy with colouring books at the kitchen table or playing snap or pairs.

Too noisy and hectic in there for his present mood, but he suspected the real reason was that Sophia might broach the subject of Maccione, quiz him deeper over his concerns about Maccione's return — he shouldn't have raised the issue before — and he wasn't sure what he'd answer. It was a subject he wanted to avoid right now.

He'd heard the strains of Oriana's piano playing from the front parlour, but it had fallen quiet now. She might want to be left alone to do her music practice. He could of course sit on his own in the lounge, but he wasn't sure he wanted to be left alone with his own thoughts either.

Tightrope. Jameson had described his situation very

succinctly. But now he felt as if he was walking a tightrope in his own home — split between possibly facing awkward questions or left to be haunted by his own damning thoughts. He decided in the end to keep Oriana company.

'So, no Scott Joplin tonight,' he commented as he walked in.

Oriana looked up from some notes she was making on a side table. 'Why? Do you like Joplin?'

'Well, he's certainly lively and modern,' Joseph answered diplomatically. Being in the company of the likes of Jameson and Roosevelt was starting to rub off. He didn't want to openly voice that it reminded him of the dance halls and clubs that street girls frequented. *The same clubs where his sister Mariella would pick up clients before she hanged herself.* Oriana was too young to be burdened by that.

Oriana smiled back indulgently, as if accepting that her father was being gracious with his comment. 'Right now I've got to concentrate on Bach, Debussy and Chopin — serious recital practice music.'

'When is that, by the way?' Oriana had mentioned that she and James had an upcoming major recital performance, but Joseph couldn't recall the exact date.

Oriana leafed through some sheet music by her notes, picked out her diary and turned some pages through to check the date. 'July the fourteenth — ten days after Independence Day.'

Joseph nodded keenly. 'I'll in turn put that in my diary, because your mother and I should...' His voice trailed off as Oriana shut her diary and he noticed its cover: *blood red.*

'Something wrong?' Oriana asked, noticing him suddenly transfixed.

It took him a second to shift the image from his mind: *the same colour as the diary they'd found in Dove's basement all those years ago.* 'Uh... I just wondered why you might have chosen such a bright colour?' he said, covering with a gentle smile.

'So many others at the music academy have black or brown diaries, and sometimes during practice they all get jumbled up on a side refractory table. This colour's easy to pick out at a distance.'

A slower nod in acceptance. Perfectly reasonable explanation, but suddenly Dove's taunting voice was playing at the back of his mind. *Ah, you see. Your daughter has chosen that colour to remind you of me. Remind you of the night I saved her life.* Maybe coming and sitting with Oriana hadn't been such a good idea. He stood up.

'I'll leave you to it. I think dinner's ready soon.'

He took slow, deep breaths in the corridor outside, closing his eyes for a second as he leant against the wall. *Tightrope.* Was there nowhere he could get sanctuary?

'Are you okay?'

Sophia's voice as she looked out of the kitchen broke him from his reverie.

'Fine, *fine*,' he said, straightening up. 'Tough day at work, that's all.'

'If you want to have a rest, I'll serve your dinner later, if you like?'

'No, it's okay. I'll eat when it's ready with everyone else.' The main time they all sat together as a family, the last thing he wanted was to disrupt that too due to his personal demons.

He managed to put on a brave face through dinner, asking Marco and Pascal how their day had been at school, smiling at all the right moments, complimenting Sophia on her beef and aubergine stew, reminding Sophia that they had to put a note in their diary for Oriana's recital performance on the fourteenth of July. Sophia hooked a thumb towards the wall behind, 'Already marked on the calendar.'

But towards the end of the dinner, his nerves were frayed at the edges. Something else had struck him halfway through. Throughout, he'd kept his darker dealings and concerns about Maccione from Sophia. But pretty soon he wouldn't be able to continue keeping it from her.

Frank Campbell's death would be in tomorrow's newspapers, but there'd be no mention of Maccione because no firm connection had been made. But a sketch artist would be seeing Betty Dalston tomorrow morning, and that sketch would appear in the following day's papers. If the likeness to Maccione was strong, he wouldn't be able to hold back any longer. *But how on earth was he going to be able to see Maccione in that time to find out what had happened without, as Jameson had suggested, it appearing as a warning?* That there was collusion between them.

Suddenly he thought of a possible way, which in fact partly involved Sophia. Though he waited until the dishes were cleared away, Marco and Pascal gone to bed and Oriana back in the front parlour with her music notes, before he broached the subject.

'You know you mentioned before about Enzio Maccione calling by the store a couple of times to see Faggiani about new lines of stock. Well, I wondered whether you might be able to arrange him coming by the store again?'

'I suppose so. When did you have in mind?'

'I was thinking very soon. Tomorrow, if possible?'

'I'm presuming you wanted to be there to see him over something.' Sophia had paused in sipping at her after-dinner coffee. Her brow creased. 'But why the urgency?'

'It appears he might be implicated in something... something serious. But I don't believe he's involved. I need to talk to him to find out.' He watched Sophia's mind wrestle with his explanation. While it was a way of meeting Maccione innocently, falling in line with his association with Maccione related to Roosevelt, '*I simply know him as an importer and supplier of provisions to many Italian stores in the city, of which my wife is a partner in one. Nothing beyond* that' — he knew that the urgency of that requested meeting might ring alarm bells with Sophia. But at least he'd stepped a toe in the territory he'd so far avoided with Sophia: possible problems with Maccione.

'I don't understand.' Sophia's brow creased heavier. If it's a suspected police matter, why don't you meet him at the station?'

Tightrope. 'Be...because there's some internal politics involved. Some suggestions — possibly originating from Bill Griffin, who I believe is still in cahoots with Tierney — that there might be collusion between myself and Maccione. I don't want to add any fuel to that speculation.'

'I see.' Sophia sank into thought again for a moment. 'I suppose the only way might be if get an urgent message passed to Anton Faggiani. He sees Enzio regularly and knows how to raise him urgently for any supplies which need speedy replenishment.' Sophia held a palm out. 'But I can't guarantee he'll come by the store tomorrow.'

'I understand. But you'll try?'

'Yes, I'll try.'

But having got Sophia's agreement to help, leaving her alone in the kitchen to wash the dishes, he felt immediately guilty. After closing the kitchen door, once again he leant against the hallway wall further along, closing his eyes for a second. While he'd finally broached the subject of possible problems with Maccione, he was still holding back on his full nightmare horrors and fears — *Maccione that night sliding his stiletto up into Brogan's brain, Falway and the many other murders he suspected Maccione was involved with, possibly now Frank Campbell as well*. Worse still, he was now using Sophia for his own devices, possibly involving her as well.

Sometimes he felt so tired with it all. Deceiving and lying to Jameson, Roosevelt and Watkins, and now his wife too. He shook his head as the strains of Debussy's *Clare de Lune* came through the wall from the front parlour. He was becoming exactly the sort of policeman he'd vowed long ago never to become.

* * *

'So, you considered Joan to be something of a favourite too,' Jameson confirmed.

'I suppose you could say.' A gentle nod from Ellie, her expression taut. 'But like I said before, Finley, we're not meant to have 'favourites'. All the girls at the Beth Jacobs are equally vulnerable, that's why they're there.'

Some raucous laughter from two tables away disturbed them for a moment. Ellie looked over and gave a strained smile, the most she could muster at that moment, and waved. A couple of girls waved back in acknowledgement, their laughter and smiles suddenly subdued. The reminder of what had just happened with Joan Bourke back with them.

Alice, one of the girls from the Beth Jacobs, had her birthday today, and this night out at a local tavern with four of her friends had been arranged a week ago, before Joan's disappearance and murder. Ellie hadn't wanted to cancel in deference of that, it would have been unfair to Alice. And she was accompanying them because it was a Beth Jacobs treat — Ellie was picking up the bill.

'No gin or strong ale,' Beth Jacobs had instructed sternly.

'Don't worry,' Ellie had assuaged. 'I'll keep them just to ale mixed with lemonade or ginger beer to wash down their pie and mash. Or just ginger beer on its own.'

What she hadn't told Beth Jacobs was that *Shelley's*, the

local tavern chosen, did an alcoholic ginger beer as strong as any ale. What Beth didn't know wouldn't harm her.

Ellie had been too distraught to talk at any length the night before when Jameson had first given for the news about Joan's body being found, so they'd agreed to meet up again at Shelley's the next night. They could talk quietly to one side while Alice and her friends enjoyed their birthday party.

'I don't think I'd be in the mood to fully join in fully with Alice in any case, and I could do with the company. A shoulder to cry on and talk things through.'

Ellie surveyed the room for a moment, as if seeking inspiration for the right words.

'I suppose it goes back to what I said before about both Lucy's and Joan's problems. In Joan's case, what might be considered by some near madness — making out a dead friends was still alive. In a way, I suppose I considered Lucy and Joan a bit frailer than most of the girls, more vulnerable. So maybe I didn't see them as fully equal.'

Jameson was reminded of a phrase from his past mentor in London, Thomas Colby, '*Equal. But some more equal than others*,' when they been debating about the 'class system' and the push of reformers to make British society more 'equal'. Jameson gently patted Ellie's arm.

'I understand. And it stands to your credit that you understood those girls more than most. Indeed, why you're so invaluable at the Beth Jacobs.'

'That's very kind of you, Finley.' Ellie forced an uncomfortable smile. 'But despite me understanding them and the protection offered by the Beth Jacobs, it still wasn't enough, was it?' She shook her head, tears brimming in her eyes. 'We let them down.'

'There was nothing more that you or the Beth Jacobs could have done.' Jameson took a fresh breath. 'But on that front, I've arranged with Joseph that a permanent Constable be assigned to the entrance of the Beth Jacobs, checking and monitoring all visitors, as well as the movement of the girls.'

'That's a comfort, Finley, and many thanks. But he can't be watching the girls' every move, every minute. And one of the joys of the Beth Jacobs is that it's a refuge, not a prison.' As Jameson gently nodded his acceptance, Ellie was struck with another thought. 'Do you think that's what could be happening here — that he's aiming for girls close to me that are more vulnerable?'

Jameson shrugged, unwilling to openly admit that, add to Ellie's unease. 'Or could be simply girls who are more free with their time and tend to go off unannounced. They're easier for him to target.'

Ellie nodded tamely, Jameson unsure whether she'd accepted that explanation or not. They fell silent, the raucousness and bonhomie of the tavern for a moment crashing in.

After a sip of her ginger beer, Ellie asked how the investigation was going, Jameson commenting that they'd got close to finding a suspect, 'But then he was found dead just this morning.'

Ellie looked across hopefully. 'So that might be the end of it?'

'Not necessarily. We fear now he was more likely to have just been a go-between with their murderer.'

'So, back to square one.' Ellie exhaled tiredly, took another sip of ginger beer.

'Again, not entirely. Whoever might have killed him could give us valuable leads to...' Jameson broke off, suddenly realizing that the background with Argenti using Maccione as a possible informant was awkward to explain. And also something else he'd noticed in that moment. One of the girls with Alice two tables away was Nancy, the girl who'd first described the young man passing a note to Joan Bourke. But because the later sightings of him had been far closer, their descriptions less vague, they'd used those solely to guide the sketch artist. They hadn't gone back to consult with Nancy.

'One moment,' Jameson said, softly tapping the back of Ellie's hand. 'One of your girls over there I'd like to speak to.'

CHAPTER SIXTEEN

Joseph Argenti anxiously checked his pocket watch. Maccione had passed a message to Sophia through Faggiani and a street boy runner late morning that he'd be at the store at 5.30 pm, before it closed — now it was 5.47 pm, and still no sign of him.

Perhaps Maccione had meanwhile seen the newspapers. Realizing there was a problem and that it might be a trap, he'd decided not to show.

Joseph was sequestered in the small storeroom at the back of the shop out of sight. Sophia had peeked her head in six minutes ago to confirm 'Enzio still isn't here yet,' then left him to it. Joseph looked around the cramped room. Eight foot by four with boxes and crates stacked along one side, there was hardly room to pace to quell his anxiety. He sat on a crate, went back to cracking his knuckles.

He was disturbed again by Sophia after a minute. He looked up hopefully. 'What — he's here?'

'No. But a young boy came by and passed a message from him.'

Joseph took the proffered message from Sophia and opened it:

> GO OUT AND HEAD NORTH ALONG VARICK STREET, THEN TAKE THE FIRST LEFT INTO KING STREET. I'LL CATCH UP WITH YOU WHEN I KNOW IT'S SAFE.

No signature and all block capitals so that his handwriting couldn't easily be distinguished. Enzio was certainly taking precautions.

'I'd better go.' Joseph tucked the note into his side pocket and rushed out.

'Be careful.' Sophia's voice trailed after him.

He'd mutely nodded, but halfway along Varick Street, the parting comment struck him as strange. Sophia didn't know the depth of his worries over Maccione, he'd purposely shielded those from her. So was it just the consternation showing on his face? Sophia knew there were serious problems, even if he hadn't admitted them to her.

Twenty yards after turning into King Street, a dark figure emerged from a side alley, started walking by his side, and at first he didn't recognize Maccione. The dark cloak of a Monsignor with a broad Homburg hat, its front rim pulled sharply down, partly concealed Maccione's face.

'I'll walk just ahead of you,' Maccione muttered. 'Follow me when I turn off.'

Seventy yards along, Maccione turned into another passageways, then another shortly after. Argenti followed him through the dog-leg of passageways until they were in a cobblestoned courtyard with three windows overlooking it.

'It's the church seminary, but classes are all finished now.'

'What about the priests?' Argenti appraised the two-storey building.

'The only person here now is the church warden, Carlo. And he's a good friend of mine.' Maccione waved one hand down his robe. 'It was Carlo who provided me with these, so my appearance here would go unnoticed.'

Argenti nodded as they walked into one of the classrooms. An exhalation that carried finality as he took a seat.

'So, you've seen the newspapers about Frank Campbell's death. That's why the precautions?'

'I hadn't when I received the message from Sophia. But then I did a couple of hours later, felt it was best to be safe.' Maccione grimaced. 'I suspect you were thinking much the same — that's why the meeting at the store rather than Mulberry Street.'

Argenti didn't answer that directly. 'You obviously managed to find Campbell, speak to him.'

'Yes, I did.' Maccione sighed. 'So, how long after I left him was he killed?'

Argenti looked at Maccione steadily. *An honest, straightforward question, or was he just trying to play clever?* 'That would depend on when you saw him.'

Maccione looked down for a second. 'Uh... that would have been late morning, just after eleven. And I was there no longer than thirty or forty minutes.'

Argenti kept his gaze steady on Maccione. 'Are you trying to suggest that Frank Campbell was fine and unharmed when you left him? That it wasn't in fact you who killed him?'

Maccione stared back indignantly. 'Of course I didn't. Why on earth would I? He said that he had nothing to do with harming these girls, was just part of setting up a distraction for the police with these blue-bonnet girls — and I accepted that.'

'You're saying that he was perfectly well when you left him approaching midday?'

'Yes, very much so.' Maccione glanced towards the religious paintings and frescoes on the wall. 'On our Lord Jesus and our Mother Mary, I swear.'

Argenti smiled to himself for a moment at the irony of a gangster like Maccione making a religious oath while in priest's garb to keep shielded from the police. *Maccione seemed sincere, or it was a very good act*. Argenti's expression as quickly clouded. He ran one hand through his hair.

'There's a problem with that though, Enzio. You were seen. The old lady across the hallway saw you go into Campbell's room, and when you left she looked across again soon after and noticed Campbell's door had been left open. That's when she found the body and the police were called.'

'That's not possible.' Maccione's eyes drifted around the classroom, as if in search of an explanation. 'Someone else must have come in there in the meantime.'

'There wasn't the time, Enzio. You left, then next thing only minutes later his body is found.' Argenti gestured helplessly. 'You can see how bad it looks.'

'Yes, I can.' Maccione looked down dejectedly.

Argenti let the full weight of the situation sink in, then: 'So maybe best you start by telling me what Campbell told you about his part in all of this. What convinced you he wasn't involved in harming any of these girls?' That had been the only scenario to make sense to Argenti initially: that if Campbell had admitted to Maccione he'd killed these girls or somehow been involved with it, filled with loathing and disgust, Maccione might have killed Campbell. He'd long ago learned that street justice was dispensed far more speedily and brutally than police and court justice.

As Maccione related the description of this other man given him by Campbell, taller, slimmer, older, lighter-haired — 'who might have been either a knife-man like myself or just a go-between' Argenti wondered whether it was all just a convenient invention. Someone who fitted in more with a

Ripper description; Campbell was too young, hair too dark, not tall enough. But then something in the account moved away from Ripper territory, struck a different chord.

'You say Campbell mentioned this man had an accent?' Argenti confirmed.

'Yes, and when I pressed him stronger on that — French, German, Italian like myself — he said no, more Swedish or Norwegian. Though a very faint accent.'

'But Campbell didn't know this man directly?'

'No. Said he'd never met him before.' Maccione sank into deeper thought. 'And the mention of the accent wouldn't have meant much to me either — until afterwards, when I'd left Campbell.'

'Why was that?'

'Well, just over a year ago at one of Abe Weimann's gala dinners in Atlantic City, Abe pointed out a gentleman across the room, Erik Larsen. Originally from Denmark, been in New York five years now, surprised you don't know him, Abe said.' Maccione lapsed into imitating Abe Weimann. 'He's a skilled knife-man like you, but from a medical background before being struck off. Abe introduced us, and he had an accent which could be mistaken for Swedish.'

Struck off? Now they were back with one foot firmly in Dove-Ripper territory. 'You say a knife-man — for hire?'

'Yes. Works independently, but has done some work for Ed Corcoran. That's why Abe thought I'd know him.' Maccione leaned forward keenly. 'But that's not the only thing, Joseph. As I was leaving Campbell's place, I thought I saw Larsen. Only for a second in a shop doorway, then he was gone again. At the time, I shook it off, thought it was just the mention of the accent that had brought Larsen to mind. But now you mention the timing of Campbell being killed, it makes sense.'

'And you're sure it was this Larsen fellow? After all, if it was only a split-second sighting?'

'Without doubt. No mistaking that tell-tale droop Larsen has below his left eye from a past knife fight.'

'I see.' Argenti let his thoughts settle. Now not only hints of the Ripper, but also a convenient — perhaps *too convenient* — explanation for Campbell's murder. He looked at Maccione sharply. 'You know how Campbell was killed, do you?'

'No. The newspapers didn't mention anything.'

'He had an ice-pick or slim stiletto slid up into his brain.' Argenti held his gaze steady on Maccione, watching his reaction. 'Sound familiar, does it?'

Maccione's eyes clouded, one hand rising to clasp and stroke his forehead. '*Madre mia*.'

Argenti watched the full weight of the situation settle on Maccione's shoulders. But a proud man, he didn't crumble, his eyes simply shifted to the religious symbols and paintings on the far wall, as if seeking inspiration.

'But that's not all, Enzio. The woman who saw you — she's giving a description to a police sketch artist now as we speak. Tomorrow your likeness will be spread across most of the newspapers.'

CHAPTER SEVENTEEN

Eugene Dove sat down with a heavy sigh in the gull-winged leather armchair at Café Mozart, one of Vienna's leading café's and patisseries.

It had been a heavy, tiring day. Out trudging across three farms to see to their horses in the morning, then most of the afternoon spent at the Spanish riding school stables. A far finer stable environment to the three working farms of the morning, but still the same mud, straw and excrement-coated cobbles of any stables .

He'd gone into the public washrooms on the corner of Maysedergasse to wash down his boots, then swapped them for the fine leather brogues wrapped in a towel in his large black medical bag. Putting his boots wrapped in the same towel at the bottom of the bag, he'd set off towards Café Mozart.

He favoured the Mozart because of its position close to the Opera house and the elegant shops of the Karntner-strasse. If anywhere was to be found Vienna's finest, including tourists and visiting gentry — which he very much considered himself — it was here. The Landtmann and Sperl, recent challenges to the Mozart's café-society crown, he found too pretentious. While certainly grand and elegant, both lacked the openness of the Mozart; from practically any seat in the Mozart, you were bathed in light and could watch the passing street activity.

He'd spent fourteen months in South-West France between Biarritz and Bordeaux, then four months in the Camargue before following the Rhone valley up towards Geneva; then finally, four months later, Vienna.

He'd quickly discovered that equine physicians, horse doctors, were much in demand wherever he went, and only rudimentary knowledge of local languages was necessary. A horse's anatomy in Latin was the same everywhere, and the rest could be filled in by pointing and basic sentences.

That being said, his French had become quite proficient in that period, so that when he arrived in Vienna, he passed himself off as a French-Canadian with a new name, Claude Laboille.

And now for the past few months in Vienna, he was keen to improve his German. For that reason, although it made for a tougher read, he would read the local newspapers — even though the Mozart was one of the few cafés in Vienna to carry the main international newspapers on its wood-spine reading rack — *Le Figaro*, *La Stampa*, *The Times of London*, *Paris Herald*, *Deutsche Tageszeitung*. His hand was just reaching for that morning's *Wiener Zeitung* when he noticed the *Paris Herald* headline, reprinted from the previous day's *New York Herald*:

Second Girl Murdered Revives Fears That Ripper Has Returned

He picked out the newspaper and, over a slice of walnut and kirsch cake, read the full article. So, another killer was working his old stamping ground in New York, and quite skilled by the look of it, copying both his mode of attack and the letters sent. 'Although forensic pathologist Finley Jameson professes strong doubts that it's the Ripper returned. "After all, myself and my colleague, Detective Argenti, clearly saw his demise before our very eyes over three years ago."

Yet both Mr Jameson and Detective Argenti as yet do not appear to have adequate explanations for both the method of murder employed with both girls and the letters sent, aside from being 'very good copies'. I wish I could feel as personally assured. An emotion no doubt shared by much of New York's young womenfolk at this time.

Dove sat back and observed the activity of the café for a moment: a young couple in an animated conversation, a tramp who was trying to get entry to beg being quickly ushered out the door by a waiter, a man in a bright crimson jacket with gold brocade and an enormous handlebar moustache — could be one of the local opera performers already in costume or a local eccentric.

His first instinct was to let things be. After all, there had been copycat murders before in both London and New York. And while he had nothing to gain by declaring himself to still be alive, the fact that was already being partly done for him by this imposter and that Argenti and Jameson were still openly denying they'd seen him two years ago — the night he'd in fact saved Argenti's daughter from the clutches of another killer — sat uncomfortably with him.

Was that denial because it might reflect on their failure to bring about his demise, or due to pressure from higher up, from the Mayor and the Police Commissioner — now no less than Theodore Roosevelt, a fast-rising young politician — both eager to avoid raising undue alarm in the City?

A fair muddle for them to sort out, he mused, smiling as he paid for his coffee and cake.

But heading from the café, halfway along Maysedergasse, he was struck with an intriguing way of putting the cat among the pigeons. Providing the ultimate dilemma for Jameson, Argenti and their bright new Commissioner, Roosevelt.

CHAPTER EIGHTEEN

'We should have been looking for two men rather than one,' Jameson said. 'I believe whoever passed the initial note to Joan Bourke was not Frank Campbell, but someone entirely different.'

'And you got this from Nancy, the girl at the Beth Jacobs who gave us our first sighting of him?'

'Yes. Her description was vague, which was why we never followed up with her. We simply concentrated on the closer, more precise sightings. When I saw her with Ellie the other night, I decided to remedy that...'

Jameson went on to relate his more in-depth questioning with Nancy. He'd managed to get a copy of the two-day-old New York Post from Shelley's bar manager, who hadn't yet thrown out that week's newspapers. 'When I pressed her about the artist's impression, she wasn't sure it was the man she saw. In fact, she was strongly inclined towards it *not* being the same man.'

'The man I saw was a bit younger than that. Two or three years at least. And his hair wasn't wavy and wild like this, it was cropped short.'

'But the same or similar colour?'

'No. It was a shade lighter.'

Argenti took a deeper draw of his cigar as he contemplated the information. One of the best Cubans, a far stretch from his daily cigarillos. But then he'd come to expect no less when he was in Jameson's company. The brandy in his other hand was also the finest Napoleon.

They were in Jameson's favourite New York gentlemen's club, *The Lotos*, Jameson informing him on their first visit there that Mark Twain was one of its founders and Charles Dickens a privileged guest when he'd visited America.

He'd felt uncomfortable on that first visit with Jameson, a world away from his meagre Hell's Kitchen upbringing and the mean streets he worked every day. But now, three visits later, he'd settled into it, felt more comfortable there. *In the same way that he now took consorting with gangsters and murderers like Enzio Maccione in his stride*. Perhaps he was changing in more ways than he realized.

Argenti exhaled a slow plume of cigar smoke. 'Even if she got his age and hair colour wrong, in that two or three days between sightings his hair wouldn't have gone from tight-cropped to wavy and unruly. So I think your concurrence might be right.'

'So, we're agreed. We should have been looking for two different men. Which then might throw a...'

Argenti cut in, 'Well, three, if we assume that both of these young men were just go-betweens. Neither of them were the actual murderer.'

'What makes you say that?'

Argenti could feel Jameson's eyes on him keenly. There was little way of him explaining without revealing his second meeting with Maccione; and already he could see that Jameson sensed he knew more than he was letting on. *Enough buried secrets*.

'I met Maccione again,' Argenti said on the back of a tired exhalation.

'You did *what?*' Jameson arched a brow sharply. 'After all we discussed last time. The risk that presented.'

'I know... I *know*.' Argenti took a quick slug of brandy to cut through the dryness in his throat. 'I didn't think he was responsible for Campbell's death, but I had to know for sure. And the only way was a private meeting... away from Mulberry Street.'

'Where did you meet him?'

'It was arranged through Sophia, so that it might look like an innocent stock-control meeting — but we ended up at a local church.'

'Oh, Joseph. I hope you know what you're doing.' Jameson slowly shook his head, took a swill of his own brandy. 'So, what did he have to say for himself?'

Jameson was quiet, contemplative as Argenti related what Maccione had told him. Towards the end, Jameson ordered another brandy for them both; perhaps sensing that relating the account had drained Argenti.

'You realize that it might just be an invented story from Maccione to cover all the questionable elements.'

'I appreciate. That struck me too.' Argenti's expression was strained. 'But he could also be telling the truth.'

'If he is, then this Larsen character does seem to be more on all-fours with the Ripper. Not just in terms of age and appearance, but expert knife-skills deriving from a medical background.' Jameson swirled his brandy balloon for a moment. 'Perhaps all the more why I fear it might be invented.'

Argenti looked at Jameson keenly. 'You think it's too convenient?'

Jameson pondered for a second, lowering his glass as he leaned forward. 'Think about it, Joseph. He knows a close facsimile is needed on the Ripper front — someone who could copy Dove's style so closely we can hardly tell the difference. But also they need to be capable of killing Campbell in a way that could be passed off as Maccione. A highly-skilled copy-killer on *two* fronts.'

'So you think he might have simply invented someone who answers both criteria?'

'If he doesn't create someone, then his neck is in the noose for the Campbell murder — so it's highly possible. But if he's telling the truth, such a skilled killer won't be easily apprehended.' Jameson sank into thought again, seemed to be struck with another thought after a second. 'One way I suppose of testing out this information from Maccione. If this second man described by Nancy also gives us a description fitting in with Larsen — then in all probability he *is* real.'

'Yes, I suppose. Except Nancy's description was vague — not enough to guide a sketch artist.'

'True. Even if it had been enough, putting his sketch on the front pages of the newspapers might have ended up a death-sentence, as it did with Campbell.' Jameson paused as a Lotos waiter passed close to them, grimacing as he took another swill of brandy. 'Although, if Maccione's account is truthful, we're a step ahead in having both a name and identification with this Larsen fellow. Does Maccione have any idea where he might be found?'

'No. Maccione says he's a particularly shadowy individual. That night with Abe Weimann is the only time he's met him. He's never come across Larsen at any other time in all his dealings in New York. But he's determined to try and find him. If for no other reason than, as you say, to save his own neck.'

Jameson gestured towards the New York Times on a side table. 'That's going to be a difficult call when a sketch of

Maccione as Campbell's suspected killer appears in the newspapers and half of New York are hunting him down.'

'Maccione says that he can be equally as shadowy as Larsen. That for three years in Sicily he was on the run from the Caribinieri without them ever finding him.'

'So, we're going to have two masters of disguise running through the shadows of this fair city.'

'It appears so.' Argenti joined Jameson in a dry smile at the thought. Another factor suddenly struck him. 'One thing with Larsen. If he is indeed our killer, at least it's not the Ripper returned — the main concern now weighing heavy on both Watkins and Roosevelt.'

'Yes, there is that benefit.' Jameson looked wistfully towards the bookshelf-lined wall to their side. 'The only problem is you can't reveal how you got that information without falling off the tightrope you've been walking these past days. Putting your own neck in the noose.'

CHAPTER NINETEEN

As much as I am reluctant to do so, I must concede that on this occasion your suspicions are correct. I am not the murderer of these two most recent girls in New York.

Of course, you would know that as soon as you receive this letter: postmarked only two days after that last girl was murdered, yet the quickest passage from New York to Austria is six or seven days. Do not trouble trying to find me. I travelled to another town to post this and have moved again since. Besides, both my name and appearance are far removed from how you knew me.

You have far more chance of catching this killer right on your doorstep — but even that seems to be eluding you. You appear to simply assert your belief that this current murderer is not me, but little beyond that.

But then you weren't as successful as you first thought in bringing about my demise, were you? Ah, it must have come as something of a disappointment when I revealed in my last letter two years ago that I was still alive. I won't go so far as saying a 'shock', because I think you always firmly suspected I was still alive. Then of course your colleague Detective Argenti actually saw me the night his daughter was almost attacked.

So why the secrecy from Detective Argenti in admitting he saw me that night? Nothing appeared in the newspapers over the following days. Fear of that final confirmation of your failure with me — after all an actual sighting carries far more substance than a mere letter — or pressure from your superiors not to unduly alarm the New York public?

It appears to me that alarm is now twofold. A killer as voracious as me in your midst, combined with the fact that I'm still alive. Could return at any time to continue my work.

* * *

There was silence as the two of them read the letter. Theodore Roosevelt had already read it three times, twice an hour ago before summoning Finley Jameson and Joseph Argenti to his office, then again just minutes ago when his secretary had announced their arrival.

Now he just watched them keenly for their reactions, his office so cloyingly silent that even the ticking of the clock on the wall to their side sounded loud and intrusive. There were only the three of them in the office; no other officers had been asked to attend, and Roosevelt had even asked his secretary to stay outside until they were finished.

As he saw them finally finish reading and look up, Argenti eight seconds after Jameson, Roosevelt commented, 'Now I've kept this meeting private today for some good and hopefully equally obvious reasons. The owner of the New York Times, who I have befriended these past few years, has very kindly let me have a copy of the letter received this morning and to run in tomorrow's newspaper.'

Jameson studied his ink-pressed copy. 'Might he hold back from printing dependent on your comments, or is he committed to its appearance?'

'He's committed to good journalism and serving the

public's interest,' Roosevelt said after a moment's thought. 'As I am with the latter. And so I could only rightfully request it be withheld if I felt its appearance posed some public danger — which I don't see here.' Roosevelt mulled his mouth. 'The only danger I see is perhaps to your personal reputations with capturing or seeing the demise of the Ripper, and how that might reflect on the police department overall.'

Jameson nodded slowly. 'Yes, sir. But that was partly already answered in his letter of two years ago in which he announced he was still alive.'

'Yes. I saw the file and read his reference to that now. But, as he says, a sighting has more substance than a letter. For instance, we now have two letters, so one of them is clearly false. But an actual sighting...' Roosevelt's gaze shifted to Argenti. 'What explanation do you have, Detective Argenti, for not making your sighting of the Ripper openly known. If his claim in this letter is correct?'

'Yes, it's correct, sir.' Argenti looked uncomfortably to one side for a second. *So many buried secrets.* Of all of them, this was the least worrying; when he'd originally got the summons from Roosevelt, he feared that it might have been to do with his shadowy background dealings with Maccione. He'd managed to delay the sketch-artist by saying there had been another sighting of a suspect near Frank Campbell's building. '*I'd like to get their description sketched as well.*' But he doubted he'd be able to delay more than another day.

'And?' Roosevelt opened out his palms on the desktop. 'What do you have to say for yourself?'

'I did in fact make it clear to both Mayor Watkins and commissioner Latham that I thought I might have seen Eugene Dove, alias the Ripper, that night.'

'And what did they say? Why wasn't that made more openly known?'

Argenti took a fresh breath, as if he was summoning

strength. 'They said that *thinking* I'd seen him was somewhat different to being totally sure... especially when possibly alarming the New York public was at stake.'

'I see.' Roosevelt lapsed into thought for a second. He'd anticipated admonishing Argenti for withholding information, but now a large part of that responsibility lay with the past Commissioner and the Mayor. 'So you weren't sure?'

'No. Not *totally*, sir. It was a busy street with an automobile display, and I was viewing him at some distance with many people in between.'

'So, they advised you to keep it under your hat, so to speak?' Roosevelt grimaced, making it perfectly clear he didn't approve of that advice. 'All in the name of the public good?'

'Yes, sir.' Argenti nodded gently. 'Unfortunately so.'

Roosevelt sighed and looked back down at the letter. 'And now we have another case of the public good being protected. On one hand the tame comfort that the current murderer is not the Ripper, but at the same time the worry that the Ripper is still alive and might return.'

Jameson smiled tautly. 'As I said, sir, that concern was already partly there from his last letters.'

'I'm not sure that's going to be much consolation for an already panicky public. Also, he's made clear reference here to us possibly covering up or withholding past information in order to protect public sensitivities and not cause alarm.' Roosevelt tapped the letter with one finger. 'You can see how bad it might look if we now compound that — especially with a major New York newspaper publisher involved — with further withholding of information.'

'I think that's been his intention now with this letter.' Dry, pained smile from Jameson. 'To present us with a moral dilemma. He's adopted much the same stance with previous letters. Otherwise, I don't think he'd have troubled to write now. There have been copy-killings before and he's ignored them.'

'I daresay.' Roosevelt stroked one temple. 'But I think we have little choice but to let this letter be published. There's been far too much secrecy and withholding of information as it is.'

Argenti nodded tamely, but as Roosevelt's eyes rested on him again for a moment, he felt his chest tighten. *How could he hope to keep secret his meetings with Maccione? And once Maccione's sketch appeared in the newspapers, the game would be up in any case.*

'One advantage with this letter's appearance in the newspapers,' Jameson commented, tapping the silver-head of his cane. 'Our current murderer won't be able to any longer credibly claim that he's the Ripper. He might be unduly unsettled by that, start to make mistakes.'

CHAPTER TWENTY

Hiding in the shadows. Enzio Maccione was more familiar with the Italian term, *sotto l'ombra*, because that's what he'd done for many years in Sicily, especially in his late teens. The term *sotto l'ombra* could mean anything from an innocent taking shade under an umbrella to more sinister, shadowy hiding away.

Though while, as he'd admitted to Joseph Argenti, he was used to the practice, having hidden away from the Caribinieri for several years, it was different now. He'd become cultured, urbane, charming, used to wearing fine dress every day. The only times he'd reverted to that shadowy existence had been the nights he'd taken out 'Geddy' Doyle, Brogan and Tommy Falway with ice-picks driven swiftly into their brains or hearts, then back into the shadows again. But that had only been for a few hours at a time, dressing as a grubby street vagrant, foundry worker or ash-picker, his face partly coated in soot or grime so that he couldn't be recognized. In no time he'd wash down and be in fine clothes again, quickly back to the existence he knew and felt comfortable with. Almost as if that quick change and slipping into the shadows was in turn slipping back briefly to some dark, past existence; and once he was back in his own clothes again, he could erase it ever happened. Or, at least, was some brief, easily forgettable interlude.

But now he'd been forced to live that shadowy, *sotto l'ombra* existence for almost two days now, and already it was beginning to tell on his nerves.

'Are you sure we're going the right way?' he commented to Nico, the young street-boy leading the way.

'Of course,' Nico said. 'I'm down here two or three times a week. It's where we do much of the share-out — away from any prying eyes.'

Away from life itself, Maccione thought grimly. At the start of the street they'd passed some merchant seamen walking up from the dockside and a few street-girls vying for their attention, but now there was only the occasional tramp curled on the ground in a doorway and scurrying rats, the buildings increasingly derelict as they headed away from the working docks and merchant ships moored in the shadow of the Brooklyn Bridge.

The most godforsaken outreach of the 4th Ward, a den of derelicts, thieves and the downtrodden, forgotten and forsaken by Tammany Hall and the rest of Manhattan many moons ago. But for many, including young street-boys like Nico, it had become a safe-haven. The one place the police didn't dare go, especially at night; the spoils of pickpocket teams or of larger robberies, some from cargo on the nearby docks, could be shared out and new plans hatched.

Maccione saw another young boy emerge from the shadows of a building to one side, as if from nowhere, and nod and touch his cap at Nico.

'That's Zack,' Nico said to Maccione as they continued on. 'He's one of three on look-out today.'

Maccione nodded, taking a quick look around; he couldn't

spot anyone else observing them. Even if the police were foolhardy enough to enter the area, they'd be long gone by the time they arrived.

Maccione had been working with Nico, his most trusted street-runner, for over two years. Now just over twelve, the first signs of brawn were evident, though Nico's main advantage was lightning speed. Being able to dodge or feint a punch or knife-lunge, if indeed his first option of running hadn't worked. Nico rarely got caught in the clinches.

Maccione was an orphan from Maccione's native Sicily, and he generally favoured Italian street-kids. Not only due to the shared heritage and language, but allegiance too. They'd be less likely to turn turtle and work for an Irish gang, or rat to the police, who were also mostly Irish.

One of the rare exceptions to that rule was Ed Corcoran, who they were on their way to meet now. But that was mainly because Corcoran was half-Italian from his mother's side, so had a foot in both camps. And that allegiance had been put strongly to the test the past two years, with Ed Corcoran — having taken over George Sheehan's gang after his murder, ordered by Tierney — caretaking much of Maccione's operations in Manhattan while he'd been in Atlantic City.

Maccione smiled to himself as they walked on. Emerging from the shadows ahead was a shiny new Duryea Motor Wagon.

Cars were extremely rare in New York, only the very wealthy could afford them, so Maccione guessed it was Corcoran's. It certainly didn't belong to the gathering of young boys and older teens gawking at it. Probably the first car many of them had seen.

One of the boys had brought out an oil lamp to get a better look at it, an old tramp coming out of one of the derelict buildings to see what all the fuss was about. One boy shoved him back, another calling out, 'Kill that lamp!'

The boy with the lamp simply moved back with it inside the nearby warehouse. A second later, Ed Corcoran — who had been hanging back in the shadows — stepped into its arc of light.

'Good to see you again, Enzio.'

'You too. It's been a while.' Maccione stepped forward and the two men embraced.

Over Corcoran's shoulder, Maccione could now see a man in his late thirties with a dark beard clutching a large sketch pad, who seemed happy for the moment to remain standing in the gloom. The artist Maccione had requested Corcoran bring with him. After a moment's mutual back-patting, Corcoran stepped back to appraise Maccione.

'Jeez. I hardly recognize you.'

Maccione forced a smile. 'That's the general idea. If you can't recognize me, the police have little or no chance.' Tonight he'd donned a heavily greying wig, a tattered black coat, his face coated with cream and chalk dust, so that he looked two-shades lighter and twenty years older. An aged tramp. 'I thought I said *discreet*.'

Corcoran waved one hand down his dress. 'I wore all black, my usual funeral garb — not that you're anywhere near dead yet.'

Maccione matched Corcoran's teasing smile. 'I meant the car outside.'

'Oh, that. That's all black too. The only colour available.'

Maccione shook his head. One of the reasons he liked Corcoran: his irreverent sense of humour.

'Don' worry,' Corcoran said, suddenly more serious. 'I killed the lights as soon as I approached. Ten yards on, it was buried in the shadows here.' Corcoran grimaced. 'As long as another o' these runners doesn't get curious again with an oil lamp, nobody knows I'm here. Anyway, to business.' Corcoran gestured towards a couple of packing crates which had been upended one side as makeshift seats.

'You've seen this morning's newspapers?' Maccione confirmed as he took a seat.

'Yeah. As has half of Manhattan.' Corcoran's pained grimace eased. 'Mind you, it's not a *total* likeness. But close enough to be uncomfortable for yer.'

'I'm sure in no time, the police will be passed information that it's me. If nobody else, then for sure the person who has set this up.'

Corcoran raised a brow. 'That's what you believe has happened?'

'Without any shadow of doubt...'

As Maccione related the full account of what had happened, Corcoran nodded slowly at intervals, lighting a cigarette after a moment. Corcoran let out a slow plume of smoke as Maccione finished, as if in appreciation of the audacity of the plan.

'So, the method of Frankie's murder and your sightin' straight after will more or less nail it?' Grim nod in response from Maccione, and Corcoran asked, 'An' your contact in the police — yer sure you can trust him?'

'I'm sure.' One of the few things Maccione was sure of right now. He didn't want to risk actually naming Argenti. While he knew he could trust Corcoran, that name could be overheard or passed to some of his men who could let it slip. 'He's taken a fair few risks giving me the information he has. Not least me asking you now to bring with you a good sketch artist.'

Maccione glanced again briefly towards the man with a sketch pad, for the moment hanging back with the young boys five yards to their side, out of full earshot of their conversation, a slow smile rising as he thought about the latest risk Argenti had taken.

Argenti had sent a note through Faggiani that some of his older 'runners' should start a fight — nothing too serious, just a scrap — in a tavern within a few blocks of Mulberry Street. Then hide himself in a back alley of that tavern while another boy ran to the police station to alert him about the fight.

Maccione had chosen O'Malley's, because he didn't want the fight connected with himself or the Italian community, and for that reason had also chosen two of his fairest-skinned older boys.

Argenti and his assistant, John Whelan, had dutifully turned up ten minutes later, by which time the two boys had scampered off, leaving one patron with a bloodied nose and another with a bruised cheek.

'You stay here and take statements from these two,' Argenti had instructed Whelan. 'I'm just going to check out the back.'

Maccione had hung in the shadows in case someone else had come out, but quickly emerged as Argenti appeared. Argenti too had commented that he'd hardly recognized him, then explained the reason for the hastily arranged meeting.

'It came from a comment I made to Roosevelt the other day when I said there'd been a sighting of another suspect nearby Campbell's murder. All I could think of to buy some time with the sketch artist.'

'So, that's how you managed to get a day's delay in my sketch appearing?'

'Yes. But then it occurred to me that this description of another suspect could indeed be of Larsen — since that's what had sparked the thought. But for obvious reasons I wouldn't be able to get you together with the police sketch-artist for that. It was then that the thought struck me of an anonymous informant — someone unwilling to come forward to provide that description for fear of their lives.'

'With Roosevelt now on his soap box about corruption at Mulberry Street, no doubt a very valid concern?'

'Exactly. Except you'll have to find a sketch artist outside of your own, then get it passed to me.'

Corcoran came in on the tail-end of Maccione's account. 'And so you asked me to arrange the sketch artist?'

'Hiding in the shadows like this, I'm not exactly best placed to arrange that.'

Corcoran nodded his understanding, beckoning towards the sketch artist. 'Howard, come and join us. Now my friend here will give you a description to sketch.' Corcoran grimaced. 'An' make sure it's a good one, because it'll be appearing in the newspapers.'

Halfway through the sketch, Corcoran commented, 'You realize that as soon as this appears in the newspapers, Larsen will go to ground. Just like you have now.'

'I know. That's why I thought it best if this wasn't delivered to the police until late tomorrow night — too late for the presses to run. That way it won't appear until the day after that.'

Corcoran nodded, assessing the timing. 'So, two days for us to try and find Larsen. Then we'll have some help from the rest of New York.'

CHAPTER TWENTY-ONE

'I know I probably said enough about the terrible risk you were taking seeing Maccione, so no need to repeat myself there.' Jameson shook his head. 'But these extra extents you've now gone to, Joseph, take things to another level. It's almost as if you didn't heed a single word of what I said before.'

'I know... and I appreciate.' Argenti held out one hand, beseeching. 'But already furnished with that description of Larsen, it began to trouble me that I wouldn't be able to pursue that without revealing my meetings with Maccione — until I hit on this possibility of an anonymous informant. Providing information secretly for fear of his life.'

Jameson smiled tautly. 'Except the secrecy this time is for fear of your career.'

'Yes.' Argenti watched Jameson close his eyes for a moment, as if summoning strength. 'Don't worry, I've taken tremendous precautions each time. Last time it was a staged fight, and I even went with John Whelan so that it would look perfectly correct on the station log. Whelan was still taking statements inside when I emerged from checking the back alley and my brief conversation with Maccione.' Jameson's eyes had opened again, studying Argenti steadily, still heavy with doubt. 'And Maccione was hardly recognizable, dressed like a rag-picker or foundry worker — far from his old dapper self.'

Jameson nodded slowly. 'You're still walking that tightrope, Joseph.'

'Yes, I know. But it's one that I feel is worth walking if it helps us find Campbell's killer.'

'You don't think it's Maccione?'

'No, I don't.' Argenti shrugged. ''Of course, if we catch up with this Larsen and he has a different account, or was out of town when the murder happened, I might revise that opinion.'

Jameson sat back, took a sip of his tea. They were in the tearoom of the Chelsea Hotel. One of Jameson's favourite Manhattan hotels and '*One of the few that knows how to serve a decent English tea*,' Jameson had proclaimed. They also did a reasonably good *espresso*, which Argenti was having.

Jameson cradled his fingers after putting his cup back down. 'One thing at least with this latest letter purportedly from Dove in Vienna — it supports my theory about these recent murders not being of his hand. Extremely close replications, but not him.'

'And nothing in response so far from the earlier letter-writer countering this latest letter?'

'No. I think he'll go quiet for a while to consider his next move, *if* there is one.'

'You think the chain of murders might stop?'

'There is that hope.' Jameson took another sip of tea, grimacing as he set his cup down. 'Or he might choose to continue killing if and when he counters Dove's letter in some way. We might have to accept that at best it will only give us a short respite.'

Argenti nodded. 'Though in that respite, if we can track this Larsen character — he could indeed also be the killer of these Beth Jacobs girls. Or, at the very least, could lead us to him.'

'Yes, there is that.' Jameson's expression lifted only briefly; he sank into a more troubled look again. 'But one thing concerns me about this being a possible set up of Maccione. Has anyone so far asked you if you recognized the sketch in the newspapers?'

'Only Roosevelt in passing myself and Whelan on the corridor the other day. But thankfully the sketch is not tremendously accurate, and is only of his face — doesn't show his trademark dapper dress. So I answered that it could be a number of people, which we were now following up on.'

'Yes. But someone else at Mulberry Street might whisper in Roosevelt's ear that, combined with the dapper dress and mode of killing on file, it appears to be Maccione. And then it might also be raised just why you were holding back on a similar conclusion?'

'I in fact considered that.' Argenti sighed. 'And if confronted with that, I'd admit that Maccione was among three or four people I was pursuing as possible suspects. Then buy more time by claiming I couldn't locate Maccione as yet, and wasn't even sure he was in New York at the time of Campbell's murder.' As Argenti watched Jameson absorb the information, gently tapping one finger against the side of his teacup, he added, 'Besides, whoever related that information internally at Mulberry Street would risk giving something else away.'

'What's that?'

'Because if this is all a set-up of Maccione, they might indeed be involved with it. Because why else would they reach such a conclusion about Maccione before me?'

CHAPTER TWENTY-TWO

Young Luca was running as fast as he could, which wasn't nearly as fast as he'd have liked. At barely eleven, despite being fast for his age, he knew that he fell far short in pace of the older teens in Corcoran's and Maccione's network of street runners.

Was it three o'clock yet? He hadn't even troubled to check the street clock as he turned the corner from Broome into Orchard Street. As soon as he'd seen the Danish man in the sketch, Larsen, he'd run flat out to tell Nico. But Nico said he'd only be with three or four others loading crates at a warehouse at the back of Seward Park, only two blocks away, until three o'clock — then he was moving back down to their east side docks hideout, at least another twelve minutes run.

By then, this Larsen man would have probably shifted. Only if he got to Nico within the next couple of minutes was there a fair chance that the man would still be inside the tailor's on Broome Street that Luca had seen him enter.

Luca hadn't been sure at first, the man had his Derby pulled down sharply on the left-hand side, as if aware of his eye injury and keen to keep it shielded at all times. But then as he'd entered the tailor's, he'd looked up briefly to tip his hat at a women coming out, and Luca had seen Larsen's trademark eye injury clearly.

'Not so handsome Larsen,' one of the older teen runners had commented when Nico had handed out the leaflets, and among some chuckles the moniker had stuck. As soon as the sketch had been completed, Enzio Maccione had 40 copies made at a back-street ink-press, handing them to Nico with clear instructions, 'Erik Larsen is late thirties with blonde hair and light-blue eyes, but his left-eye has a trademark droop from an attack when for once he got on the wrong end of a knife. We've got only two days to find him before his pictures in the newspapers and the rest of Manhattan's on his tail too.' Nico had then shared it among a wider gathered group of street runners. 'Good payday on this one! Four dollars directly for whoever spots him first, another twenty dollars to be shared among the group.'

They'd gone in every direction, searching and scouring every possible street in Manhattan, with Luca first to have sight of Larsen.

'I've just seen him,' Luca announced breathlessly as he approached Nico halfway through lifting a crate with another boy. '*Larsen*!'

'Where?'

'Going in a tailor's on Broome Street, just a few blocks away. Hopefully he's still there.'

'*Hopefully*.' Nico set down the crate and pointed to the other boys. 'You two continue loading. Gerry, you head to Faggiani's with an urgent message for Enzio that we're on Larsen's tail on Broome street. And Paulo and Mack, you come with me.'

If they got close in the clinches, Nico didn't think Larsen would try his luck with four of them. And Mack at fifteen was one of the larger boys, already close to six-foot, and handy himself with a knife and Billy club.

They ran off, Luca taking the lead.

As they turned into Broome Street, Nico spotted Gill, one of Corcoran's street runners, thirty yards along on the opposite side. Nico beckoned him over.

'You seen this Larsen guy on the street here?'

'No.' Gill looked vague. 'Whereabouts exactly?'

Luca hooked a thumb behind them 'Maybe at that tailor's back there, about eighty yards along.'

Gill shook his head, pointing ahead. 'I been heading this way. Coupla more betting slips to pick up, then I'm done for the day.'

'Looks like he could still be inside,' Luca said hopefully.

'Yeah.' Nico held a keen eye towards the tailor's, waving Gill off with a 'Thanks' as they moved towards it. As they got closer, he urged Luca ahead. 'You look in casually as yer passin', see if he's still inside. Better than us all gawping in.'

Nico and the other two hung back waiting, tense, as they watched Luca slowly stroll by and glance in the shop window.

Luca appeared to falter for a second, as if he was having trouble looking inside with the window's reflections, or was unsure of what he'd seen.

As Nico looked intently towards Luca, a man sixty yards further along coming out of a tobacconists struck a chord. The corn-blonde hair and his height a few inches above most passers-by was the first thing to draw Nico's attention. And as the man tamped a cigarette against his silver case and leant down to light it, Nico was sure. He caught sight of the man's left-eye droop. Only for a second, but enough!

'He's there. Over *there*!' Nico hissed, loud enough for Luca to hear but not reach the man beyond.

Luca jolted in recognition and started his run, now just two paces ahead of Nico who was already into his stride.

The man turned and headed away from them. Quite briskly, Nico noted. *Had Larsen picked up on them pursuing him?*

If not now, then he would any second. So as an added diversion, Nico pointed to the tram that had just trundled past.

'If we hurry, we might catch it at the next stop!'

The same brisk stride away from them, only a half-glance back at one point. *Deadpan*. Nothing of any significance registering either way.

Even if Larsen did cotton on that they were chasing him, he couldn't possibly know their intent. His sketch wouldn't be in the newspapers until tomorrow. At best, or worst, he might think they were a gang of young footpads out to rob him.

But then, as if belying that, Nico watched Larsen take the next turn off into an alleyway. Why head into an alley away from public gaze if you feared you might be about to be set upon? Especially one that headed back towards the dockside — more their own territory, along with half the footpads of the area.

As they came alongside the alleyway, Nico had his first clue as to why. Larsen wasn't in sight, and there were two or three alley turn-offs each side. Larsen could have ducked into any of them.

They proceeded in cautiously, Luca just ahead of Nico with the others following behind, peering keenly into each alley as they went, hands on waistband-tucked coshes and knives.

As they came to the second right-hand side turn-off, Luca caught a flicker of movement deeper in, as quickly disappearing. He called back to the others, 'I think he's up here.'

Luca led the way, Nico and the other two close behind. At the end of the alley thirty yards ahead, they could see the flat wall of a building, another alley leading off left and right. *Which way had Larsen headed?*

As if in answer, Larsen suddenly emerged from a recessed doorway as they came alongside the last building along, grabbing Luca firmly and holding a knife to his neck.

'Now I suggest the rest of you take a step back unless you want to see your friend's throat cut.'

A long, slim blade, Nico noted, and from what he'd heard this Larsen was deadly proficient with it. He held his palm up to keep his sidekicks at bay, keep their calm.

Mack behind him had his Billy club out, brandishing it threateningly. 'Yer could pick someone your own size.'

Larsen tilted his head to one side, as if in consideration. 'Yes, I could I suppose. A fair observation.' With a sudden thrust, he flung Luca back towards them. 'You fancy taking your chances, then? One on one. You look the largest of your group.'

Mack paused for a second, suddenly realizing his bluff had been called. Then he edged forward, Billy club raised in his right hand, knife out now in his left, sidling gradually towards Larsen like a double-clawed crab.

'I'll fokin' have yer — you'll see.'

Mack swung with the Billy-club, but Larsen side-stepped easily. The following knife-lunge, Larsen also leaned away from easily. And as the next Billy club swing came, Larsen feinted to one side, then drove his knife swiftly and hard into Mack's upper-arm.

With a scream in agony, Mack's Billy club clattered to the ground.

While Larsen was pre-occupied, Nico seized the opportunity to swing in with his own smaller cosh. A last-second feint the other way, and it glanced off Larsen's shoulder. Then, swinging back with the same arm, Larsen flung Nico back like a rag doll into the brick wall two yards to their side.

In one fluid motion, Larsen took a step back, bracing one arm hard around Mack's neck as he held his knife point just above his throat. The same position he'd held little Luca a moment before.

'I have a clear message for whoever sent you. In future, tell him to face me himself like a man — not send little kids to do his dirty work.'

Nico was still winded from hitting the wall, eyes watery and stinging, feeling as if something had been dislocated in his back. The other two held back uncertainly, a knife waved with one, a cosh with the other; but lacking any conviction after Larsen's display with Nico and Mack.

The three of them looked on helplessly as Larsen raised his blade to slit Mack's throat.

* * *

Lawrence pulled sharply on the reins as he turned the Hansom sharply at the end of Pike Street and swung into the dockside, wheels rattling on heavier cobbles.

'Just up ahead,' Luca nodded. 'Forty yards on the right.'

The young boy was wedged between Jameson and Argenti. Surveying the dockside to their right, it was little different to where Joan Bourke's body had been found, half a mile upstream on the East River docks.

'That building there,' Luca pointed.

Lawrence drew the horse to a halt and they stepped out, Luca half-running ahead of them towards a dilapidated warehouse. Lawrence followed a few paces behind them, carrying a black leather medical bag.

'They're in there,' Luca said, beckoning them towards a partly open weathered door half off its hinges.

As their eyes adjusted, the only light inside from a single

oil-lamp, Jameson didn't need to be pointed towards the boy that needed medical attention.

A burly lad in his mid-teens sat on a crate, blood seeping heavily through a makeshift blue cotton shirt wrapped around his face and neck, with as much blood again spilled down his own shirt-front. Two other boys stood to one side, one of which was Nico.

'Okay. Let us tend to this,' Jameson said, kneeling by the boy and waving Lawrence over. He delicately opened the bandage. 'Now this is going to hurt somewhat.'

Almost as if a measured, practiced routine, Lawrence had taken a wad of cotton wool from the bag, soaked it in iodine, then put it into Jameson's outstretched left hand.

Jameson dabbed at the wound as the boy hissed sharply, gritting his teeth. Two more iodine cotton wool wads and he'd cleaned the general area, inspecting closer.

'Well at least it hasn't gone through any major veins,' Jameson remarked, sighing. 'Most of it's a facial cut on this left-hand cheek. And even where it slices an inch or so down into your neck, it has missed the jugular by a good two inches.'

Nico looked at Jameson keenly. 'What? You mean he's going to be alright? His throat hasn't been cut.'

'It certainly doesn't look like it.'

Argenti added, 'And if it was who we think it was from the description' — he gestured towards Luca — 'I don't think it was his intention to cut your friend's throat, just send a clear message. He was lucky.'

Jameson grimaced sourly. 'If 'lucky' is indeed an appropriate term for such a heavy facial wound. It will need serious cleaning, stitching and dressing to ensure infection is kept at bay. And you'll carry the scar for life.' He grimaced again, looking at Mack directly. 'But you'll live.'

Mack returned the smile crookedly. Relief that he wasn't

going to die combined with coming to terms with the scar; at least it might make him look meaner, warn people off from messing with him in future.

Nico nodded slowly. 'I thought for sure he was going to slit Mack's throat.'

Nico recalled the sense of helplessness as Larsen had raised his knife, then suddenly run it down rather than across and thrown a blood-soaked Mack towards them as he'd run off.

'But you got a good look at him?' Argenti enquired.

'Sure did,' Mack said. 'When a guy's about to slit your throat from only inches away, yer don't' forget him.'

'Just like the sketch,' Nico said soberly. 'It was the sketch in fact that first put us on his tail on Broome Street...'

As Argenti took details from Nico, Mack and Luca of what had happened, Jameson and Lawrence treated, stitched and bandaged Mack's knife wound.

Then, almost as if on cue as their collective account finished, a faint rustling came from the deeper shadows at the back of the warehouse, and a man in dark ragged clothing, his face grimy with grease and coal dust, stepped into the arc of light from the single oil lamp under which they'd tended to Mack.

Argenti recognized him straightaway, though it took a second longer to dawn on Jameson. *Enzio Maccione*! Jameson bristled, standing up.

'I shouldn't be here.' He looked at Argenti sharply. 'You didn't tell me he'd be coming.'

Argenti gestured helplessly. 'I didn't know myself that he'd be here.'

'It's enough of a risk that you've been seeing him. Without involving myself in your clandestine activity and possibly —'

Maccione held a hand up, cutting in. 'Gentlemen...

gentlemen. I didn't tell Joseph that I'd be here today. In fact, the only one who knew in advance was young Nico — but I felt it was my duty to be here now.' He gestured towards Mack. 'After all, I was responsible for this. If I hadn't set Nico and his boys on finding Larsen, this wouldn't have happened.'

'As may be,' Jameson said curtly. 'But I think you fail to appreciate the terrible risk Detective Argenti is taking in continuing to see you, with you now a murder suspect and half of the city's police hunting you down. A risk I've admonished him about and strongly advised him against taking — especially now with our new Commissioner, Roosevelt, focused so heavily on anti-corruption.'

Maccione smiled dryly. 'I'm flattered that I'm due such consideration at Mulberry Street. And I do much appreciate the risks Joseph has taken in seeing me.' His countenance became more serious as he looked at Argenti meaningfully. 'If it's any consolation, I took all due precautions. Nobody saw me coming here today, even if they could recognize me dressed like this. And your own arrival here today, Dr Jameson, was purely for medical tending to a young boy. Nothing untoward or suspicious.'

Jameson looked from Maccione to Argenti and back again, not wholly convinced. 'Still, I like to be informed in advance of such things. So I can make up my own mind whether I wish to take such risks or not.'

'As you can see, there was little other way.' Maccione glanced towards Mack and Nico. 'You needed to tend urgently to a medical situation. And even if there had been time for me to warn either of you in advance, that could have spelt more collusion on your part.'

'He has a point.' Argenti looked at Jameson, sighing. 'As much as I'm reluctant to agree. Because I too would like to have been warned in advance.'

Maccione observed the two of them settle into reluctant

acceptance. 'At least now hearing these accounts and seeing this boy's injuries, you know that my sighting of Larsen that day and my concerns about him are *real*. He could well be not only Campbell's killer, but also the Ripper-style murderer of these Beth Jacobs girls.'

* * *

Jameson and Argenti were silent for a moment, each with their own thoughts, as Lawrence sped the Hansom away from the dockside.

Argenti was looking blankly through the window his side, hardly paid attention to the tramp curled in a doorway clutching onto a small briefcase. Only slightly scuffed, the briefcase didn't fit in with the rest of the tramp's ragged dress; and perhaps if Argenti had paid more attention to the tramp, he'd have noticed that he was in a similar position as they'd entered the dockside, and might have thought the case was a recent acquisition from the street-robbery of a city gent. But he had other things on his mind right now. He looked back at Jameson.

'Do you think that was Maccione's main intention in turning up now? To make the point that Larsen was real, not just an invention of his?'

'Perhaps. But difficult to arrange all the rest to suit.'

'Yes, I suppose. So you think overall Maccione is telling the truth?'

Jameson sank into deeper thought, glancing out for a moment as they turned from Pike Street into Madison street.

'Against my better nature, *yes*, I do. That facial wound was too heavy to get someone to agree to put it on for show.' Jameson sighed. 'Also, the accounts of all those young boys tallied.'

Argenti held one hand out, playing devil's advocate for a moment. 'Maccione could have coached them all.'

'Difficult with a group like that. Also their responses were quite rapid-fire, natural. If they'd been coached, I think there would have been more gaps between their answers while they ensured they got their facts straight. All their ducks in a row.'

Argenti nodded thoughtfully. 'So Maccione's account about Larsen being Campbell's killer might well ring true? And possibly these Beth Jacobs girls too.'

'It's a distinct possibility.' A heavier rumble took over from the clatter of their wheels as they stopped at the Broadway junction for a tram to go past. As the brighter lights from Broadway reflected on Jameson's face, he was struck with another thought. 'Unless of course Maccione has some other conflict with Larsen he's not telling anyone about. And so this is his way of using his little street-boy army to track-down Larsen, while at the same time exonerating himself of Campbell's murder.'

CHAPTER TWENTY-THREE

At first when Finley Jameson looked at Sulee above him, it looked like tiger's stripes across her naked body...

And for a moment she transformed completely to a tiger in woman-form, her breathless guttural groans of pleasure suddenly sounding like a tiger's low, threatening growl.

He shook his head to clear the image from his mind, his own breath falling short with his own pleasure rising.

But instead of clearing, the image suddenly morphed into Ellie above him, reaching back to tie a ribbon around her flowing red-brown hair to stop it swaying and whipping between them.

'Something wrong?' Sulee enquired between caught breaths.

'No, nothing... nothing,' he offered equally as breathlessly, forcing a smile.

Perhaps he shouldn't have partaken so heavily with the opium pipe earlier. He'd been good for a while, hadn't visited the opium den and Sulee for a massage for almost four months now. And when he had visited before that, he'd cut back on his opium consumption and taken only briefly to the pipe. Enough to get him to relax, but not anywhere near the edge of oblivion, as he used to.

But with the pressures of this renewed Ripper case and now getting involved with Argenti's cover-up over Maccione, he felt he needed a touch of oblivion again.

Or could it be because earlier he'd tried to explain his concerns about Argenti to Ellie. His worry that Argenti was 'getting involved with the criminal fraternity in a way that might threaten his career.'

'What? In a dishonest way?'

'No, not dishonest — that would be against his principles. And I'm sure he means well and his intentions are good — it's just that they might not be viewed as such by others at Mulberry Street, if they come to light.'

Ellie had picked up quickly. 'He's covering for someone that he shouldn't?'

'You could say.'

But he'd held back from sharing Maccione's name and the finer details, feeling a twinge of guilt that he didn't feel he could fully share this with Ellie. Or *anyone* for that matter.

And her reassuring and holding his hand across the dinner table, in the same way that he'd reassured her over Beth Jacobs attacks, hadn't helped.

That feeling of some distance between them. As if their affection and care shown for each other could only go so far. Afraid that if they took their relationship to the next level, both emotionally and physically, he'd be somehow taking advantage of her. Reverting her to a bygone day of being a street-prostitute which she'd spent the last few years — and he'd helped her in that quest — trying to escape from.

So there'd be that hand-holding across the table, a softening and compassion in her eyes along with a spark running between them — which Jameson was sure Ellie felt as much as he did — and as quickly that hand would be pulled away before the gesture might be misread or crossed a certain unspoken line between them.

And sometimes, like tonight, he'd take out that pent-up frustration by visiting Sulee. Because their relationship had been forged on little else but raw lust and sex. No crossed lines; in fact, they'd have been crossed the other way if he *hadn't* partaken of Sulee's pleasures. Sulee might have felt insulted, asked him 'What's wrong?' in the same way as she had now as she'd momentarily transformed to Ellie above him.

As he re-focused, he could now see that the tiger pattern was from the oil-lamp behind a palm tree to one side. The dark shadows of the palm fronds playing across Sulee's naked body.

Always the same routine. After an opium pipe in the adjoining 'den', he'd retire to the backroom for a massage with Sulee. She'd rub sweet-scented oil gently into his body, then soon after would move her naked body against his, a gliding motion with the oil — verging finally into lovemaking, the two almost seamless.

And he wondered whether he slipped easier into that routine with Sulee, not just to protect Ellie for fear of sullying her by reminding her of her street-girl background, but for himself too.

He could abandon himself with Sulee without fear of the complications of a relationship. Without having to bare his soul and physical emotions. He could keep them separate.

What was he afraid of Ellie seeing by opening himself fully to her?

* * *

The figures in the first photos were quite distant, their faces too hazy and indistinct for Theodore Roosevelt to make out.

Taken from beyond a Hansom cab pulled up on a dockside, its dark frame filled almost a third of the photos one side, dilapidated warehouses beyond.

But as the figures moved away from the warehouses and closer to the Hansom, they became clearer: Argenti and Jameson, followed not far behind by Jameson's assistance, Lawrence.

Only two photos, as if the photographer had to rush and scurry off. Then another of the Hansom passing, clearly Argenti looking absently from its side window. Then another two photos from the same position of a stocky man in ragged dark clothing, his face smothered with black grime and soot, walking alongside a young boy.

Roosevelt had to beckon over again their Mulberry Street photographer, Eric Morrison.

'And you think the man in this photo holds a resemblance to the sketch we produced two days ago?'

'Yes, I do. Not a complete likeness by any means — but if you look beyond the grime and adjust for the poor lighting, there's certainly something there.'

Roosevelt nodded solemnly. The photos had arrived anonymously that morning with a note: *Thought you might be interested in these. Detective Argenti and Finley Jameson meeting up with none other than Enzio Maccione.*

He'd asked Morrison into his office soon after to compare the photos with the sketch.

'And you don't think the photos have been re-touched or tampered with in any way?' he asked now.

'No way of knowing for sure, I suppose. But I don't think so.'

'Also, why don't the subjects seem aware that their photos are being taken?'

'Ah, it would appear to be some sort of concealed camera.' Morrison beamed, *his area of expertise*, leaning over and pointing to two photos. 'Note the faint shadows at the edges here and here, probably from a cloth surround or some sort of casing.'

'Yes, I see. Thank you.'

Roosevelt sat with his own thoughts for a moment, then reached for the telephone. One advantage of these new-fangled contraptions. They'd taken over from the telegram in spelling urgency.

Though he'd have to set the meeting for an hour's time to allow for Jameson to get to Mulberry Street. He wanted to see both of them at the same time.

* * *

Argenti felt Roosevelt's eyes on him keenly as he and Jameson studied the photos. Only one set, so they passed them back and forth between them.

After a moment, Roosevelt eased out a tired, impatient breath and asked, 'Do you recognize the man in dark clothes with soot and grime on his face?'

Argenti felt Roosevelt's eyes on him keenly. The question was directed at him. He looked up finally. 'I didn't at first, sir. It took me a moment to recognize him with the darkness of the photo and the grime on his face. And still I'm not fully sure — but it could be Enzio Maccione.'

'Indeed.' Roosevelt interleaved his hands on his desktop. 'But I daresay you might easier identify both yourself and Dr Jameson — since neither of you have any such markings on your faces.'

'Yes, of course, sir. We're far clearer in the photos.'

'With the question then raised: what on earth were you and Dr Jameson doing in the same place as Enzio Maccione, no doubt perhaps meeting with him?'

Argenti nodded slowly, picking up on the 'perhaps'.

Because the photos were taken at different times, none actually showing them with Maccione, obviously Roosevelt couldn't be a hundred-percent sure they'd met with Maccione. 'We went to that dockside area primarily for Dr Jameson to tend to a young boy. Also, both he and another boy who witnessed the attack felt sure it was this Larsen character — the other suspect in the Campbell killing. So I went along to take statements. It was all in my report the other day.'

'Yes, I read your report.' Roosevelt sighed. 'But that wasn't what I was asking. So I ask you again, in plainer language this time: did you at the same time of seeing these young boys also meet with Enzio Maccione?'

Argenti felt his face flush, feeling uncomfortable with a direct lie. 'As I say, sir, we went there initially to tend to this young boy and get statements from him and the other boys. It was only later that —'

Jameson cut in, 'That we heard a noise at the back of the warehouse. But we never in fact saw anyone there. We only had a single oil lamp by the patient, and they were in shadow at the back of the warehouse, never presented themselves.'

'I see.' Roosevelt looked at Jameson doubtfully. 'And did you not enquire who it was?'

'Of course.' Jameson smiled in deference, as if that was an obvious action. 'But the young boys said it was probably just a tramp stirring at the back of the warehouse. Many tramps and vagrants use those empty warehouses for shelter. We thought nothing more of it.'

'So, you're saying this person — whether a tramp or Enzio Maccione in ragged clothes — never presented themselves to yourself and Detective Argenti?'

'No, they didn't,' Jameson said firmly.

Argenti just nodded numbly in support as Roosevelt's eyes shifted to him for confirmation. Still not trusting himself to speak and openly lie. But he wondered whether the heavy flushing in his face might have given him away.

Roosevelt's eyes stayed on them keenly for a moment, then with a huffed breath, one hand held out, 'We also have to ask ourselves what on earth Enzio Maccione is doing dressed like a tramp. That in itself, skulking away in the shadows like that, would tend to indicate guilt.'

Argenti nodded a tame accord. 'It would certainly explain why I've had trouble tracking him down. But it could also be that he fears he's being blamed for a murder he didn't commit.'

'Then why not come forward and say so? He would surely have some proof that would discount him as a suspect?'

'You'd have thought so.' Non-committal response that wasn't an open lie. Argenti swallowed as he felt Roosevelt's eyes linger on him for a moment.

Jameson interjected, 'Perhaps part of that proof rests with this second suspect, Larsen. Simply put, if an evidential case is proven against Larsen, then Maccione couldn't have been guilty of Campbell's murder. So perhaps he's keeping a low profile until such time.'

Roosevelt pondered for a moment. 'So do you think that's why Maccione was present at that time. He wanted to hear first-hand what these boys had to say about their confrontation with Larsen?' Roosevelt offered a taut smile. 'That is, without showing himself.'

'Possibly,' Argenti answered. 'Also, he might have felt partly responsible for the boy's injuries in confronting Larsen.'

'And of course, Maccione wouldn't show himself openly to a detective,' Jameson supported. 'Knowing that immediately he did so, he'd be liable to arrest.'

Another tame nod of support from Argenti. Jameson had obviously also picked up on Roosevelt's doubting tone, countering in a way that he himself wouldn't have been able to without again crossing that *open lie* line.

Roosevelt looked at the two of them steadily. 'Remind me again: when is Larsen's sketch due to appear in the newspapers?'

'Tomorrow, sir,' Argenti answered. 'We missed last night's presses.'

Roosevelt's brow furrowed. 'So, what on earth were these street kids doing chasing after him before his sketch has even appeared in the press?'

Argenti felt his face flush again as he considered. 'Well, uh... the information about Larsen did come through a gangland informant — so I daresay it travelled faster on that grapevine.'

Roosevelt nodded after a moment. 'I suppose all will become clearer in due course.'

Meeting Roosevelt's gaze, Argenti could still sense heavy doubt there. He was still walking that *tightrope*, had momentarily slipped off only to cling on by his fingertips. But would he be able to cling on and survive the next fall?

'What we should also perhaps be asking ourselves,' Jameson remarked, 'Is just who took these photos and why they were sent anonymously to you, Commissioner Roosevelt. That could be equally telling.'

* * *

'Thank you for helping out there,' Argenti commented as they walked along Mott Street.

'I didn't see much option. I feared you were about to say something that would have been irreversible.'

They'd been silent, both with their own thoughts, as they'd come out of Mulberry Street police station. Jameson had waved on Lawrence, who was sitting in the Hansom.

'Take the horse on slowly for a stretch. We want to walk for a little while.'

Argenti had waited until they were almost a hundred yards into the first turn off on Mott Street before offering his thanks; as if afraid that any closer, somebody from Mulberry Street might hear.

Jameson looked at him questioningly. 'Were you in fact about to admit to meeting Maccione?'

'I fear perhaps I was in a way.'

'In a *way*? Jameson looked at him sharper.

'What was in my mind to say was that I was unsure at first it was Maccione with the grime and soot... and when I *did* realize and said he'd need to come in for questioning, he ran off followed by one of the young boys.'

Jameson nodded slowly. 'Except that Roosevelt would have asked why it wasn't in your report of the other day?'

'Yes, it would have been more awkward, without doubt. My only defence would have been that I wasn't totally sure it was him. And with him running off so suddenly, it might have reflected badly on me that I hadn't apprehended him.'

Jameson grimaced. 'It would still have meant that you were covering something up, keeping a secret. And Roosevelt might have thought: if you can withhold *one* thing from him, then why not others?'

'I know. It would have been far from ideal. Just that I felt uncomfortable telling an open lie.'

'So, you settle for half a truth and keep the rest hidden. I can understand that.' Jameson nodded ponderously for a second. *But then the memory suddenly resurged of his own mother's madness shielded from him for years, until she was virtually on her deathbed*. 'But one day you'll come to realize, Joseph, that holding back on truths, not revealing them, can be as bad. Sometimes worse.'

CHAPTER TWENTY-FOUR

Joyce Bennett had a reputation for being something of a 'fantasy queen' at the Beth Jacobs refuge.

Barely eighteen, she'd enthral them all with tales of princes and royalty she'd met. 'One in fact was a boyfriend at one time. Says his family were originally from Bohemia and that they originally owned a castle there, with turrets, servants and everything...'

But after a while with the various stories, most of the girls had concluded that Joyce was in fact 'making them up'. The number of princes and nobility she'd met along with the fine family she'd come from were simply too many for a dozen lifetimes, let alone one. So, they'd simply nod and smile back at her. 'Sure, Joyce. That's a grand story.' They'd got used to humouring her, because many of her stories were in fact entertaining, but they hardly believed a word of them.

Ellie had become protective of Joyce for that reason, watchful that the other girls didn't become too hard on her because of her stories. Challenge her over them, become difficult or give her the cold shoulder.

Thankfully, there had only been a handful of incidents in

the three years Joyce had been at the Beth Jacobs, and Ellie had quickly calmed the waters once Joyce was out of earshot. 'Just indulge her, if you can. She means well. It's just her way of escaping from a tough past.' Taut grimace from Ellie. 'I daresay all of you have that to contend with. Just that you deal with it in different ways.'

But the reason Ellie was so protective of Joyce was that she knew part of her story about her family background was in fact true. Joyce's father, Stanley, had been one of New York's original railway barons. But he had died suddenly at the age of forty-one without leaving a will or trusts for his children.

Joyce's mother had died giving birth to her four-years-younger sister, Nancy, and when two years later their father remarried, neither Joyce nor Nancy got on with his new wife, Eleanor, and the feeling was reciprocal.

A rift that Eleanor drove to heartless advantage after Stanley died. Within a year, she'd ejected them both from the family home, claiming she couldn't abide them any longer and were 'not her responsibility' anymore. Their father's funds were directed entirely towards keeping Eleanor and young Jason, the son she'd had with Stanley, in the style they'd become accustomed to.

At the age of only twelve, Joyce found herself on the streets with her eight-year-old sister, Nancy, to fend for. For a while, they got by with begging, but eventually it had become too difficult to scrape together enough for anything more than a few food morsels each day, and within fourteen months Joyce had turned to street prostitution.

Then one winter's night only ten months into her street trade, she'd stayed longer with clients than she'd planned. The temperature had dipped sharply below zero, their night's shelter in a dilapidated warehouse insufficient to fend off the bitter cold.

Nancy developed a heavy chest infection which within three weeks turned to pneumonia and claimed her life. Joyce was all alone, and on top of her abject loneliness was burdened by guilt over young Nancy's death, felt she was responsible.

The fantasies and wild tales became an escape from her dark, insufferable street-life. Not just harking back to real memories of her privileged, glittery life before her father died, but continuing those in her mind, as if her father had never died. Life had just continued the same.

In a way, Ellie felt for Joyce more than many of her other girls. Yes, with most of them, they'd endured terribly tough young lives; but in a perverse way, that had given them an antidote of what was to follow. Their tough existence built up in stages, so that they in turn toughened-up and were more prepared.

In Joyce's case, her early life had given no preparation for that. Cosseted, loved and protected one minute — then the next abandoned to fend for herself and her young sister, with no preceding years of tough street-life experience — like so many other of the Beth Jacobs girls — to prepare for that. Develop a tough skin.

Ellie could understand why Joyce fantasized as a protective device against that. The reality had simply been too hard and sudden for her — for *anyone* — to face.

When Joyce had been just fifteen, collapsing one night on the streets with cold and exhaustion, she'd been taken into the Beth Jacobs refuge, and started to entertain the other girls with her bright and glitzy tales of a world they'd never known and could barely dream of.

At least one thing in Joyce's favour, Ellie consoled herself; she'd lived that life for a while, whereas the others had never experienced anything like it.

Joyce had quickly become one of Ellie's 'unspoken'

favourites. And while she and some others at the Beth Jacobs encouraged Joyce's stories — taking them with a pinch of salt for what they were, 'protective escapism' — Ellie was equally protective of Joyce from others who might have tired of the stories and would give Joyce a hard time over them.

So when that morning, Joyce announced that she'd just seen the 'man with the droopy eye' a hundred yards or so along the road from the Beth Jacobs, some of the group of girls around her were doubting.

'Come on,' protested Cathy, one of the strongest doubters. 'His sketch has been in the newspapers barely two hours, and suddenly you've seen him.'

'Yeah,' another quickly supported. 'You've come out with some wild stories in your time, Joyce. But this one takes the biscuit.'

'Why would he show up near here, especially with his sketch just in the newspapers. This is the *last* place he'd want to be seen.'

Joyce looked from one to the other helplessly. 'I tell you. I've just seen him. Just along the road!'

'Did Fenton in front see him?' Fenton was the Constable who'd been put on temporary 'watch-duty' in front of the Beth Jacobs.

'No, he didn't. He's just gone on his lunch break.'

'Was he with the tooth fairy, or father Christmas?' Another girl ribbed.

They burst into a collective guffaw of laughter, but it only made Joyce more desperate to prove her point.

'The newspapers have only just come out — so perhaps he hasn't seen them yet. And he... he was trying hard not to be seen. He had the brim of his hat pulled down sharp and was wearing thick glasses. But as he turned to one side, I saw that tell-tale droop in his eye. I'm *sure* it's him.'

They fell silent for a second, a couple of them starting to sway, have doubts, but Cathy stuck to her guns.

'Yeah, sure, Joyce.' She smiled and shook her head. 'I much preferred your stories about Prussian princes — at least they were entertaining.'

'*Girls*! That's enough of that!'

They turned as Ellie's sharp voice came from behind. She'd been drawn from her office by their rising laughter and mocking.

'If Joyce says she's seen him, then she's *seen him* — and that's the end of it!' She looked sternly at them, then flapped her hands out, as if she was shooing away a gaggle of geese. 'Now away to whatever you were doing before this.' She watched them reluctantly disperse, then with a nod of finality as she turned back towards her office, 'A bit more civility in future, girls.'

Ellie got lost for a while in mundane paperwork — checking laundry rotas and lists, clothing inventories — so when the phone on her desk rang almost half-an-hour later, it jolted her. Her phone rarely rang, but it was the breathless alarm in Joyce's voice, barely coherent, which startled her.

'I told them I'd seen him!.... He's *here*!'

'Where, Joyce.... Where?'

Joyce didn't answer directly. 'He had a knife at my throat, and he's coming after me still... he'll catch up any minute and be here! You've got to get someone to help me.'

'I can't send help if I don't know where, Joyce. *Where?*' Ellie's shouted last word finally broke through Joyce's frantic stupor.

'Uh... I'm at a phone booth on the Bowery. Just by...' Joyce's train of thought was suddenly broken. 'He's here again! Though I don't know if —'

Sudden clatter, then the line went dead.

* * *

Twenty-eight minutes before

'I'm just going to grab a breath of air,' Joyce remarked to one of the other girls as she made her way out of the Beth Jacobs Refuge. 'I won't be long.'

First and foremost, she was annoyed, so felt she needed a quick break to clear her head. Although the other girls had shuffled off to other part of the main hall, she could still feel their eyes on her at moments: questioning, doubting, making fun or her, or maybe snide remarks about her again as she saw a couple of them whispering to each other and then one of them smiling her way.

She had to get out!

And although she was pleased that Ellie had broken things up, she was almost as bad. Simply saying flatly that if she'd seen him, 'That's the end of it.' More or less saying that the other girls had to humour her and accept what she said. But if Ellie had truly believed her about seeing Larsen, she'd have asked more questions: 'Where did you see him? If we can't wait for Fenton to return, then maybe we should call the police.'

Nobody believed her anymore!

As her feet hit the street outside, she found herself instinctively looking to where she thought she'd seen Larsen, a hundred and twenty yards or so along. And if Ellie had believed her and come outside with her, as she should have done, Joyce would have pointed to where she thought she'd seen him.

'He was by that shop doorway for a moment, but then as he looked my way, he ducked back in again. Or is that an alleyway there, I'm not sure?'

The words played in her mind as she found herself unconsciously drifting that way, trying to discern if it was a recessed doorway or alleyway she'd seen him duck into.

Maybe she should have waited for Fenton to return, but she was sure he'd be gone by then; perhaps Larsen even timed it to appear when Fenton had gone for lunch. The big rush on the street had finished hours ago, most people were still at work, so she had a clear view for most of the hundred yards ahead, only a dozen or so stragglers also on their lunch-breaks in-between. She couldn't see him again now.

No doubt he'd moved on, or perhaps it had been an apparition all along. A figment of her imagination. *That was what most people said about her stories, wasn't it?* If she could see him again and point him out, this time they'd know she was telling the truth!

But the patch of street ahead where she'd originally seen him was empty now, except for a young couple ambling along, nobody who looked remotely like...

And then suddenly, as if answering her wishes, he was there again! Just beyond the young couple. She had to blink for a second to make sure that it wasn't in fact an apparition. Make sure she wasn't just seeing things.

He was staring straight ahead at first, as if contemplating something directly across the street, and there was no mistaking that droop on his right eye, just below the rim of his glasses. Then he turned to look directly towards her, as if picking her out among the half-dozen people in between, seemed to meet her eye for a fleeting second before falling back as quickly into the shadowed recess he'd emerged from.

An alleyway or a doorway?

As she got closer, moving faster now to catch a glimpse of him again, confirm that it wasn't just an apparition after all — she could see that it was a small alley.

But from her position and angle — the young couple now walking past her — she couldn't see him the first yard or so.

She moved closer. Still nobody apparent, and she began to think again that she had been seeing things after all, or he'd appeared briefly as a tease, then as quickly slipped away again.

It wasn't until she was almost upon the alley that she finally saw him, emerging from its deeper shadows. They met eyes, and a gentle smile teased one corner of his mouth.

'Are you interested in cats?'

Now she'd seen him, perhaps she should just turn and run. But there were people walking close by, so she didn't feel threatened. And she was intrigued by the strange question. 'Well, I suppose... why?'

He looked thoughtfully at her, then just past her shoulder, as if he was seeking inspiration from someone unseen. 'Because two phrases come to mind: 'curiosity killed the cat'... and the 'cat and the canary.'

His action was so quick, it made her gasp — reaching out and pulling her into an embrace, as if they were lovers. Then he turned and fell back with her through a recess to one side of the alley. An eight-foot passage that led to the back of a building. Suddenly they were out of sight of the main street and the alley.

It hit Joyce then that he'd been looking past her shoulder to time people passing, and had chosen a moment when nobody would have seen his sudden action.

She caught the glint of a blade in her side vison and felt its cool press against her skin.

'What are you going to do?' she asked breathlessly.

'What do you think?' She felt his warm breath against her other cheek. 'What does the cat normally do to the canary?'

CHAPTER TWENTY-FIVE

Constable Fenton was still at lunch, so Ellie's first instinct was to rush out and grab a Hansom to the Bowery.

But if Joyce's claim that it was Larsen was real — which perhaps she should have taken more notice of before — then she would need some help. And the telephone was right there at her hand.

She phoned Finley Jameson first. Although he was slightly further away from the Bowery, she recalled his number off by heart: *Manhattan 1334*. At the time he'd applied for a phone, allocation numbers were only up to the 1100's, but Finley told her he'd wanted one that others could easily remember, so had requested 1334, the same as his house number on Greenwich Avenue, 'As long as it's still four digits, that's fine according to the phone company,' he'd shared his phone ordering saga with Ellie. And, as he'd rightly surmised, the number had stuck in her mind.

Jameson cut in halfway through her breathless account. 'Do you know which phone kiosk she was calling from on the Bowery? There are two or three along that stretch.'

'I don't know. The line went dead before I could find out.' She contemplated for a second. 'I suppose the closest would be the easiest guess.'

'Perhaps. But also perhaps not the right guess.' Jameson appeared to be struck with an afterthought. 'Any noises in the background you can think of that might indicate her position?'

At first, Ellie couldn't think of anything. But then she suddenly recalled something which had made Joyce's voice difficult to discern for a moment.

'There was a shunting noise in the background at one point, like a heavy engine, then a sharp whistle. I thought nothing of it at —.'

'Bowery East Station!' Jameson cut in breathlessly. 'Must go! I have to raise Joseph...'

For the second time in the last few minutes, Ellie found herself holding a dead line.

* * *

Joyce felt the cool press of the knife against her left cheek. Then it lifted a fraction, her body tense, breath held as to what would happen next.

The sound of a Hansom cab suddenly pulling up in the street directly by the alley entrance. More pause for thought from her slope-eyed assailant. The sound of a door opening and closing, then another.

And she felt herself being pulled back slightly towards the alley, Larsen leaning out for a glimpse of which way the passengers were heading.

If they made their way up the alley, they'd have a clear view of Larsen with a knife at her throat.

As Larsen leant furthest from her glimpsing out, seemingly distracted, she seized her opportunity. She sank her teeth as hard as she could into his hand gripped around her, screaming out loud as she wrenched free.

'Help... *help*! It's the Ripper!' She burst past the elderly couple who'd just got out the cab. 'Stop him... *stop him*!' she pleaded desperately as she ran on. But they looked too frail to be able to stop anyone.

Larsen was about eight yards behind her, shouting, 'Thief... *thief*!' Obviously he'd picked up on her 'victim gets the attention' cry and also needed an explanation of why he was chasing her.

Except his plea was supported by him partly nursing his bloodied hand as he ran, and she also noticed that he'd quickly tucked his knife away.

The few people they passed simply looked perplexed, not sure who to believe or who they should try and apprehend. Or perhaps they were simply loath to get involved — because whoever they stopped, a thief or the Ripper, they were bound to be armed.

Joyce's breath caught in her throat, her heart pounding hard. He was catching on her, only six yards behind now — he'd be upon her any minute!

She glanced back frantically, caught sight of a tram approaching behind Larsen. If she could just keep her pace up until it pulled alongside them? She put on an extra spurt, heard its rumble and rattle reverberate off the road and buildings each side.

Five yards... *four* behind her. And at the last second, she darted to the side, seemingly right in front of the tram, heard its screech of brakes and just cleared its far side by only inches.

'Keep your eyes open in future!' the driver shouted after her, the brakes as quickly released as the tram trundled past.

But she was fast away the other side, hardly paying attention, glancing back only to catch a quick glimpse of Larsen the far side of the tram, peering between the gaps in passengers to see which way she'd gone.

Her ploy had worked! He hadn't had the time or space to follow. The partial-braking had also made the tram's passing more ponderous. She darted up the street and took the next left-hand turn, eager to put as much distance between them as possible.

A short cross-street, no more than sixty yards — she hoped to be at its end before Larsen turned into it, so that he wouldn't know which way she'd gone.

But just eight yards from its end, she heard his rapid, frantic stride turn into the street — a quick glance back to ensure it was him. *Damn*. No way of disguising which way she was headed.

Unless... *unless*.

As she burst into the wider main street, she spotted another cross street just twenty yards away on the opposite side. Hopefully she could get to it before he reached the main street. That way he'd be looking each direction with no sight of her. Some more time and distance bought... *or maybe she could lose him entirely*.

This side street was longer, a good 100 yards before the next main street ahead. Joyce was split between running as fast as she could along the street and making her step light so that her rapid feet-patter wasn't discernible from too far behind, otherwise Larsen would know from listening out which way she'd run.

Thankfully, halfway along someone had come out to empty their ash into one of two barrels in the street, the clatter of their bucket against iron to ensure they got all the contents out masking the noise of her running.

She was breathless as she approached the end of the street, but thankfully there was no sign of Larsen behind. Obviously, he'd got lost with direction for a moment in the main street behind.

Which way to head at the end? Billows of smoky-steam to the left made the decision for her. They seemed to merge with the day's faint mist which hadn't been fully burned off by the sun. The combination of smoke and mist would help obscure which way she'd gone.

She ran towards it, realizing twenty yards in that she was on the Bowery, and the smoky steam was from the train that had just passed on the raised parapet she was now running beneath.

She looked frantically ahead for a policeman. *None in sight*! The only one she'd seen so far had been 300 yards along on the last main street she'd crossed and heading away from her. Larsen would have been on her in a quarter of that distance, before she'd even got the copper's attention.

But now with the billowing smoke and steam, there was little visibility beyond eighty yards. Good for masking her own movements, but not for trying to pick out coppers.

Then beyond the next patch of swirling steam, she saw the telephone. She fished in her pocket for a nickel as she ran towards it.

* * *

With the billowing steam, it took Jameson a moment to spot Argenti with John Whelan ahead. They stood at the side of a police Hansom; among the numerous black Hansoms ahead, it would have been impossible to pick them out otherwise.

Ellie was at Jameson's side. They'd picked her up on the way to the Bowery.

'Any sign of her?' Jameson asked as Ellie scoured the street-scene ahead.

'No... not as yet. But apart from Broadway, she could hardly have chosen a busier street.'

Jameson nodded grimly. 'Probably why she chose it. That and the train steam obscuring vision. Far easier to get lost in it all.' But right now, she wasn't only lost to Larsen, but them as well. No hope at all of picking her out if Ellie hadn't been with them.

As Argenti came to the side of their Hansom, Jameson was struck with an afterthought. 'Joseph. Ellie here is keenly looking for this Joyce — but can't see her right now. Meanwhile, we could make ourselves useful by keeping our eyes peeled for Larsen or anything unusual — particularly anyone running.'

'Good thinking,' Argenti agreed. 'I'll head on with Whelan a few hundred yards...'

'And we'll head back a similar distance,' Jameson picked up. 'In case she's gone that way' As Lawrence swung the Hansom around, Jameson called out of the open window, 'First of us to see something, stand up high on the cab driver's seat and wave frantically. 'That should be visible amongst all this steam and smoke.'

* * *

The smoke billowed into any windows left open and the train would rattle and shake any rooms adjacent to the tracks. As a result, the Bowery had increasingly become an area for shops, warehouses and run-down hotels and lodging houses. The only residents those so down on their luck that a room at half-price — even with the walls vibrating every fifteen minutes — was better than no room at all.

While most of the smoke and steam billowed up — or

sideways depending on the wind — much of it would also slowly drift down in the wake of the passing train. The Bowery's own intermittent cloud cover, barely clearing before the next billowing train arrived.

It was through that mist that Ellie first caught sight of Larsen about eighty yards away. She wasn't even sure at first if he'd already seen her, or was just generally peering through the mist in her direction.

But as his eyes locked on her and he jolted into a run towards her, she knew! She dropped the phone mid-sentence on Ellie the other end.

She darted away frantically, glancing back at intervals. She couldn't see him at first, lost among some steamy-mist swirls — and when she did catch sight of him again, he seemed to have gained twenty yards on her already.

She looked around desperately for anyone who might help her, putting voice to her thoughts breathlessly as she ran.

'Help... *help*! It's the Ripper after me!'

But all that returned were stark, vacant looks from down-and-outs, a leer from a passing tramp, a drunkard on the ground tucking in tighter to a doorway away from the disturbance to his sleep.

She looked frantically each side for places she could run into, but this stretch seemed nothing but closed-door warehouses and small lodging houses. Not anywhere large enough for her to get lost in, get away from Larsen. In any case, she'd need to dart in a doorway in a patch of mist, so that he wouldn't know where she'd gone.

But Larsen was fast catching on her, there were hardly enough steam patches between them to obscure. And then suddenly ahead she saw a more respectable couple: a stout middle-aged man with a broad, bristly moustache with a woman with a furled-up pink umbrella, using it as if it was a walking-cane.

She tried again. 'Please, please... *help me*! It's the Ripper.'

The couple turned to look at her, alarmed.

But Larsen, rapidly approaching, called out, 'She's a thief, *a thief* I tell you! She took my wallet and cut me.' He waved his bloodied left hand to illustrate.

The couple looked from Larsen to herself, as if unsure who to believe. And then as the woman's brolly point came up towards her, as if to fend her off, she realized that Larsen's account held more water with them. After all, the Ripper was a rarity, whereas thieves were thick on the ground, especially in the Bowery.

No time to argue, Larsen would be upon her any second, and she'd need something to fend him off. At that moment, proving the cry of 'thief' seemed to be the lesser of two evils. Joyce grabbed the woman's brolly, wrenched it from her hands and ran on.

Larsen was rapidly closing on her, calling out 'Thief!' again, now echoed by the stout man not far behind him. *With two of them shouting the same, who now among the people she passed would believe her?*

But no matter. She knew that with the brolly in her grip, she could fend off Larsen effectively. Before joining the railways, her father had been fencing champion in New York's Eleventh Regiment, one of the best swordsmen in the State. And up until his death, she'd have regular fencing sessions with him. She just hoped the skill was still there, that she hadn't lost it over the years.

At the point of no return, as Larsen's rapid stride closed in on her, she turned and went into an en-guard position with the brolly.

Larsen looked at her curiously, as if she was mad.

He lunged towards her and she swirled and cut around, prodding him hard in the chest. Larsen tried again, and she swung below this time and hit him solidly in the stomach. On the third lunge from Larsen, she struck him in the neck, drawing an angry red welt.

Larsen scowled, losing all patience. He drew his knife out, and she could see that its blade was long, ten or eleven inches. She'd have to be more cautious.

At the sight of the blade, the stout man behind shrank back. Obviously, it had struck him then that her 'Ripper' claim might be true.

Joyce fended off the first few knife lunges, but the next one caught part of her dress by the shoulder, ripping it, a small welt of blood appearing. Although she managed to get in a few sharp prods in between, the last to Larsen's face, in turn drawing a trickle of blood.

Larsen was so wrapped up in his knife lunges that he didn't notice the two burly workmen approaching behind him, the first one appearing to take outrage at this attack on a young damsel and fancy his luck.

He came in quickly to brace Larsen from behind, and whether from his approaching footfall or the fleeting shift in Joyce's gaze to past Larsen's shoulder — Larsen became aware of him at the last second, leaning down and away. Larsen as quickly swung back with his knife, slicing a savage stripe across the man's cheek.

Blood welled up, rapidly dripping down, one of the workman's hands going to his damaged face.

'Yer fucker, I'll have yer!' He stumbled forward, as if oblivious to the pain.

'The next will take out your gullet,' Larsen said icily, finally bringing the man up short as the long blade was waved threateningly, his friend behind also looking uncertain.

Joyce seized the stand-off moment to dart towards the run-down building to one side. It looked larger than most of the lodging houses she'd so far passed; hopefully large enough to get lost in.

* * *

The frantic running was the first thing to catch Jameson's eye, a hundred yards ahead through a shifting steam patch.

'Is that her... Joyce?' he asked Ellie.

Some shifting mist and steam obscured for a moment, but then as Ellie saw the girl ahead take a fencing posture, she was sure. Ellie recalled some of Joyce's past fanciful stories involving hers and her father's fencing prowess.

As Ellie breathlessly exclaimed, 'Yes, *yes*... that's her!' Jameson called out the side window for Lawrence to get Argenti's and Whelan's attention.

Lawrence took a slower cant as he stood and frantically waved with one hand.

'I think I've alerted them,' Lawrence said as they picked up pace again after a moment.

But fifty yards away, they saw another two men get involved in the affray. And as Larsen struck out at one of them with his knife, they saw Joyce rush away into a building to one side.

'Joyce!' Ellie shouted out, but her voice was drowned out by the sounds of the street and the shunting of a passing train.

Then seconds later, realizing what had happened, they watched Larsen race into the same building in pursuit.

Pulling up by the building, they had to wait only a moment for Argenti's and Whelan's Hansom to catch up.

'She's gone in there,' Jameson announced to Argenti. 'Larsen not far behind her.'

'The Albion.' Argenti grimaced tautly. 'She could have chosen better places. As many thieves and cutthroats as vagrants. If Larsen doesn't get her, *they* will.'

'Or maybe they'll be better equipped to deal with Larsen,' Jameson said hopefully, glancing towards the workman who

Ellie was now tending to, pressing her hankie tight against his torn cheek.

'Maybe,' Argenti said with more guarded hope in his tone. He took the Remington .44 from inside his jacket and signalled Whelan to do the same. 'But at least with it being Larsen, *we* came equipped.'

CHAPTER TWENTY-SIX

The darkness inside the building was the first thing to hit Joyce. After some brief light by the unmanned entrance hall, she was rapidly swallowed up in pitch darkness as she got deeper into its corridors.

While it might help hide and obscure her from Larsen, it didn't help being able to see where she was going, and in any case he'd be able to hear the rapid patter of her steps. She couldn't hear anyone else running on the corridors — but then thankfully after a moment came the rumble and shunt of a passing train, seeming to rattle the whole building and drown everything out. Her step became more open and rapid as it passed, taking a couple of dog-leg corridor turns to hopefully obscure which way she'd gone to Larsen following.

Then as the noise of the train finally passed, she paused for a second, breath held, listening out for his pursuing footsteps.

Something faint thirty or so yards away on the corridor dogleg she'd just come from, the step shuffling for a moment, uncertain — as if unsure which way she'd gone.

But then another footfall superimposed, coming from the

other way towards her, and she was suddenly uncertain herself: could Larsen have gone around in a corridor loop, and now was heading back towards her? But if she ran from those fresh footsteps, she'd bring herself closer to those steps behind. *Which one was Larsen?* Her breath caught in her throat, the footsteps ahead now closer, almost upon her.

The footsteps behind were also advancing, and she felt herself still frozen in indecision. No side corridor in-between she could escape into — her caught breath only finally releasing as an old lady materialized through the darkness ahead.

The old lady attempted a smile at Joyce, but it came across more as a mordant grimace. Joyce gave a taut smile back and ran past her. Not worth trying to summon help from; she looked too frail and decrepit to be able to halt Larsen for even a second.

Scant light from the next corridor she turned into — a half-boarded-up grimy window at its end. But it wouldn't help if Larsen came into the same stretch of corridor in pursuit — he'd see her clearly.

Two-thirds of the way along were some rough wooden steps. She headed up, taking them two and three at a time, and at the end turned right, finding herself immediately in a darker corridor again.

But suddenly there was light ahead in this corridor too; though different to the steady, subdued light of the corridor below. This was a stark, flickering glare.

As it came closer, she wondered whether to run the other way from it — but then suddenly beyond the flickering glare she could make out two figures: vagrants or ash-barrel sifters, their clothes rough and faces grimy, the first man holding up an oil lamp as they squinted towards her for a better look.

But they looked burly enough to be able to hold Larsen off; or at least give her a place to hide away.

'*Help me*!' she hissed, keeping her voice low so that it wouldn't carry too far. 'I'm being pursued by the Ripper.'

'Are yer now?' The first man looked to the other, as if he didn't quite believe her.

'Can you hide me away... at least until he's gone?'

Again they exchanged a glance before the first man commented, 'Suppose we could, at leas' for a while. Our room's right here.' He hooked a thumb to a door behind them.

Brief nod and smile in thanks and they hustled her quickly into the room — her caught breath only releasing as the door shut behind them. Hopefully Larsen hadn't seen or heard them.

But as she felt herself pinned back against the wall behind and the knife at her throat, she wasn't sure she'd made the right decision.

* * *

Larsen had heard faint voices on the floor above when he was at the bottom of the stairway. Sounded like her voice among a couple of mumbling male voices. Then seconds later, a door opening and closing. No voices anymore, though he was pretty sure he could pick out where that closed-door sound had come from. Well, within a couple of doors each side.

He knocked on the first possible door. No answer. He leant closer to it: no sounds from within.

He tried the next. Chair screeching on the floor, footsteps approaching. A mid-thirties woman, face worn, hair greying before her time, opened the door carrying an infant boy on one hip, a girl of six or seven at her side looking up with wide eyes.

'Sorry to disturb you,' Larsen said. 'But has a young woman just come by your door?'

'When might that be?'

'Oh, only moments ago.' But Larsen was already looking past her at the room behind, starting to think it was unlikely — no men in sight — as she shook her head.

'No. Nobody's come by here in a while. The last was days ago.'

But as she said *days ago*, Larsen picked up the mumbled shriek from beyond the next door along, and held up one hand hurriedly.

'Thank you... *thank you*.'

The door was barely shut before he rushed to the next door. *Knock first or simply kick it in*? For a moment he was undecided.

* * *

'That's a nice necklace you're wearin',' the man said, the cool of his blade pressed just above it. 'Any jewels in it?'

'I'm not sure. It was a present from one of my father's friends. He was a...' Her voice trailed off. The last thing these men wanted to hear were stories about Counts and noblemen. Besides, she knew that the necklace was just costume jewellery. Nevertheless, she'd had to save her pennies for it and had bought it in a flea market because it reminded her of a necklace her mother planned to give to her, which no doubt had ended up with her stepmother along with everything else. Although as attached as she was to the necklace, it was worth parting with if it might save her life. 'But take it by all means.'

The knife-wielding vagrant smiled and she could feel and smell his fetid breath against her cheek. 'I don' think we need yer permission now, do we?'

His friend mirrored his smile, then reached out and yanked the necklace from her. As he placed it on a trunk to one side, she noticed some stopwatches, rings, a bracelet and a couple of pocket books laying there. She swallowed. She'd wandered into a thieves' den in the hope of saving herself from Larsen. *Out of the frying pan into the fire*!

'Such smooth skin too,' the knife-wielder said, stroking her bare neck.

Then as his hand drifted down and pulled her dress off one shoulder, she realized with horror that they might want more from her than just whatever valuables she had on her. She swallowed harder and her body started to tremble.

'My, my. Like a frightened little deer,' he said.

If only he knew, she thought. Among the many men she'd slept with, a number had been as filthy and fetid. But that now seemed in another lifetime, almost another person; and it was fear of getting dragged back to those horror memories that was making her tremble, not her inexperience with men.

As he yanked her dress down further on one side and reached inside her petticoat to roughly grasp her left breast, she let out a shriek, quickly muffled by his knife hand.

'Now can't have yer disturbin' the neighbours, can we?' he said.

His friend gloated. 'Especially a nice neighbourhood like this.'

Two sharp raps on the door interrupted their chuckling halfway through. They quickly fell silent again.

'Who might that be?' The knife-wielder ventured after a second. Then in the silence following: 'Toby, is that you?'

No answer. Only a heavy kick against the door after a few seconds. Then another, and the door burst open, part of its rotting frame splintering.

Larsen stood there, his long-bladed knife held out, part-guarding, part-threatening as he assessed what he was facing.

The knife-wielder shoved Joyce brusquely to one side, realizing he'd need a clear aim and swing at this intruder. His friend quickly reached for the long billy club against one wall as he moved in to back-up his friend; almost as if this was a choreographed routine they'd enacted before.

To his credit, Joyce watched the knife-wielder get in a half-decent lunge high up on Larsen's left arm, drawing some blood, just a second before Larsen sliced through his jugular with a backswing.

His friend on the tail-end of that backswing landed a solid blow to Larsen's right shoulder as his knife-wielding colleague sank to his knees in a pool of blood.

Joyce shrank back from the fight, trembling gripper her deeper at the impossibility of her plight. Once Larsen had dispensed with the club-wielding thief, she'd be next; even if by some miracle, clubman won out, she'd no doubt be raped or possibly even murdered as well. And no possible escape — their life or death tussle was taking place by the doorway, the only way out.

Suddenly it felt as if her trembling was getting even more intense, before she realized it was the rumble of a passing train shaking the room.

Clubman seemed to be keeping Larsen more at bay with the reach of the Billy club, but as Larsen drove his knife in hard to clubman's right shoulder, she knew it was only a matter of time.

Clubman took a step back and bravely transferred the club to his left hand rather than drop it. But how effective might he be with his left hand?

And as Joyce looked desperately around for escape routes again, she saw the train carriage the other side of the window, grime-stained from years of smoke and soot from passing trains.

It was surreal. She felt she could almost reach out and touch the passengers the other side. A couple of them looked absently towards the building, but with the grimy window and only a single oil lamp, she doubted they could see into the room clearly; whereas outside, it was broad daylight.

She tried the window, but it appeared to be jammed solid. She looked around frantically for something solid.

Larsen glanced towards her trying the window, but the distraction caught him a club blow to his shoulder and side of his head. Larsen leant back and then swung in again, driving his knife into the clubman's left shoulder. But it didn't connect cleanly this time, only drew some superficial blood. The club was still held threateningly, swinging quickly towards him again.

Joyce spied the iron scuttle in the corner, half-full of coal. She didn't bother to empty any out — she wanted the extra weight in any case — just swung it as hard as she could against the window.

The club blow only glanced off Larsen's this time, and he swung quickly underneath it and sunk his blade into the man's stomach.

The window shattered cleanly on impact. Joyce leapt through it and ran towards the closest train carriage door.

The man clung onto Larsen for a moment, then took a step back to swing his club in again. But half the strength was gone from the swing this time, and Larsen parried easily, driving home a far heavier knife lunge to the stomach to finish the man.

Pushing the bloodied figure brusquely to one side, Larsen leapt through the shattered window as the train outside started to move.

CHAPTER TWENTY-SEVEN

The sound of the window shattering galvanized Jameson, Argenti and Whelan into action. Still on the floor below, they ran up the stairs and into the room with its half-open, splintered-frame door.

A six-carriage train, the last of the carriages was just passing the window. Jameson looked frantically out as Argenti's voice came from behind.

'It's moving too fast for us to catch it now, Finley.'

'I know. But they're on it,' Jameson said, peering keenly towards the receding train. 'I just caught sight of the back of Larsen two carriages along.'

Jameson looked desperately around for options, saw the steps down from the station platform thirty yards along. He beckoned towards Argenti and Whelan. 'Come on. We might still be able to catch them!'

They clambered out of the window, ran along the platform and down the steps. By the time Jameson had summoned Lawrence, the train was over two hundred yards ahead. Jameson and Argenti went with Lawrence, while Whelan followed with Ellie in the police Hansom.

'When's the next station?' Jameson asked Argenti.

'A mile and a half along, north end of the Bowery.'

'Hopefully we'll catch up with it by then.'

Lawrence was driving the Hansom at break-neck speed. Looking up at the train on its parapet above, Jameson could see that they'd already gained almost a hundred yards on it. But they weren't close enough to pick any people inside the train. He bit at his lip. If Larsen got to Joyce before they reached the train, no doubt he'd knife her and be away at the next station.

Jameson called out the window, 'Can you go any faster, Lawrence?'

'I'm almost at full pelt, but the train has gathered momentum too. It will no doubt start slowing in its approach to the next station.'

'No doubt.' Jameson bit at his bottom lip. By then it might be too late. But as they got to within sixty yards of it, he thought he saw the back of Larsen again, moving hurriedly through, now at the start of the second carriage along. 'I think I can see him again. *Larsen*!'

'Any sign of Joyce?' Argenti asked. He was leaning and craning his neck from his side of the Hansom to get a clearer view.

'Not yet, I...' But then he thought he caught some recognizable movement towards the end of the same carriage — a girl moving hurriedly through. *Could that be Joyce?* 'I can see someone that could be her — but they're too distant to make out clearly.' Another thought suddenly hit Jameson. If that figure was Joyce and Larsen caught up with her before the final front carriage, she'd have nowhere left to go! Unless the train reached the next station before then and she could leap out and make good an escape.

His breath seemed to catch in his throat with the unfolding drama on the train on the parapet above, now only forty yards ahead. Some drama ahead now too as Lawrence had to swing around a brewery cart which was going ponderously slow.

As they swung back in again, Jameson caught sight of a ticket guard ahead of Larsen holding one hand out in a stopping motion. Obviously, Larsen had pushed brusquely past one too many passengers, and the guard was intent on putting a stop to it.

Jameson's hopes rose that Joyce would get away — then as quickly sank again almost in time with the guard sinking to his knees in front of Larsen. The action with the blade had been so deft and quick that Jameson had hardly noticed it, but there remained little doubt that Larsen had run the guard through. *Now there was nothing to stop Larsen getting to Joyce*!

'We've got to stop him!' Jameson exclaimed. 'He's just stabbed a guard, and he'll be upon Joyce any moment. Can you get a clear shot at him? You need to be this side.'

Jameson was already in motion and swapping positions, Argenti taking his gun out as he sidled across.

'It's difficult,' Argenti said as he finally spotted Larsen walking rapidly past the collapsed guard. 'Moving train and still passengers in between. I could catch them by mistake.'

Jameson leant down and peered up at the train, catching sight of Joyce at the start of the front carriage, Larsen now two-thirds of the way through the second carriage. 'We've got to try something! Aim high, hopefully that will warn him off.'

Argenti took aim at a point just above Larsen's head in a clear patch between passengers. The shot zinged off the metal roof of the train, so he aimed a bit lower — saw it shatter the top part of the glass window towards the end of the second carriage.

Larsen looked startled, looking towards the source of the shot and finally picking up their Hansom racing along below. But it only held him up for a moment before he raced on with fresh determination, now scurrying a bit lower to make himself a more difficult target.

He was out of sight for a moment as he went from the second carriage to the first. And as he reappeared, they could see Joyce just over halfway down the carriage look anxiously back at him.

'*Try again*!' Jameson implored. 'We've got to stop him or warn him off.'

Argenti's first shot fired hit the glass high up, but didn't shatter it — but the second did, half of a glass pane exploding inward. Larsen only faltered for a second in his stride, but the main result was him hunkering down even lower. The carriage was half-full, and most of the passengers were also now bent low away from the shots; in a perverse way it gave Larsen a clearer passage towards Joyce.

Jameson noticed the train start to slow as it approached the next station 400 yards ahead — now they were practically alongside it and had a clearer view of the drama being played out between Larsen and Joyce.

'*Another*!' Jameson shouted out.

Joyce was almost at the end of the carriage, looking back desperately at the rapidly approaching Larsen as the shot came — the shattered window between them making her step falter for a second as much as Larsen's.

Jameson looked anxiously between them and the upcoming station, and his heart began to sink. It didn't look like the train would reach the station for her to be able to get out and away before Larsen reached her.

* * *

As the train guard had come in between them, Joyce's hopes had lifted. Someone had come to her rescue! She was going to be able to get away.

But then as she'd watched Larsen run the guard through, those hopes had plummeted like a stone, far worse than even before. Until then, she'd held out some slim hope that someone would intervene, put a stop to Larsen and save her. But now that hope was gone: if he could knife a train guard, then nobody else was likely to stop him.

That fact evidenced by the number of people in the carriage in-between who hastily kept out of Larsen's way or held up their hands. *Not me. I'm not going to get in your way*. Or simply averted eye contact with either Larsen or herself, as if the two of them were invisible. The drama being played out before their eyes wasn't happening.

The shots being fired seemed to detach them further from the drama — most passengers sinking down further in their seats and shielding themselves. Of course, it had the opposite effect on her — *another possible saviour*! Though it took her a moment as she scampered frantically through the carriage with Larsen in pursuit to be able to spot the Hansom almost level with them in the street below where the shots had come from.

The man closest to the Hansom window firing his pistol seemed familiar, but it wasn't until she saw Finley Jameson leaning across beyond that she could place him. She'd seen Jameson a number of times visiting Ellie at the Beth Jacobs, and with the recent murders Detective Argenti had accompanied him on a couple of occasions.

The train was slowing. Without pausing her frantic stride, she glanced out the window. The station was still too far away. Larsen would be upon her by then.

Only four more yards to go before the carriage end, and Larsen was only ten or eleven yards behind her. Another shot came then, taking out a side window between them, and Joyce was suddenly struck with a thought. Perhaps her only hope. If she backed into the recess of the last carriage door along closest to the road and the Hansom, then Larsen would be more visible then and hopefully present a clearer target.

She backed away as Larsen approached, looking frantically between the upcoming station, the Hansom and Larsen. The train slowed more, now doing no more than 20 mph. But the station was still a hundred or so yards away and Larsen was almost upon her.

As she backed against the last door along, he was only five yards away, a faint cruel smile rising in anticipation, his knife brandished openly, the guard's blood still visible on it.

Four yards, *three* — the train slowing more, about 15 mph now — and as Larsen lifted his right arm with the knife, the anticipated shot came.

Her breath held in that frozen moment, her heart pounding uncontrollably as she saw him stagger a fraction to one side, as if off balance. But then she realized with horror that his knife arm was still raised, poised to come down as he got his balance back.

The shot hadn't hit him cleanly, only caught the top part of his left shoulder as he'd swung towards her. Another shot came quickly, but it zinged just above them, hitting a ceiling light fitting — and in that instant, as the knife swung down, she made her snap decision. She turned the handle behind her, tumbled out of the open door and onto the trackside.

She felt a wrench to her right ankle and a jarring pain short through her knee and hip on that side as she hit the ground.

But it wasn't as bad as she'd feared. The train had only been doing 10 mph, and there was wooden boarding below her rather than rocks or shale.

She saw Larsen tempted to follow her for a second, but then another shot fired quickly warned him off. He dived for cover out of firing line on the far side of the receding train.

She scrambled to the side rail and levered up on it, both

to take the weight off her damaged ankle and lift one hand in acknowledgement to her saviours.

Argenti and Jameson were now standing by the side of the Hansom, looking up at her with concern, and she could now see Ellie Cullen running towards them from another Hansom which had pulled up behind.

'Are you okay?' Ellie shouted up at her.

Her whole body shaking, she nodded numbly, hardly trusting her voice to speak.

'We'll be up to you in a minute,' Jameson reassured. 'But don't worry, you're safe now.'

Another numb nod in gratitude, an uncertain smile in return. Wondering if she dared believe that was true.

But as she saw the last of the train pull into the station ahead and caught sight of Larsen on the opposite side of the tracks twenty yards short of the platform, moving steadily towards her, she realized that once again her brief faith had been an illusion. She wasn't safe.

CHAPTER TWENTY-EIGHT

Erik Larsen looked around the room. A drab and dilapidated warehouse floor, a trestle table opened up at its centre as a makeshift desk, an oil lamp at its end the only light. His second meeting with the man behind the desk, the first had been in a far more salubrious setting. But he supposed with half of New York's police now hunting him down, he could expect no less. *Beggars can't be choosers.*

As before, the man's henchman was at his side. No doubt in case the meeting went the wrong way and Larsen was tempted to add him to his long list of knife victims.

'Quite the drama,' the man said, glancing to the newspapers to one side on the trestle-table. 'Guard and Bowery-bum killed, a couple of others injured...'

'There was little choice,' Larsen said flatly, matter-of-fact.

'But even after all of that, the girl got away.'

Larsen could feel the man's eyes on him more intently, accusing. 'Yes. She started to clamber over the side rails, and if I'd got too close the cop below would have had a clear shot at me.'

The man nodded, as if he knew who that might be, or at

least accepted Larsen's account. 'Still, you managed to get away, that's the main thing. Ready to fight another day.'

'Yes. Life has its compensations.'

The man smiled wryly, not sure whether Larsen was being ironic, or this was what passed for philosophical thought in Denmark. He wasn't too surprised that Larsen had managed to lay-low and not be detected appearing as he did now. He wore a strange top hat with straggly grey hair falling out of it to his shoulders, along with face make-up which made him look twenty years older. His sloping eye was covered with dark glasses and he carried a white stick. '*That of an old blind man*,' Larsen had enlightened. '*Who could appear less threatening than that? Let alone a skilled knifeman able to stalk his victims*.'

A simple nod in response, accepting the rationale. But apart from the white stick, Larsen's appearance had struck the man more like an ageing wizard or magician.

'As may be,' the man said. 'But could give us problems with continuing.'

'What? You think we should stop... at least for a while?'

'No. I think we should continue.'

'Oh, I see.' Although Larsen clearly didn't. And as he observed a wry smile rise from the man at his momentary confusion and heard a faint rustling in the shadows at the back of the warehouse beyond the glow of the single oil lamp, he felt a twinge of anxiety. What was that? *Someone in the shadows behind, or a rat scurrying?*

'Just that I thought you might need some help this time,' the man said. 'Someone to provide look-out and back-up.'

'Yes, I suppose.' Larsen's brief apprehension eased. 'That girl will be watched very closely now.'

'That she will certainly be. But I'm actually proposing a fresh girl as target. Which your new accomplice has the details of.' The man looked to one side expectantly, and footsteps advanced from behind.

The rustling Larsen had heard earlier. But it was surprise more than apprehension that Larsen felt as the man came clearer into view in the glow of the oil lamp. Not only that a knifeman as skilled as himself would be chosen simply to be an *accomplice*, but also that, like Campbell, he was another Italian. He wondered if there was some pattern and purposeful reason for that?

'Here are the details of your next target.'

One hand lifted from the trestle table in offering as the man behind advanced and passed Larsen a sheet of paper.

* * *

'One heck of a fiasco,' Roosevelt said, glancing back at the newspapers on his desk before staring steadily across at Argenti and Jameson. 'Guard and a vagrant killed, passengers complaining of being hit by flying glass and being shot at by the police. And still after all of that, our man got away.'

'If I hadn't fired the shots, the girl might have been killed,' Argenti defended. 'Larsen was very close upon her at that point.'

'Yes. And we did manage to save the girl,' Jameson supported. 'The first to have been saved in this current bout of killings. That factor should not be overlooked.'

'That has indeed been taken into account,' Roosevelt said. 'But I have to look at the overall picture and the mayhem meanwhile caused to New York citizens. Were you aware that one of those complaining of being shot at was no less than Max Werner, Curator of the Metropolitan Art Museum, out for a day with his wife and daughter?'

'No, I didn't sir.' Argenti looked down briefly in supplication.

Jameson glanced briefly across at Argenti, appeared unsettled by him bowing so readily under Roosevelt's admonishment. Jameson didn't feel so inclined, possibly because he wasn't under Roosevelt's direct command, so he could risk being bolder.

'I'm not sure it would have helped much if Mr Werner had witnessed young Joyce being run through in front of his family. Given that alternative, I think a bit of flying glass would be of far lesser concern.'

Roosevelt's taut smile lasted only a second before he became more serious again, contemplating the two of them levelly.

'Your efforts in bringing about the girl's final safety are appreciated, but we do have certain codes of practice to be observed by the New York Police department. And one of those is not to endanger the lives of citizens while in pursuit of a criminal.' Roosevelt drew a fresh breath, as if he was summoning patience. 'After all, firing at a moving train like that, there was no guarantee that you might not have killed two or three innocent bystanders, and Larsen would *still* have got to the girl and killed her.'

Argenti simply nodded, sensing this was a bone Roosevelt wasn't easily going to let go of. But Jameson wasn't so easily deterred.

'Then I have to take main responsibility for that, Commissioner. It was I who urged Detective Argenti to fire at Larsen to warn him off the girl.' Jameson tapped the silver head of his cane, as if he was at the same time impatiently telegraphing the message. 'And it worked — particularly at the last moment as Joyce was by the side rail with Larsen advancing upon her. He realized then that Detective Argenti would have a clear shot at him, and so hastily retreated. And at that moment, I might add, there were no other people nearby at risk of being hit by a stray bullet.'

Those final seconds had been excruciatingly tense as they wondered whether Larsen would nevertheless take the risk and attempt to finish Joyce off. She'd started to climb over the side rail as Larsen moved closer, with Jameson directing from below, 'Clamber down as far as you can, then jump the last bit onto the Hansom roof.' He waved Lawrence into position directly beneath, but the distance between the last hand and foot holds was still a good twelve feet shy of the Hansom roof. If she'd already sprained her ankle, then a drop like this would surely break a leg or two. But it was the lesser of two evils than Larsen running her through.

Then with Larsen only yards away and Argenti firing another shot which zinged just past his shoulder, Larsen appeared to think better off it and pulled back and darted away.

Meanwhile, John Whelan had continued on to the station and up the steps to the platform to move in on Larsen the other side.

'But even though Larsen was warned off by a final shot,' Roosevelt commented, 'with Whelan trying to head him off — *still* Larsen managed to get away?'

'Yes, sir,' Argenti said. This was merely confirming details. Safer ground. 'Larsen didn't head back to the station ahead. He simply smashed and went through a window in the adjacent tenement block — as Joyce had earlier in gaining access to the train.' Argenti sighed. 'By the time Whelan got to the building, Larsen had disappeared into its warren of corridors, then no doubt swiftly out the back. Whelan checked the two main back alleys from the building, but there was no sign of Larsen. Long gone.'

'I see.' Roosevelt cradled his fingers on the desk top. 'And the girl's injuries — are they serious?'

'No. Sprained ankle and a few bruises.'

'The main damage has no doubt been psychological,' Jameson added. 'I doubt we'll see her venturing out of the Beth Jacobs for some while.'

'Might make these girls easier to watch over,' Roosevelt commented, looking pointedly at Argenti as he sensed he was about to make a comment. 'On which front, I've approved *two* police Constables for its entrance. So there'll be no future vulnerable lunch and dinner periods. They'll take their breaks at separate times.'

'Thank you, sir,' Argenti said. The first moment of reasonable accord between them since the meeting started.

'Perhaps should have been done earlier,' Roosevelt said with a pained grimace, as if partly reprimanding himself. 'But at least this girl is safe from now on.'

Safe now. Jameson nodded grimly. He recalled saying those same words to a trembling, uncertain Joyce as they'd got to her by the train railings, and an uncertain smile returning, as if she no longer trusted such assurances. They'd gone back to the Beth Jacobs for he and Lawrence to tend to her minor injuries, and halfway through he'd sent Lawrence out to get something from a local store. Lawrence returned minutes later with a bottle of champagne, and Jameson had boldly proclaimed a toast.

'*I think you deserve a drink after what you've been through, Joyce. And to celebrate the fact that you successfully got away from Larsen's clutches. The first to do so.*'

Again that uncertain smile as Joyce sipped at the champagne, Ellie looking anxiously around that Beth Jacobs wasn't watching them break the 'no alcohol' rule. But it wasn't until Ellie got talking more with Joyce that the smiles came easier. Perhaps the champagne, perhaps the fact that, as Ellie had related to Jameson afterwards, '*I think she's just realized she's got something to add to her stock of wild and fanciful stories. Although this time it's for real.*'

'Though of course that will only remain the case,' Roosevelt added as an afterthought, 'while these girls remain inside the Beth Jacobs. We can't assign constables to each and every one of them every time they decide to go out.'

'Yes, of course, sir,' Argenti said. 'We've already advised them to only venture out in pairs in future.'

But as their meeting wound to an end, a connected concern struck Jameson. He shared it with Argenti as he was about to get into his Hansom outside.

'With the Beth Jacobs Refuge now guarded so heavily, the venue and the girls might change. At least while it was focused there, we knew both the girls being aimed for and the proximity. If we no longer know that, we'll be at a disadvantage.'

'Either that or Larsen will have to be far more inventive to get to them.'

'Yes, I daresay.' But Jameson found that equally troubling.

CHAPTER TWENTY-NINE

His first thought was that she was too young, pristine and clean to be a lady of the night. Certainly, there were girls on the street as young as thirteen or fourteen, particularly in this area, but usually they were more grubby, their dresses stained or soiled; or, more often than not, they were just in rags.

This girl appeared superbly clean, her dress bright white and shining like a beacon amongst the drab surroundings. The neck and hem of her dress had been ordained with blue brocade. She looked quite sultry too, long black hair contrasting with her white dress. Girls this young who looked like this were usually safely at home in middle-class, respectable households — not out in the dead of night on the edges of the 4th Ward.

She'd been in the same prominent position on a street corner for a while now; so either she was waiting on someone or trying to lure clients. He decided to observe a while longer from across the street.

A couple of men stopped briefly to talk to her, then moved on. Either not the person she was waiting for, they were not seeking a street girl or not their type. Street girls being choosy about their clients was a rarity.

Finally, another man stopped in workmen's clothes — looked like a dock handler or porter — stopped and talked with her, then finally they headed off together.

But now he was curious. He decided to wait and watch out for her — a bit of pacing back and forth, a couple of cigarettes smoked to kill the time — but always one eye on that same corner. He'd wait an hour; most street girls turned their clients around in thirty or forty minutes. If she hadn't returned within an hour, his first assumption had probably been right: not a lady of the night.

So when fifty minutes later she returned to the same corner, he wasn't sure if he was disappointed that his first thoughts about her had been wrong, or pleased because he wouldn't have the delay of seeking another girl.

But just as he was about to cross the road towards her, slip into the first lamplight that would have made him visible to her, another man came from the street beyond the corner and started talking to her.

A brief nod in acquiescence from the man — slightly more respectable this time, wearing a clerk's or bookkeeper's brown suit — and then they went off together.

For a moment, he thought of choosing another girl. But this young girl had now intrigued him. Perfect for his purposes in so many ways. He decided to follow them at a discreet distance.

* * *

As soon as Kiara ushered the man in the brown suit out of her door, she went to check on her little brother, Toby. Only five years old, she'd promised him a hot chocolate before bedtime, but he'd fallen asleep straight after dinner reading a picture book, and it had got forgotten.

She'd heard him stir behind his door while the man had been on top of her, but like the good boy Toby was — and following her instructions — he hadn't knocked on the connecting door and disturbed them.

'What's that?' the man had asked, picking up on the faint noise.

'Probably just my cat. Or rats if the cat's asleep.'

The man had laughed briefly before resuming his grunting rhythm on top of her, and twenty minutes later she was ushering him out of her door and grabbing the key to open the connecting door to Toby.

Little more than a large larder with a makeshift bed on two wooden pallets, Toby blinked up at her as the light from the oil lamp spilled in.

'Sorry if I disturbed you,' he said in his soft, squeaky voice.

'No, you didn't disturb me at all.' She leant down and ruffled his hair. Her heart broke. He was such a good boy, worried about the slightest noise which might disturb her, when she'd have all manner of men the other side of the locked door, wheezing and grunting and sometimes worse. But then she'd explained to little Toby that it was only to put food on the table. Nothing more. These men weren't harming her. 'Now, how about that hot chocolate I promised,' she said brightly.

After taking Toby his hot chocolate and settling him back down by reading from the picture book with him for a moment, she put the gas lamp on a side table and checked herself in the mirror for a moment.

Only faint smudges to her eye make-up. She refreshed with some coal dust in a small petri dish. She'd become so expert at it, she was sure most clients didn't catch on that it wasn't real mascara. She then dipped another finger into the paste made from boiled red berries in the adjacent petri dish and gently rubbed it on her lips. As with mascara, lipstick was too expensive.

She liked her make-up fairly heavy, so that clients would think she was older; hopefully fifteen or sixteen rather than the two months shy of thirteen that she was.

Her make-up finished, she went over to check on Toby. He was fast asleep again, looking peaceful and angelic. She softly closed the door and locked it again. He'd be okay now for the night.

She'd made sure to stay in her dressing gown as she did her make-up, not wanting to risk getting any coal dust on her white dress. She had two exactly the same and was proud of their creation. Made from little more than white linen sheets, she'd sewn on the blue brocade trims herself. Obviously, she'd inherited her mother's milliner's skills, who'd died just over a year ago from consumption, leaving her and Toby to fend for themselves.

She'd rotate the dresses in boiled washes each day, but as she'd held today's dress up for inspection, turning it front and back, it would probably do for one more client tonight. It wasn't soiled or stained.

Her nerves bristled. A shuffling noise from outside her window, the sense of being watched. She put the dress back down on the side, took the oil lamp over and looked out.

Nothing. The oil-lamp glow petered out after only a few yards, pitch-darkness beyond. And as she listened out keenly, there was no rustling sound now.

She wondered for a moment whether it was a signal that she should call it a night, not go out. But then she reminded herself that she'd promised young Toby they'd be having beef stew tomorrow, one of his favourites from their mother's cooking. And the extra client would help buy a bit more beef and some carrots.

She shook off her concerns. Here she was joking with clients about cats and rats in the next room, while forgetting herself that both were numerous in the alley outside.

She changed into her white dress and slipped back out into the night, clicking the front door softly so that she wouldn't wake Toby.

CHAPTER THIRTY

When you try and thwart me, it always ends up worse, you should know that by now.

You and Argenti probably thought you were clever, patting yourselves on the back for saving that last Beth Jacobs' girl. But you know of old that there's a set list of girls and a sequence of symbols marked on internal organs to be observed. And if it couldn't be this last Beth Jacobs girl, then another had to be sought.

Oh, and what a find she was. Not high-class like that girl at the opera years ago, but special in her own way. So young, no more than thirteen or fourteen, yet keeping herself pristine clean and virginal looking despite the filth and squalor of her surroundings.

She was taking care of her little brother too. Out on the streets no doubt simply to put food on the table for the two of them. Oh, yes, special in so many ways. And you and Argenti are responsible for her death. If the chain of symbols hadn't been disturbed by you saving that last Beth Jacobs girl, then this new girl wouldn't have had to be sought. She'd still be alive.

But now you are also faced with something of a conundrum. I claimed in my last letter that I wasn't directly the killer of the last two girls, but what I didn't impart was whether I was guiding the hand of their killer or not. Carrying on my work, so to speak. You might even find that this killer now is not the same as last time, or indeed I've returned from Austria to take care of her myself. Displeased with the failed attempt on that last Beth Jacobs girl. Ah, so many choices for you now.

But just to show you I'm not heartless, this young girl was left only yards from her door so that you'd easily find her, if you haven't already done so. But what you might not know is that she keeps her little brother locked in a back room for safety. The key should be in her pocket.

You'll need to get to the boy without delay. Left too long without food or drink, he could perish. I wouldn't wish another death on my conscience; *or yours, for that matter.*

* * *

The body was laid flat on its back, one leg at an awkward angle. The face had a mottled grey-maroon pallor to it, but it was clearly Erik Larsen.

'Strange,' Jameson commented, leaning closer over the body. 'This facial discolouration.'

'Why's that?' Argenti countered. 'I've seen that same pallor on many a corpse before.'

'No doubt you have.' Jameson smiled cautiously as he straightened up. Reminded that in a city like New York, Argenti would no doubt have seen as many corpses as himself. 'But you might have observed that pallor more at autopsy stage, or if you arrived late at a murder scene or the body wasn't discovered until the next day. Not upon discovery of a fresh corpse — as this is meant to be.' Jameson looked keenly towards Bill Griffin, standing two yards the other side of Larsen's corpse with his assistant and two Constables. Griffin was drawing hard on a cigarette and stamping his feet to warm himself in the cold night air. 'How long were you with the body before we arrived?'

'Uh, an hour or so, no more.' Griffin nodded towards the Constables. 'These two were first to discover the body. This one stayed with it while this one here ran the five blocks to Mulberry Street to raise me.'

Jameson nodded, shifted his gaze to the Constables. 'So you'd have come across the body, say, half an hour beforehand?'

They looked at each other for a moment. The one who'd stayed with the body answered. 'I suppose so. About an hour after dark, it was.'

Jameson looked back at the body again. 'Could you do me the honour of lifting the body slightly on this side?'

'Go ahead.' Griffin gestured as the two Constables looked his way. They were under his command at this murder scene, but he had no intention of getting his suit crumpled by helping them. 'Just make sure not to disturb the note and the stiletto.'

Jameson smiled dryly at Griffin stating the obvious, then when one side of Larsen's body was clear of the ground by four or five inches, he crouched down and peered underneath.

'As I thought,' he said after a moment, signalling for the Constables to let the body settle back down. 'No blood stains beneath, either fresh or dried-up. I don't think this was the actual murder scene.'

Griffin appeared to shuffle his feet stronger then, Argenti noticed. *Uncomfortable*, or still fending off the cold? They were only half a mile from where they'd tended to the boy in the warehouse and Maccione had emerged from the shadows. Argenti wondered if that was significant. He looked each way along the dockside.

'I suppose we could have guessed that from the site itself.

Not exactly the most concealed location — especially if the murder took place in daylight a few hours earlier.'

'I'm thinking even earlier than that,' Jameson said. 'But I won't know for sure until I get the body back to the lab and inspect closer.'

Argenti nodded. They'd had a day of it at the autopsy lab. Although the girl's body had been found in the morning, because of a busy situation at Bellevue morgue, a full autopsy with Jameson and Lawrence while he'd observed and taken notes hadn't taken place until late afternoon. They were just finishing up early evening when the message came from Mulberry Street that Larsen's body had been found. That's why Bill Griffin had been first on the scene with his assistant, Tom Henderson. Normally, Argenti would have been first to be notified.

One of Bill Griffin's first questions when he'd arrived on the scene had been, 'Do you by any chance recognize that handwriting on the note and the knife?'

'I'm not sure,' Argenti had answered. Although he'd recognized the handwriting straightaway. *Enzio Maccione*! The note read, *In repayment for the girls at the Beth Jacobs*. The knife too looked similar to Maccione's favoured stilettos. But he needed to get his thoughts clear on just why Maccione might take out this sort of macabre retribution for the Beth Jacobs girls murdered. He'd felt Griffin's eyes linger on him a moment after he'd answered.

He'd also noticed Jameson's eyes on him briefly in that instant, though Jameson waited until the Bellevue wagon had taken Larsen's body away and they were walking back to the Hansom, out of earshot of Griffin and Henderson, before he mentioned anything.

'You need to come clean about Maccione at some stage, Joseph.' Jameson eased out a heavy breath on the night air. 'This can't keep on.'

'I know.' Argenti nodded sombrely. 'But I need to talk to him about this stiletto-pinned note first. It just doesn't make sense.'

'Doesn't it?' Jameson looked at him sharply. 'It appears as if Maccione spun you a story about Thompson, so what's to say he won't do the same over Larsen now?'

Argenti closed his eyes for a second in supplication. 'I understand, and what you say might well be true. But I need to hear his account directly myself before taking it to the next stage of an arrest.'

'Maccione is obviously embroiled in this in some way, and you risk it tainting you too.' Jameson shook his head. '*Tightrope*, Joseph. Having almost slipped from the wire twice, what makes you feel you might survive a third fall?'

* * *

'As I suspected,' Jameson said, swilling a mixture of blood, body fluids and formaldehyde from his hands in the morgue sink. 'I don't think the dockside was the original murder scene.'

Argenti's brow creased. 'But I thought you said that blood lividity supported that the position of the body at point of death was laying on its back — the position indeed we found it by the dockside.'

'Yes, blood lividity supports that. But with the note pinned to the chest by a stiletto knife, we might expect that. If the body had, say, been moved onto its side, the knife or note might have been disturbed. It was obviously important to the murderer that these be seen in their original position when the body was finally discovered.'

'So the main clue has been the lack of blood found beneath Larsen's body by the dockside?'

'That was the first indicator, certainly. As his body was

lifted into the morgue wagon and I had a clearer view — it became even more evident that there had been no blood seepage there, fresh or old.' Jameson moved towards the petri dish on a side bench, which Lawrence had spent the last ten minutes examining. 'Any change in the acidic process we discussed earlier?'

'No. There still appears to have been a change of rate in the dissolving process,' Lawrence commented, prodding with a probe at a few particles in an acrid soup-consistency mix.

'These are the contents of Larsen's stomach,' Jameson enlightened. 'Now under normal circumstances, as stomach acid settles after death, there's a fairly even pattern to stomach contents dissolving. But in this case, it isn't even at all — it appears as if the process has been disturbed halfway through. The stomach contents shaken up.'

It took Argenti only a second to pick up on the intimation. 'You think this was the point the body was moved?'

'Exactly. Moving the body, and then a shaky Hansom ride would have had this effect.'

'How far?'

Jameson held a hand out. 'Distance wouldn't have been a particular factor, or at least would be difficult to measure. Even a very short journey over cobblestones, such as found at the dockside, would have resulted in the same.'

Argenti sank into thought for a second. 'If we can't accurately judge distance — what about the timing involved?'

'Yes, somewhat easier.' Jameson looked at Lawrence, still prodding in the petri dish. 'What are your thoughts on that, Lawrence?'

'I would say the body was moved anything from four to five hours ago, judging by the dissolving rate in the latent particles.'

Argenti did a quick mental calculation. 'So, only about an

hour or two before the two constables first discovered the body?'

'Yes, appears as such.' Jameson nodded his concurrence. 'Which then ties in with it being such an open area. Any longer and it would surely have been discovered earlier.' Jameson exchanged a quick look with Lawrence before adding, 'But far more telling, from both blood and organ lividity, is when Larsen's murder first took place.'

'Why's that?' Argenti enquired.

'Because it appears to have been between twenty-five and thirty hours ago.'

So that explained the skin pallor, Argenti considered. But then as the other significance hit him, he asked pointedly, 'Are you sure?'

'Without any shadow of doubt,' Jameson said. He knew that the autopsy made earlier on the young girl, in which he'd stated clearly the time of death had been at most '*eighteen to twenty hours* ago' was still fresh in Argenti's mind. 'Erik Larsen couldn't have been the murderer of that young girl last night, because he was by then already dead.'

CHAPTER THIRTY-ONE

The shadows in the courtyard were heavier than Argenti recalled last time. Had the closest street gaslight gone out or been broken, or was it just the different time of day? Far later at night, not the time for doing Bible studies.

Argenti leaned in close to the main seminary classroom and peered inside: no sign of Maccione, either in a Monsignor's robes or any other garb; but then he could pick out only half of the room. The shadows at the back were too heavy; though perhaps how both he and Maccione would like it, given the circumstances of their meeting.

Argenti moved along to the window of the next, far smaller classroom. Nothing visible there either at first, but then there was a brief flickering light from towards the back, as if some had lit a match — and in its brief glare Argenti saw Maccione looking his way, beckoning urgently. The fleeting light was as quickly extinguished.

'You were careful coming here?' Maccione questioned after they embraced briefly in greeting and took seats each side of a classroom desk.

'Of course,' Argenti said; although he'd been far from

careful. An integral part of his plan now. 'I could ask the same of you.'

Maccione smiled tautly. 'Nobody would be paying much attention to a Monsignor going into a church seminary, even in the dead of night. A police inspector is a different matter.'

'I daresay,' Argenti said, his expression quickly becoming stern, grave. 'You've no doubt seen this morning's newspapers about Larsen's murder?'

'Yes. Along with the rest of New York not in hiding in the same way as me.' Maccione gestured. 'Is that why you've hastily called for a meeting with me now, Joseph? To tell me that the saga with these girls' killings is over? That Larsen rather than me is also seen as responsible for Campbell's death and I can come out of hiding now?'

'I can see how those headlines might have indicated that.' *Erik Larsen, suspect in the recent bout of 'Ripper' style killings and that of fellow knifeman, Frank Campbell, has been found dead by the East River docks.* Argenti smiled briefly at the irony before becoming stern again. 'But I'm afraid tomorrow's headlines might tell a different story — at least in regard to Campbell's death, and indeed Larsen's for that matter.'

Maccione's brow creased. 'I don't understand.'

Argenti observed Maccione's expression keenly — that brow creasing and worried frown settling deeper — as he explained about the note pinned by a stiletto to Larsen's chest. 'Identical to another murder attributed to you.'

Maccione raised an eyebrow. 'Attributed to me? By whom? As we both know, the police never fully investigated Tommy Falway's murder. He was just another villain fished out of the East River.'

'Yes, I appreciate that. But there were strong rumours at the time.'

Silence settled with the stand-off. Argenti knew that Maccione would never openly admit to Falway's murder any more than the person who had first discovered the body, Michael Tierney, would declare that to anyone outside either. After all, Falway's body had been found in a high unfinished floor in Tierney's newly built Manhattan skyscraper — and the note left had been an open challenge to Tierney's gang leadership. Showing the note to the police could have also implicated Tierney in the murder of dock Custom's officer, Paolo Calvi, a close friend of Argenti's. So Tierney had no doubt simply removed the knife and note and had Falway's body dumped in the East River. But rumours among the underworld and police informants had been rife.

Argenti took a fresh breath. 'This time it's different. The police were first to see the note and the stiletto knife.'

'Were you first to see it?'

'No. It was Bill Griffin with a couple of Constables. I was at the time busy with Jameson finishing the autopsy on the young girl killed two nights back.' For a moment Argenti wondered why Maccione had asked. *Did Maccione think that in respect of their friendship he might bury the note and knife, if he'd been first to see it?* 'But even if for now only I recognize your handwriting, it won't be long before others identify it.'

Argenti slipped the close-up photo of the note taken by Eric Morrison from his jacket pocket and passed it across.

'I didn't write the note,' Maccione said flatly before even fully looking at the photo. 'Or kill Larsen or Campbell.'

Argenti looked keenly at Maccione again as he studied the photo, watching every nuance of expression. *The right amount of surprise, or just replicating what he thought would be expected?* After all, Maccione was a master-gangster, used to such Machiavellian games on almost a daily basis.

'A good copy, no more,' Maccione commented after a moment. 'My writing of capital letters has less of a slant to it. Looks like someone assuming that my normal writing in caps would have the same strong slant to it.'

Argenti nodded as he took the photo back. *Or Maccione trying to disguise his writing slightly so that he could later come up with that argument?*

Maccione shook his head. 'Also why on earth would I leave the note openly like that, put blame immediately back at my own door?'

'Because, like last time, you probably didn't think the police would be first to find the body.' Argenti looked at Maccione steadily. 'The body was found directly in front of dockside warehouses that Tierney controls. And only two blocks away is Tierney's new skyscraper. If he'd looked from his penthouse with binoculars, he'd have clearly seen the body.'

Maccione cast his eyes down for a second. 'Still doesn't make much sense. If the intention was leaving Tierney some sort of message, then why wasn't the body left within his building?'

Argenti noted that Maccione had carefully left *I* and *me* out of his comment, kept Larsen's murder at arm's length, *remote*. In deference to their little game, if that was what it was, he did the same. 'Because whoever killed Larsen, unlike the situation with Tommy Falway, Tierney's building is now finished. Difficult to get past the front desk porter and security.'

Maccione leaned across the desk, looking back intently. 'But you're the detective, Joseph. What earthly motive?'

One of the main things to trouble him, Argenti had applied thought to the question in advance. 'Outrage over the Beth Jacobs girls. Gaining retribution and also waving a banner of protection for myself and Jameson — as you've done in the past.'

Maccione nodded slowly, some pieces falling into place. 'But trying to leave Larsen's body as a message to Tierney?

That would assume the killer attached some level of blame for his bout of murders with Tierney.'

'Both Campbell and Larsen had worked for both you and Tierney — so blame could be laid at either of your doors.'

'...Or at Corcoran's or Don Mahler of the Hudson Dusters, or any number of people, including the original Ripper, who might have chosen to hire them.' Maccione stared the message home, but after a moment with little more than a blank stare in response, he conceded. 'A reasonable point, nonetheless.' His eyes searched the shadows of the small room for a moment, as if he was feeling suddenly cornered. 'But this retribution and waving a banner of protection you mention? That would have been more for you than Jameson — yet the Beth Jacobs girls were associated very much with Jameson. The only girl that might have been associated with 'protective banner waving' for you was that young girl killed by the Fourth Ward the other night — because she might have been a reminder of your sister Mariella and your own tough background. But she wasn't mentioned in that note.'

'No, she wasn't.' Argenti regretted now having shared his background about Mariella with Maccione; raised when they were in the clinches of a confrontation. 'But there's a good reason for that.'

As Argenti went on to explain the findings of the recent autopsy on Larsen and the young girl, he watched Maccione's body jolt in shock, eyes darting rapidly. Either Maccione didn't know, or he was a very good actor.

Maccione stared back incredulously. 'But if Larsen didn't kill that last young girl the other night, who did?'

'I'm sorry, Enzio. But with both Campbell and Larsen dead, there'll be only one natural conclusion.' Argenti stared back impassively, and felt sorry for Maccione in that moment as he watched the realization dawn, that shock worming deeper.

'*Dio mio*, Joseph.' He held one hand out, imploring. 'Surely you can't believe that...?'

'Not me, *no* — although I'm sure many at Mulberry Street will be eager to claim my blind belief in you is because of our close association. But among many in the police and the public at large, unfortunately, *yes*. Especially when the story runs in tomorrow's newspapers about Larsen not being responsible for that last girl killed and the note with your hand-writing found on his body.'

Argenti watched Maccione sink in on himself, closing his eyes again for a moment and shaking his head in disbelief before looking back directly at Joseph. 'So, you're saying that I have only until tomorrow before the final curtain in this staged tragedy comes down?'

'Yes. That's why it was urgent I see you now, warn you what's coming.'

Maccione nodded sombrely, looking aslant for a moment. But then another jolt seemed to run through him, as if he'd suddenly struck on something among the dark shadows of the room.

'*Gianni*,' Maccione muttered, as if it was an incantation, a prayer. 'Gianni Campanelli.' As he watched Argenti's eyes knit quizzically, he added, 'Frank Campbell's brother. Gianni kept the original Campanelli family name. He passed a message through my main street runner Nico the other day that he needed to see me urgently. Said he had information that another killer would continue with these girls after Larsen.'

Argenti held a palm out. 'So, why didn't you meet up with him?'

'The message only came to Nico late yesterday, and, apart from there not being much time, I didn't know at that stage that Larsen was dead, or that he wasn't the killer of that last young girl. Also, I feared it might be a trap — Gianni's not the most reliable of individuals, combined with the suspicion that I might have killed his brother.' Maccione shook his head. 'But now his message makes some sense.'

Argenti nodded slowly. He'd thought the main feast were the surprises and warnings he'd be bringing for Maccione, but Maccione was firing back with some surprises of his own; and he began to have a twinge of doubt and guilt about what he had planned now. Unless, as before, this was simply another invention of Maccione's? Pulled out of the hat when he realized he was in a corner; in the same way that he'd pulled Larsen out of the hat when he'd initially been suspected of Campbell's murder.

But then he'd personally seen Larsen trying to kill Joyce Bennett, fired shots at him on the Bowery train — so that part had at least seemed real. One thing he certainly shared with Maccione in this moment. *Confusion* over what was real or imagined any more — that confusion appearing to run deeper in Maccione's eyes as they darted past Argenti's shoulder.

Argenti caught the flickering light on the far wall first, then half-turned as the glare of four or five lanterns moved rapidly towards them. Maccione was quickly on his feet as the door burst open behind Argenti, eyes rapidly scanning for escape routes; but the room was small, the only exit where the five policeman were now standing, Bill Griffin at the forefront.

Maccione had raised his knife almost automatically, but now with three pistols levelled at him, he slowly lowered it.

Argenti smiled wanly at Griffin. 'I wondered when you might show up?'

Griffin lamely returned the smile.

But Maccione, eyes darting frantically between the two of them, misread their interaction. He glared at Argenti.

'You betrayed me! I trusted you as a friend... and you *betrayed me*!'

'No, *no*... you've got it wrong,' Argenti pleaded. But his voice was lost among the burst of voices and commands as Maccione was handcuffed and led away by Griffin's team towards a black wagon.

CHAPTER THIRTY-TWO

Roosevelt drew hard on his pipe as he listened to Bill Griffin's account the other side of his desk. Roosevelt had said little so far, merely punctuated Griffin's monologue by lifting and pointing his pipe stem — as if it was a conductor's baton — as he clarified a few points. Then would wave it down and resume puffing as Griffin continue.

Roosevelt's brow furrowed at one point. He lifted his pipe stem again.

'I follow the general motive you're suggesting here,' he said. 'That much of this has been to divert the police department here from local gangland activity...'

'And corruption, sir,' Griffin interjected. 'That's why it has come so hot on the heels of your announcement about clamping down on police corruption. What better diversion than a reprisal of the Ripper case — which has occupied this department's time more than any other this past five years?'

'I understand that,' Roosevelt said impatiently. 'That part is quite clear. But what I don't follow is why one city gang-leader, Enzio Maccione, would try and lay blame at the door of his main rival, Michael Tierney?'

Griffin held a palm out, smiling wryly, as if at his own ingenuity. 'Don't you see, sir? Both men hired to kill these girls were independents — but linked more to Tierney than Maccione. But as they were identified and came more to the police's attention, Maccione had to dispense with them — fearing they might through plea deals inform that it was Maccione who had hired them, not Tierney.'

'But Maccione was actually identified by one eye-witness after Thompson's murder.'

'Yes. But he then very craftily through an informant identified Larsen, the next knifeman he'd hired.' Griffin mulled his mouth for a moment. 'Though I suspect that information might have been passed directly from Maccione to Detective Argenti.'

Roosevelt looked at him sternly. '*What*? You suspect Detective Argenti might have met up with Mr Maccione before — not just this last night when you caught them together?'

'Yes, I do, sir.'

Roosevelt nodded, the silence in his office heavy, the pendulum tick of the grandfather clock in the corner suddenly noticeable.

'And do you think laying blame on his rival Tierney was Maccione's intention from the outset?'

'I'm not sure, sir. The ruse of the Ripper might initially on its own have been enough of a diversion. But once it had been uncovered that it wasn't the Ripper, not least from the Ripper writing his own note — laying the blame on his rival became the obvious option. Perhaps that card was in fact up his sleeve all along.'

Roosevelt sank into thought for a moment. When he'd previously questioned Argenti and Jameson about being photographed by the dockside and Maccione emerging from the shadows and running off — it hadn't completely rung true. How long in fact had Detective Argenti been playing this game of subterfuge with Maccione?

As Roosevelt got to the final element troubling him, that of why Maccione would incriminate himself by leaving a hand-written note on Larsen's body, he listened intently to Griffin's explanation of where the body had been found, right in front of Tierney-controlled warehouses and only two blocks from his newly-built skyscraper.

'Maccione didn't expect the police to discover it first. It was meant as a warning message to Tierney, nothing more. After all, he's done this before.'

'Oh, has he now?'

'Yes, very much so, sir. And Detective Argenti was complicit in that previous action as well.'

* * *

The first thing that Argenti felt seep into his bones was the darkness, then the cold. He was in one of the 'holding' interview rooms for serious crimes in the basement at Mulberry Street. When he'd voiced his surprise at being led to the room by the two Constables escorting him, Bill Griffin just behind them had commented, 'Commissioner Roosevelt himself ordered that you be kept here.'

'For how long?'

'Now that would be up to him, wouldn't it?' Griffin smiled at his obvious discomfort. 'You're lucky. Your friend Maccione has been taken straight to the Tombs.'

Argenti knew all too well the routine of the 'holding' interview rooms. For the first few minutes, the gas-lamps would be kept on full, and if it was a suspect they wished to expedite quickly, a detective and assistant would come in within that time to question them. But if it was one they wished to languish for a while, the gas-lamp would be dimmed from a control outside, as if only that brighter light was necessary while an interview was in progress.

But Argenti knew that it was also a psychological ploy. It gave time for suspects to consider their possible fate, and the darkness of the small room and the bars on its door — through which a Constable would peer at intervals — was an uncomfortable reminder of the fate awaiting them if the interview went the wrong way.

A Constable had peeked his head inside the door after the first twenty minutes. 'Commissioner Roosevelt sent the message that he'll call for you shortly.'

Argenti had in turn asked if the Constable could pass a message to Commissioner Roosevelt. 'It's important,' he'd stressed. But from the Constable's nonplussed agreement to do so, Argenti wasn't sure whether the message would have been passed on.

That had been over an hour ago. Argenti shook off a faint shiver as the chill of the room got to him, and shortly after he'd started to pace the room impatiently to further ward it off when the heavy bolt slid back again and the door opened.

'Commissioner Roosevelt will see you now.'

* * *

'Did you get my message, sir?'

'Yes. Something about Detective Whelan vouching for you.'

'Well, not vouching for me directly, but certainly vouching for my *actions*,' Argenti clarified. 'Because, before I left Mulberry Street, I told John Whelan where I was going and what I'd be doing.'

'I'm not sure I see the distinction.' Roosevelt's brow knitted. 'All that would mean is that Whelan is in collusion with you regarding a clandestine meeting with Enzio Maccione that *shouldn't* have taken place.'

'Except that I told Whelan clearly that it was my intention to have Mr Maccione arrested.'

Roosevelt fell silent at that, thoughtful. Then, after a moment, 'So, if that was the case — why did you go on your own to this meeting?'

'Because I wanted to hear Mr Maccione's explanation privately before he was arrested. As we well know, gang members so often clam up, say nothing once under official arrest — and that's particularly true of the new Italian Mafia fraternity. I thought that only some time alone with Maccione would get us closer to knowing the truth of what's happening. I asked Whelan and his team to give me an hour before coming to arrest Maccione.'

'I see.' Roosevelt appeared to be swaying a fraction, but Argenti could still sense reserve doubt. 'But still Inspector Griffin and his men got there before Whelan and the others. How do you explain that?'

'Yes, sir. That was the other part of my plan that I hoped would work. And it *did*.' Argenti allowed himself a faint smile, but still subdued, no hint of arrogance as he explained about passing a message also to a young street runner, Ralphy. 'I told Ralphy that I had a private meeting with Maccione in an hour's time, and that I wanted him to keep a look-out on the nearest corner for me. I'd used Ralphy for some messages before, but nothing juicy or incriminating. Yet I knew that Ralphy also ran messages for Griffin and Michael Tierney — and this would be too irresistible for him not to pass on. Would probably earn Ralphy a good ten bucks — five times what I was paying him.'

Roosevelt nodded thoughtfully after a second. 'And you think this Ralphy passed a message to Griffin or Tierney?'

Argenti held a hand out. 'How else would Griffin know I was there at that time?'

A slower nod this time, Roosevelt's gaze drifting to the side wall and the map of Manhattan there, as if for inspiration. *Which of the gang leaders vying for control of his fair city to believe?* Or perhaps neither of them. He took a fresh breath.

'You appreciate that you firing back with a defence of Griffin being in collusion with Tierney straight after the same being levelled at you over Maccione — might appear too simplistic and obvious to many. Not just me.'

'I appreciate that, sir. But my plans declared in advance to Whelan to arrest Maccione stand against any such collusion.'

Roosevelt looked steadily at him for a moment before nodding a tame concession. 'Yes, I understand that. And I'll be speaking to Whelan as well shortly.' Roosevelt's pipe had laid forgotten in an onyx ash-tray to one side since the start of their meeting, but now he reached for it again. 'The thing is, Inspector Griffin has provided quite a convincing explanation of Mr Maccione's motive with this current wave of girls murdered and his collusion with you.' He re-lit the pipe and drew the first few eager puffs. 'So now I'd like to hear your account?'

Argenti had spent the day before brainstorming with Jameson about possible motives, and many of them ended up laid uncomfortably at Tierney's door. Jameson had his suspicions from when the dockside photographer had snapped both them and Maccione after tending to the wounded boy, and suggested the ruse with Ralphy. '*If Griffin and Tierney take the bait, then we'll know almost for sure my suspicions are correct. But in case I'm mistaken, you'll need to plan an intended arrest of Maccione privately with Whelan or others — otherwise it will simply look like more collusion between the two of you.*'

Argenti had nodded his accord, though one part of that

plan made him distinctly uncomfortable. '*But it will appear to Maccione as if I've betrayed him.*'

Jameson had shaken his head. '*You're not doing him any favours by simply continuing clandestine meetings while he's still a fugitive. Indeed, if Maccione is being set up — which I fear is the case — the more he's still free out there, the more girls' deaths can be blamed on him. He'll just be putting his neck further in Tierney's noose.*'

But Argenti was anxious as he explained his theory about Tierney being behind the set-up. Without fully knowing Griffin's account, there might be vital information and angles he'd omit. His own neck would be tighter in that noose of suspected collusion. *Six to eight years in The Tombs.* He knew all too well the sentence for police corruption; and jail time for coppers surrounded by hardened convicts was often far tougher.

Roosevelt seemed to puff harder, looking at him steadily as he finished talking. Roosevelt waved his pipe to one side. 'You do appreciate that your explanation is little more than a mirror image of Griffin's account — only with Michael Tierney behind it all rather than Maccione. So why should I necessarily believe you over Griffin?'

'You have no reason to, sir.' Argenti nodded in acceptance. 'In fact, you have every reason to doubt *both* accounts equally. But I would argue that if indeed a diversion from police corruption is the main motive, then Tierney has far more to gain from that than Maccione. Tierney is far longer established with many more tentacles both in Mulberry Street and Tammany Hall. Maccione has in fact spent more than the last two years in Atlantic City, with his interests here caretaken by others.'

'That is indeed the one area where yours and Griffin's accounts totally coalesce: an intended diversion from police corruption.' Roosevelt held his gaze steadily on Argenti. No sign of concurrence either way, not even a faint nod. 'But that could be simply Maccione, once he'd been seen just prior to Thompson's murder, attempting to shift blame to Tierney. And using you as a stooge to do so.'

'Or indeed the other way around, sir. Tierney keen to put Maccione more in the frame in case Thompson talked and his ploy was uncovered, and in turn using Griffin as his stooge.'

Throwing the term from his own shoulders onto Griffin's made him feel slightly easier. *Slightly*. Roosevelt's stare remained intense, doubting. *Six to eight years in The Tombs?* The chill of that possibility resurged.

'Imitation is the sincerest form of flattery,' Roosevelt commented, smiling thinly; his first since Argenti had entered the room. But his expression as quickly clouded again, became severe. 'Even if I was to accept your account of this recent dalliance with Maccione, my deeper concern is that this has been going on for some while. And so I ask you directly now — did you know a certain Paolo Calvi before his death?'

'Ah, yes I did, sir,' Argenti answered hesitantly. No point in subterfuge. There were bound to be records on file of his dealings with Calvi at the East River Customs depot. But suddenly he felt as if he was on the tightrope again, and it was starting to shake. He braced his trembling hands on his thighs.

'And you're aware of the circumstances surrounding his death?'

'Yes, sir, I am. I was in fact the lead investigating officer.' Argenti knew what was coming. However hard he braced his hands, the tightrope shook stronger, *the darkness of long years in The Tombs looming below*.

'But it's the retribution of his murder I'm most interested

in. I understand you know or suspect who was involved in that, don't you?'

'Yes, I believe I do, sir.' Feeling himself suddenly frozen on the tightrope as it shook uncontrollably. *No more subterfuge, nowhere left to go...*

'And I believe you know too the manner in which that retribution was carried out?'

'Yes, I do, sir.'

'And that it's almost identical to this murder of Larsen now?'

Argenti simply nodded numbly, feeling himself falling...

CHAPTER THIRTY-THREE

'How was it?' Jameson asked Lawrence as he finished eating.

'Very good.' Lawrence raised a quizzical eyebrow. 'Much the same as last time, in fact.'

'Yes, I had noticed you tend to have the same each time we eat here: the Saddle of Lamb.'

'That's because I like it.' The quizzical eyebrow remained.

Jameson smiled gently. It was obviously lost on Lawrence that to many it might seem odd having the same dish each time. Though he knew that with Lawrence's compulsive behaviour, Lawrence was thinking entirely the opposite: *if you'd found a dish you liked, why not have the same each time?*

They'd been late coming out of their meeting with Rabbi Morais, so Jameson had elected they go to his gentleman's club, The Lotos, for an early dinner. They could let their thoughts settle and discuss the meeting 'in more congenial surroundings'. *Saddle of Lamb* had in fact been on the Lotos menu ever since they discovered nine years ago that it was the favourite dish of their illustrious guest and after-dinner speaker, Charles Dickens. It had even been named after him, *Dickens' style Saddle of Lamb*.

'Well, if you must know,' Lawrence commented, as if Jameson expected more than simply, *Same as last time*, 'It did appear to have more rosemary and sage in it this time. Which actually was a slight improvement. Brought the flavour out more.'

'Good to know — that at least some things are not in decline here.' Jameson smiled primly and cast a glance towards the worn armchairs the far side of the dining room, as if the Lotos proprietors were loath to change the upholstery since Mark Twain and Dickens had sat in them. He raised his glass, took a sip of wine. 'So what thoughts on Morais's findings?'

'Well, he does seem to have at least narrowed it down to two possibilities, Azrael — Azriel as he is known in Hebrew — or Adriel.'

'Any others you can think of he might have overlooked?'

Lawrence was lost in thought for a moment. 'No. No others that immediately come to mind.'

Over three years since their first visit to Rabbi Morais, to identify the Hebrew symbols marked on the internal organs of past New York Ripper victims and decipher what they spelled. Returning to him now with this fresh wave of girls and Hebrew symbols, there was insufficient from the past two markings, but now with this third one, it had been narrowed down to two possible fallen angels.

'Remind me?' Jameson prompted. 'What was this last Hebrew symbol which has steered towards these two?'

'*Lamed*, the Hebrew equivalent of our letter L,' Lawrence said.

'So now with no other apparent prospects outside of these two...'

'None that I can immediately think of,' Lawrence interjected.

'... Azriel or Adriel — what thoughts? Any particularly leaning towards the most likely?'

Jameson could practically see Lawrence's mind spinning through the *Pseudomonarchia Daemonum*, the main encyclopaedia of over 1,500 demons and fallen angels. While Rabbi Morais's knowledge of Hebrew was absolute, it was Lawrence's more agile, eidetic memory which four years ago had pinpointed the correct demon, Asmodeus, after only two days' reference with the encyclopaedia. And now Jameson could see Lawrence mentally sifting through for any possibilities or useful references.

'Both of course equal death and destruction,' Lawrence said at length. 'But if I had to favour one, it would be Azrael, because of its link to retribution.'

Jameson nodded pensively. 'I would have hazarded the same, except that most of the retribution with the Beth Jacobs girls appears to have been aimed at myself and Ellie. If Tierney, who appears to be increasingly suspect, is behind this — then why hasn't that retribution been aimed equally at Argenti?'

'Well, we do have the young girl the other night. Dark hair, somewhat Italian-looking, and from the Fourth Ward — an area more akin to Argenti's background.'

'Yes, but it's a far more tenuous link,' Jameson said. 'In addition, that girl appears to have been a last-minute replacement, because Larsen failed to get to her.'

'You have a point.' Lawrence held a hand out. 'But we also have the framing of Maccione. He is, after all, Tierney's main rival, and also somewhat linked to Argenti.'

'Yes, but it's still not a direct form of retribution — as it appears to have been with myself and Ellie.'

'Except if we consider Argenti's current plight: his career threatened because of possible collusion with Maccione.'

'I considered that too.' Jameson nodded, took a sip of

wine. 'And the only problem there is that Tierney would have had no way of knowing that Joseph would respond in that way. He might have simply arrested Maccione from the off, rather than try and help or consort with him in any way.'

'It seems that you already have it all worked out.' Lawrence smiled primly. 'You can see why I indulge purely in facts rather than summation. I leave that to you.'

Indeed, the backbone of their association: Lawrence dealt with the myriad of facts and details in a case — the finer points that Jameson would sometimes overlook — while Jameson would surmise and theorize. But now Jameson wondered whether Lawrence was having a back-handed swipe or simply being defensive.

'I wasn't critiquing your input by any means,' Jameson said. 'It has indeed been very useful in clarifying my own thoughts, plus drawing attention to any areas which might be found wanting.'

'My pleasure,' Lawrence said blandly, but Jameson could tell that his thoughts were still mostly elsewhere. 'Of course, we also have the factor that Tierney might have suspected that Argenti would react in the way he did. Would try and defend Maccione, leave arresting him as a last resort.'

'Yes, there is that. But while I concede this plan has obviously involved some quite elaborate scheming, that might be granting Tierney with too much aforethought. Again, he would have no guarantee that Argenti would act in that manner — and Tierney doesn't strike me as someone to leave much to chance.'

Lawrence was pensive for a second. 'What, some sort of support plan?'

'Perhaps. But with how things have ended up for Joseph, it doesn't look as though that plan will now be needed. So we'll never get to discover what that plan might have been.'

* * *

Argenti sat in the dark, although this time it had been of his own choosing. He'd been on his own almost an hour before Sophia opened the door and a shaft of light spilled in from the hallway. She looked surprised to see him there.

'I'm sorry. I thought you'd gone to bed already.'

'I just needed some time alone with my thoughts,' he said. He was sat in the back parlour which Oriana used as her music room. Oriana's last piano playing had stopped almost two hours ago, not long after dinner when Pascal and Marco had gone to bed. The sounds of music, laughter and joy from the house gradually dissipating, the last the soft clink of pans and plates from the kitchen and Sophia gently humming; now the room and the house beyond was eerily silent.

'I did notice you preoccupied over dinner.' She was pensive for a moment. 'Was it something you wished to share with me?

He looked at Sophia levelly. *Three years of keeping secrets from her and he was still hoping for a few extra hours or days*. But now there was no time left, and in the end there probably never was going to be a 'right time' to broach the subject.

'There are some decisions being made at Mulberry Street about my future career, so I'll be at home for a few days.'

'Oh, I see...' Sophia took a seat in the corner across from him.

She returned his look steadily, almost mournfully, as if partly taking the weight of the problems she sensed burdening him. She didn't switch on the light, and so they sat there in the subdued light spilling in from the hallway as he filled in all the gaps in his relationship with Maccione that he'd so far held back from her.

Sophia nodded slowly as he finished. 'So is this to do with the meeting with Enzio you asked me to arrange last week?'

'Yes, partly. But Maccione turned up unexpectedly when Jameson and I were seeing a street boy by the dockside who had been seriously wounded... then another meeting since.' Argenti cast his eyes down for a second. 'And on that last meeting we were found together, and Enzio was arrested by Griffin and his team. I was also held and questioned for a while, and now there's a pending charge of collusion between us.' Argenti grimaced awkwardly. 'Almost as serious a charge as murder given Commissioner Roosevelt's current drive against police corruption.'

Sophia shook her head. 'So, knowing this, why take the risk with these meetings with Enzio?'

'Because when I saw Enzio as a suspect for both Campbell's and then later Larsen's murder, I simply didn't believe it. As I'm sure you don't.' That had always been the gap in their perception of Enzio Maccione: Sophia saw him simply as a kindly Italian importer, taking a tough line to protect local Italian shopkeepers, like her own store partner, Anton Faggiani, against the rigours of Tierney's street protection and extortion gangs. Whereas Joseph suspected and sometimes knew that 'tough line' had verged into murder — but had never openly admitted it to Sophia. Whether because he didn't wish to tarnish that gracious image in Sophia's mind, or his own allegiance and appreciation of Maccione's protection of the Italian community — possibly a last line of defence against Tierney — he wasn't sure. 'And I wanted to hear his account personally before he was arrested.'

'But Griffin and his team got there before John Whelan?'

'Yes. But that was also partly engineered by myself and Finley — to help prove our suspicions about Tierney and Griffin.' He watched the trace of a smile ease Sophia's worry lines for a moment as he explained about street-boy Ralphy and the message passed in advance.

'Seems like Tierney and Griffin aren't the only one's adept with set-ups?'

'Perhaps.' Argenti's expression remained serious, sombre. 'But there are linked elements now which might be inescapable.'

'In what respect?'

'Regarding the murder of Paolo Calvi's suspected killer, Tommy Falway. This murder now with Larsen is identical. Similar stiletto wound piercing his heart, and the note pinned to his chest is in Enzio Maccione's handwriting.' He watched the worry lines return to Sophia's forehead. 'There's now the claim that not only did I know that Maccione was responsible for Falway's death, but that with Paolo Calvi being a good family friend, I actually *ordered* his murder.'

* * *

When minutes later the front door knocker went, Joseph was put out at first; it was late for a disturbance, and he hadn't fully finished his account to Sophia. Though a part of that he also saw as a saving; he'd started to get into uncomfortable ground about the depths of his association with Maccione and what he suspected Maccione might be guilty of. *Still, after all these years of guarded secrets, he still hadn't been able to admit to Sophia, or anyone else for that matter, seeing Maccione slide a stiletto up into Brogan's brain that dark alleyway night.*

As Joseph opened the door, Sophia a step behind him in the hallway, Jameson and Lawrence stood there. Jameson touched the brim of his hat.

'Sophia... Joseph. Sorry to call so late. But Lawrence and I earlier today saw Rabbi Morais, and we've since been discussing the matter. So I wondered whether you might have a moment?'

Joseph ushered them in, and Sophia offered them tea or

coffee. They said they'd like tea, 'Thank you.' Another hat-brim touch from Jameson, and they took seats in the music parlour where moments ago Joseph had sat with Sophia. Jameson shared the conversation he'd had with Lawrence over dinner while Sophia prepared their teas in the kitchen.

Joseph nodded thoughtfully as they finished, sitting back deeper in his chair. 'Makes sense, I suppose. Although I have no idea what any support plan from Tierney might have been.' Joseph held out a hand. 'Surely this is bad enough? Three days forced leave while Roosevelt deliberates — the closest he could come to 'house arrest' without appearing too obvious — meanwhile my career hanging by a thread.'

'But do you think Roosevelt might have accepted your account about Griffin and Tierney's association?' Jameson questioned. 'That it's more likely Tierney is behind this than Maccione?'

'I don't know... I don't know.' Joseph shook his head. 'Both are such close mirror images of each other, that at times even I'm not sure. And if things go the wrong way against me, I'll not only be facing the end of my career, but an eight-year stretch in The Tombs.'

'Remind yourself of why we took the action we did with Griffin,' Jameson said, trying to lift Joseph's forlorn spirits. 'Yes, we weren't sure at all, so we ran that test. If Griffin hadn't shown up when he did, then we would have remained unsure. Roosevelt's an intelligent man, I'm sure he'll see that.'

'Perhaps. But it still might not be seen as conclusive enough.'

'In which case, nothing would be found conclusive in your own case, Joseph.'

Joseph shook his head again. 'You think that would be any better? While I might escape a sentence in the Tombs, I'd still have that shadow hanging over me in the police force. I doubt I'd last more than...' Joseph broke off as Sophia came in with their teas and another coffee for Joseph.

'It's good to see you, gentlemen,' she said to Jameson and Lawrence as she set the tray down. 'You should visit more, perhaps have dinner one night.'

'That's very kind of you, and I look forward to the invitation.' Jameson stood and bowed slightly and Lawrence followed suit as Sophia took her leave of them, commenting that she was retiring to bed now.

Joseph lapsed into thought for a second after Sophia left. 'There's one thing which might make matters more conclusive in my favour.'

'What's that?' Jameson prompted as Argenti paused, giving his initial thought some deeper consideration.

'Just before Griffin and his team barged in to arrest Maccione, he was surprised at first when I revealed that Larsen wasn't responsible for killing that last Fourth Ward girl — then Maccione was suddenly struck with a fresh thought.' Joseph explained about Gianni Campanelli, Frank Campbell's brother, passing a message to Nico that he had urgent information he wanted to pass to Maccione that another killer would continue killing girls after Larsen.

'So why didn't Maccione meet up with this Gianni Campanelli?'

'He feared it might be a set-up, some sort of retribution for Frank Campbell's killing. But then with the news I brought him that Larsen was already dead, so couldn't have killed that last Fourth Ward girl, he began to suspect there might be far more to it.'

'Something which might pin things more to Tierney's camp?'

'Yes, very possibly.' Argenti sighed. 'Except it appears that Gianni has gone to ground, so might be difficult to unearth. And my chances of doing so while I'm on forced leave are zero. Roosevelt made it very clear that I mustn't involve myself one iota in this investigation until he's made his final deliberation.'

'Makes perfect sense, I daresay. But that doesn't extend to myself or Lawrence.' Jameson smiled slyly, glancing across at Lawrence. 'Possibly Nico would be a good start point to try and find this Gianni Campanelli.'

CHAPTER THIRTY-FOUR

Gianni Campanelli peered from the shadows of the shop doorway towards the alleyway entrance sixty yards along on the opposite side of the street. From his position, he could see anyone coming in and out of that alley, and he knew there were other approaches to the building at its end — a foundry which had been derelict now for the past two years. So there should be no other visitors in and out of that alleyway — just the two people he was looking out for.

It seemed he'd been doing little more these past days than duck and hide in the city's shadows. Ever since that night when he'd seen Erik Larsen meet up with Michael Tierney and his henchman, Liam Monahan in that dilapidated warehouse.

In fact, he'd been keeping an on and off tail on both Maccione and Larsen for the past week — the two main suspects in his brother's murder. Not an easy task trying to tail two men hiding in the shadows themselves. But then since he'd been doing the same the past ten months, he had a decided edge on the police. Knew all the dives, haunts and hideaways where those keen not to be seen might be found.

His own bout of hiding had started with a dockside warehouse raid gone wrong. Part of a gang of nine, they'd been halfway through loading crates of whisky newly arrived from Scotland when a police wagon turned up. One of his gang was shot and killed and a policeman knifed in the neck, who miraculously survived.

But Gianni had been one of three out of the five that escaped — two were arrested — identified by the police. Facing a likely fifteen years in The Tombs for armed robbery and being an accomplice to attempted murder, he'd been on the run since. Within a week, he'd hightailed it to Baltimore to stay with a cousin, returning only recently to New York with the news of the murder of his brother, Frank.

Gianni had to admit — both Maccione and Larsen were good at hiding in the shadows. He'd only been able to latch on to them and trail them a couple of times, and that hadn't thrown any extra light on what was going on. Then after hearing street rumours that Larsen might be in Tierney's pocket and Argenti was using Maccione clandestinely as an informant — he decided to trail the other way around. He'd managed to spy Argenti meeting up with Maccione, who was disguised as a Monsignor, yet hadn't been able to get close enough to hear their conversation, glean anything.

But with the meeting between Tierney, Monahan and Larsen, he had more luck. A dilapidated warehouse floor, he'd been able to sneak in the back and hear and see much of what prevailed. At first, he hadn't recognized Larsen — with the top hat, long hair and a white stick, he looked like an old, blind wizard.

Gianni was concealed behind some forgotten packing crates and boxes at the back of the warehouse floor, and that area was also heavily in shadow. He couldn't be seen. The beginning of the conversation between them was a bit muffled, he didn't catch all of it, but the latter part was clearer:

'Just that I thought you might need some help this time,' Tierney was saying. 'Someone to provide look-out and back-up.'

'Yes, I suppose,' Larsen responded. 'That girl will be watched very closely now.'

'That she will certainly be. But I'm actually proposing a fresh girl as target. Which your new accomplice has the details of.' Tierney looked to one side expectantly, and Gianni was alarmed to realize that someone else had also been concealed in the shadows of the warehouse floor, yet on the opposite side to him.

Gianni's throat was suddenly dry, tight. *Might the man have seen him*? But then as the man advanced closer into the pool of light cast by the single oil lamp on the trestle table Tierney sat behind, Gianni's nerves eased a fraction. *If he hadn't been able to see the man in the shadows at the back, then the man in turn wouldn't have been able to see him*!

'These are the details of the new target,' the man said, handing Larsen a piece of paper.

Gianni couldn't see the man's face clearly. When he'd been alongside at the back of the room, the man had still been heavily in shadow; and although now he was in the pool of light from the oil lamp, his back was to Gianni.

Larsen had barely started reading what was on the slip of paper handed to him, his eyes lifting in surprise, before the knife drawn swiftly by the new man was plunged through the note, pinning it to Larsen's chest.

Larsen tumbled back, and the man leant over him, working his knife — a thin stiletto — home that final inch as Larsen gasped in his death throes, blood trickling from his mouth.

Gianni's chest cramped, his heart pounding hard. Not just

from the surprise and horror of what he'd just witnessed — but because as the man straightened up, he recognized him.

Like himself, a ghost that had been hiding in the shadows the past ten months.

Gianni would have hastily left then — not least because of the shock murder he'd just witnessed — but the conversation that followed between Tierney and the knifeman held him transfixed. Explained a lot — in particular why the knifeman, known simply as *Sombra*, he hadn't seen for the past ten months, ever since that fateful night by the dockside when he'd witnessed Sombra stab that policeman in the neck. The event which had added seven years to his own likely sentence if he was caught, and probably more for Sombra.

Quite a fitting name, *Sombra* — a derivation from shadow in Italian — for someone who like himself had been hiding in the city's shadows the past ten months. Although he knew that *Sombra* was only a quarter Italian on his mother's side, his father had been a Spanish gypsy. But as he overheard the unfolding conversation with Tierney, he learned that Sombra's shadow-hiding since that fateful night had been aided.

'...I've kept you successfully hidden the las' while, haven't I?" Tierney gestured towards Larsen's prone body. 'Now after this tonight — one last job and we're square. I'll arrange that passage I promised. Down to New Orleans, then a boat to Jamaica. Like I said, I gotta cousin there — you'll be safe. The police won't find yer.'

'I thought there was only *one* job you wanted me to do before you arranged that,' Sombra said.

Tierney's tone was sharp. 'If it hadn't been for yer knifing that copper that night — none of this duckin' and hiding yer away would have been needed. Did I *ask* you to knife him?'

'No, you didn't.' A more subdued, penitent tone.

'Tha's right, I didn't.' Tierney looked back at Larsen's

body. 'And this now wit' Larsen came up unexpectedly — he got sloppy and was seen, so had to be taken care of.' A sly smile curled Tierney's lips. 'But this next target yer gonna like in any case, trust me.'

Hearing the conversation had already taken part of his breath away, kept him spellbound. *Sombra* had always been a knifeman enforcer associated with Maccione and Corcoran — so he'd assumed the dockside raid had been ordered by them. But not only had Monahan somehow enticed Sombra away from them, he'd also obviously engineered the raid that night. And as Gianni heard who that target was, the last bit of his breath went. *It was one thing knifing a copper, but this...*

Although his mind was as quickly shifting to how he might be able to use the information. *Perhaps it might be enough to do some sort of deal with the coppers, reduce his likely sentence?* Stop this endless hiding in the shadows, a fifteen-year sentence hanging over his head.

Sudden scurrying noise a couple of yards to his right. Three sets of eyes moved towards it, then Monahan's gaze shifted to his position, buried in the darkness at the back of the warehouse behind stacked packing crates.

'Jus' rats, probably,' Tierney said.

Sombra nodded his agreement.

But Monahan's stare stayed fixed his way, Gianni's heart rising into his throat. *Surely he hasn't seen me in the shadows behind these crates?*

'Maybe,' Monahan said, not fully convinced. 'But thought I saw one of those crates the other side move a fraction. And don't know any rats big enough to do that.'

As Monahan took a few paces his way, Gianni held his breath even tighter, his heart pounding hard. Without realizing it, he'd obviously moved a fraction against a crate his side, startled by the scurrying of the rats.

A suspended moment as Monahan stopped hallway, eyes

darting a yard each side of Gianni's position, holding one hand up as he listened intently.

But as Monahan started towards him again, lifting his gun out of his jacket at the same time — *Monahan would be on him in only a few paces* — Gianni gave up any remaining hope.

Gianni barged the crate behind him out of the way as he lunged desperately for the door behind — the tumbling and banging of the falling crates merging with the first shot fired by Monahan, splintering the top of a crate only a foot to his side.

The second shot was even closer, missing him by only inches as he burst through the door, bits of wood from its frame spitting past him.

Then he was frantically scrambling down the fire escape he'd come up, taking the steps two and three at a time the two floors to the back alley.

* * *

Another shot rang out, clanging off the iron railings close-by.

There was a gas-lamp by the alley entrance, but it's light dissipated quickly and cast only a faint glow at the bottom of the fire escape.

Monahan's thundering step behind him paused for a second to fire another shot — hitting the cobbles a yard away as he jumped the last part, stumbling frantically away from the light cast by the gas-lamp.

Gianni didn't pause to look back as he ran into the darkness ahead, his breath falling so heavy it all but drowned out the next shot from behind. It whistled past, Gianni's breathing and step hardly faltering.

He knew that Monahan was firing mostly blind now, his only hope a lucky shot. Gianni was lighter and more sprightly than Monahan, and each split-second pause to fire a shot —

another zinging past him near the end of the alley — was holding Monahan up even more, that gap widening.

But still Gianni ran frantically on, taking a left at the end of the alley, then a sharp right into the next alley on the opposite side, then a left two along, then a right...

Zig-zagging his way haphazardly through to minimize Monahan's chance of getting a clear shot at him.

Only when he'd run four of five city blocks did he pause for breath, tucked into the shadows of another alley, looking desperately across at the mouth of two alleys across the road for any signs of Monahan or any sound of his advancing footsteps. Monahan was a heavy man. His step would carry on the night air. *Nothing*.

* * *

And now he was looking on expectantly at another alley entrance to explain what he'd seen and heard that night with Tierney and Sombra.

'I'm not sure I'll be able to get Joseph along to meet you,' young Nico had said. 'He's in a bad situation now over Maccione...'

Gianni had seen Nico and another young runner go into the alleyway eight minutes ago — but no sign of Argenti yet.

If Argenti didn't show, he wasn't sure he'd feel comfortable sharing this information second-hand. *After all, what earthly assurances and possible plea deals could Nico even talk about, let alone offer*? Even if he did show, there were still heavy risks: from what he'd heard on the street that last meeting with Maccione had been a set-up. Argenti arriving for a personal meeting, then soon after a police entourage showing up.

What if this was the same now? *A trap*. Or even if he met

with Nico alone, Argenti could turn up with a police team minutes later.

Gianni was in the same position, conflicting thoughts raging through his head, when a minute later he saw a black Hansom pull up close by the alley entrance.

A smartly-dressed man with a cane and top-hat stepped out, his driver in tweeds and a brown Derby stepping down to join him.

Gianni seemed to recall the man in the top-hat vaguely from past Ripper reports in the newspapers. Some sort of forensic associate of Argenti's — though Gianni couldn't recall his name.

But what on earth were they doing here instead of Argenti? He stayed in his shrouded doorway position, still undecided, as he watched the two men walk into the alleyway.

CHAPTER THIRTY-FIVE

Michael Tierney had only been to the Opera once before — the guest of the architect for his Fulton Street monolith, Louis Sullivan — and he hadn't enjoyed it.

But it served his purposes now. One thing he'd noticed during that visit with Sullivan two years ago was that only the front row of the Opera box they were in was visible from the main auditorium or from the balcony and boxes opposite.

The back of the box was in pitch darkness, the people there couldn't be seen. He'd recalled at the time one of the Ripper murders from a year before his visit had been committed at the back of one such box. And he could see why when he'd scanned the boxes opposite at the Metropolitan Opera House that night with Sullivan. Nothing but vague shadows could be made out — certainly no faces were clear.

So that's what he'd arranged now for his meeting with Bill Griffin. With things heating up, he couldn't afford to be seen with Griffin. So he'd arranged to take a private box with Monahan while Griffin had purchased — and dutifully kept — his receipt for a seat in the main auditorium. A couple of nods from Griffin towards gentry he knew while the lights were on, and Griffin would stay in his seat until the interlude — then head out as if to use the washrooms.

Except Griffin would make his way swiftly to Tierney's third floor box and sneak into a back seat unseen.

Tierney only half-turned in acknowledgment as the door opened and clicked back shut behind Griffin.

'Tell me some good news,' Tierney said, his tone edgy. 'Tell me what I hear on the street is not correct — that Argenti is out free!'

'He was in a holding cell for at least two hours, and now...'

'*Pah*! Two hours!' Tierney cut in, holding out one hand. 'Not much of a result when we expected him to still be held in a cell and awaiting time in the Tombs — is it?'

'No,' Griffin conceded after a second with a defeated tone. He attempted a brighter edge. 'But that could still happen once Roosevelt has made his final deliberation.'

'Might it now?' Tierney's tone still doubtful. 'And meanwhile?'

'As... as I was saying.' Griffin took a second to regather his thoughts. 'Right now Argenti isn't exactly free. He's under orders to stay home and not get involved in the case anymore, or any other investigations for that matter.'

'Is that so?' A moment's pause as Tierney considered the information. He gave a small nod and Monahan shifted from his position at his side and went to take a seat next to Griffin. 'From what I hear, it's hardly more than a nice little holiday fer Argenti at home with his wife and kids.'

'It's a bit more than that,' Griffin offered, suddenly uncomfortable with Monahan taking a seat at his side. *If the Ripper could run through a girl unseen in the shadows of one of these boxes, then certainly Monahan could reach out and snap his neck*. 'He's not meant to go out anywhere. It's the closest to 'house arrest' without charges actually being made.'

'I see,' Tierney mumbled over his shoulder. He hadn't in fact looked directly at Griffin since his arrival. He'd signalled for Monahan to sit at Griffin's side purely because anyone looking from the boxes the far side might wonder who he was talking to. With Monahan now behind him, that question would be answered. But, now sensing Griffin's discomfort, he wasn't about to offer that explanation. The more Griffin was on edge, the better. The more he might get out of him. Below, the auditorium was beginning to fill again. Griffin would have to return soon.

'One spark of hopeful news from all o' this,' Tierney commented. 'I hear that Maccione was none too pleased when your little entourage turned up — caught him and Argenti together.'

'Yes, that's right. He thought that somehow Argenti had arranged it — betrayed him.'

'*Betrayed* him.' Tierney repeated the words, as if they were golden syrup on his tongue. 'Now there's a strong term between two supposed friends. Pray tell me — what exactly was said between them in those final moments?'

* * *

Find him, find him... find him!

Ever since a forlorn Monahan had returned from chasing Gianni Campanelli along that warehouse back-alley to report to Tierney, 'Unfortunately, he got away,' Tierney had repeated that barked order practically every day. The only saving grace was that Monahan — as the frantically running figure had fallen into the faint alley-end light at the bottom of the fire escape — had recognized who it was.

'Gianni Campanelli,' Tierney mused thoughtfully. 'So maybe he's more curious about his brother's death than we reckoned on.'

'Looks like it,' Monahan agreed. 'But, as with Sombra, having spent the last long months hiding away, isn't going to make him an easy find.'

But Tierney hadn't realized how much events would turn such a fateful circle with Sombra until he'd heard those magic words, 'Betrayed him.' He looked absently through the Hansom's side window as they left the Opera house.

Tierney's first interest in Sombra had been hearing Monahan proclaim his skills as a knifeman. 'One of the few to match Maccione's skills, word has it on the streets. With similarities too in their methods and preference for stilettos.'

Hearing Sombra and Maccione compared so closely had made Tierney sit up. But the problem was Sombra at that time was working for Corcoran, who was allied with Maccione in many enterprises. Two such skilled knifemen working on the same side could be worrying; indeed, extending that thought, he could do with someone like Sombra on his own side going up against Maccione. *But how could he lure Sombra over?*

It was then that he realized Sombra probably didn't know about Maccione's clandestine association with Argenti. It seemed unlikely, given Sombra's own history with Argenti.

Just over six years ago a jewellers and watchmakers on 2nd Avenue had been robbed. An eye-witness picked out Sombra at an identity parade and Argenti, leading the case, pushed it to trial — despite Sombra claiming he wasn't guilty of the robbery and providing an alibi. Argenti and the prosecution argued that the alibi was of little worth, because it had been supplied by a fellow criminal. Sombra was found guilty and got five years.

Tierney and many others in the criminal fraternity felt this was one occasion where Sombra had been telling the truth — not least because they knew who was actually responsible for the robbery in question. Sombra apparently cursed Argenti every other day of his sentence in The Tombs, and that repeated curse took on a darker 'blood vengeance' edge when three years into his sentence, Sombra's young sister died — who he'd vowed to their mother to take care of.

Tierney made sure that a little birdy whispered in Sombra's ear about Maccione's secret association with Argenti. From that point on, Sombra was easy to lure away, Tierney providing him with two lucrative robberies and a murder-contract before that fateful night when Sombra had stabbed a copper and gone to ground. But with those robberies and the murder-contract being over only a two-month period and kept heavily under wraps, most people on the street — and indeed within Mulberry Street — thought that Sombra was still working for Corcoran and Maccione.

Betrayed him. And now everything had turned full circle, the ideal opportunity presented for Sombra to get the revenge he'd craved all these years against Argenti.

The only possible remaining fly in the ointment was Gianni Campanelli. If he'd overheard their conversation in the warehouse that night, then he'd know their clandestine plan; along with the fact that Sombra no longer worked for Corcoran and Maccione.

* * *

Find him... Find him! That shout seemed to be echoing emptily back at both himself and Monahan.

Until early evening the day after their Opera meeting. Roddy, one of the young runners they paid for inside information on Nico's little gang of street runners, sprinting frantically into their Pearl Street brewery.

'Just seen Gianni Campanelli,' he exclaimed breathlessly to Monahan and Tierney in the first-floor office. 'Hanging in a doorway, eyes peeled on an alley across the way where Nico's planning to meet him.'

'How long ago?'

'Four or five minutes, no more. I ran straight here.'

Tierney looked sharply at Monahan. 'Hopefully we'll get lucky — he'll still be there.' From that moment on, Tierney was on fire, barking orders to Monahan and a back-up team of three.

And a minute later - Billy clubs tucked into belts, guns being loaded and primed — they were thundering out of the yard in one of the brewery's express delivery trucks, Roddy in the back pointing the way.

CHAPTER THIRTY-SIX

Nico had put two of his best runners, Benny and Aldo, watching activity either end of the street the alleyway led off from.

Aldo was the first to spot Gianni Campanelli hanging in the shadows of a shop doorway sixty yards along. The doorway was almost twice as far from the other corner, so he doubted Benny had seen him.

As the minutes ticked past the assigned meeting time, Aldo wondered what was holding Gianni back. When Gianni was still tucked into his shop doorway as Argenti's toff sidekick and his accomplice turned up, Aldo was in a quandary what to do. He knew that Argenti's toff was expecting Gianni to already be there.

Should he alert them that Gianni was hanging just across the street from them? He couldn't risk running directly across, but he pondered too whether he could risk the two minutes lost to run around the block and in the back of the warehouse? He might miss something vital in that two minutes — though of course there was still Benny watching from the other end of the street...

Aldo was still weighing up the pros and cons when three minutes after the toff and his assistant had gone into the alleyway, Gianni finally shifted from his shop doorway position and headed across towards the same alley entrance.

* * *

Young Benny, on look-out at the far end of the street, only saw Gianni as he came out of his doorway recess and crossed the road towards the alleyway.

As Gianni disappeared fully into the alley, he saw Aldo lean out and signal from the other end of the street, pointing to his eyes then holding up three fingers. *I saw him three minutes ago*.

Benny nodded and answered with a solid hand waved across his own eyes. *I didn't see him*.

But barely six minutes later, Benny was first to see the wagon thundering up the road towards them. From two hundred yards away he could clearly make out Monahan in the passenger seat, at least two or three huddled behind him in the open wagon.

Pulled by two sprightly horses and empty of its usual load of beer barrels, it rattled and bounced along — *would be upon them any minute*!

Benny turned and sprinted towards the alleyway.

* * *

Jameson was aghast as Gianni Campanelli related his account. 'Are you sure you heard what you think you heard?'

'Of course I'm sure.' Gianni held a palm out. 'That warehouse was deathly silent — not too different to this place now. And I was only eight or ten paces from them, hidden behind some crates.'

'I'm sorry. I'm not doubting you.' Jameson's expression was taut. 'It's just that it's unusual to involve family like this — even among the criminal fraternity.'

'Maybe not so unusual in this case.' Gianni shrugged, filling in the rest of the details about Argenti's early prosecution against Sombra and Sombra's younger sister dying while he was in prison. 'Obviously, Sombra was unaware of Maccione's association with Argenti early on. But looks like a little birdy told him at some stage.' Another, more resigned shrug. 'Maybe that was Tierney — who knows?'

'Would explain how Tierney might have lured this Sombra over and got him to do his dirty work now.' Jameson nodded slowly. 'And you mentioned a red diary — how does that tie in?'

'Sombra said he had no idea what Argenti's daughter looked like — so Monahan said that he'd been watching her and she could be easily picked out by the diary she was carrying. A blood red diary.'

Jameson had a sudden flashback to the Ripper choosing some past victims because of a garish display of red. A jacket, a ribbon around their necks, bright red-lipstick... *but now it appeared to purely serve the purpose of identification.* Argenti's daughter, Ariana, had also been targeted by a killer two years ago. *Might that be what had inspired Tierney's move now?*

Jameson's thoughts were broken. Heavy patter of feet approaching in the alleyway, the warehouse door at the end bursting open.

'Monahan's comin' up the road with some men,' Benny said breathlessly. 'Just seen him now!'

'How many men?' Jameson asked.

'Three or four, maybe more.'

Jameson took a quick assessment. With Nico's team of four boys, himself, Lawrence and Gianni, they weren't necessarily outnumbered — except that most were young boys and

Monahan probably had his top heavyweights, heavily armed. Jameson looked sharply at Gianni and Nico.

'Look. You two head off — it's no doubt Gianni they've come for. Your other two boys as well — myself and Lawrence will hold them off.'

'Are you sure?' Nico questioned, taking one step towards Benny.

Jameson nodded firmly, and Benny shooed Nico back with a waved hand. 'No, *no*... not this way. We wouldn't make it in time.'

Already the rattle of the speeding carriage could be heard from the nearby street.

'*Okay*,' Nico said, darting towards a single door at the back of the warehouse. 'Out the backway here... there's another alley leading off.' He looked back briefly at Jameson as he held the door open and the other three ran through. 'Where best should we go? Our usual dockside hideaway?'

'No. Tierney might take the precaution of staking that out.' Jameson glanced back anxiously. The sound of the carriage now pulling up at the end of the alley. 'Detective Argenti will need this information as quickly as possible. Head to his home!' Men jumping out, starting to run their way. 'And one of you go to Mulberry Street and alert John Whelan that we're here. Now go... *go*!'

Nico sprinted off, and five seconds later a burly man burst through the front door of the warehouse, Liam Monahan just behind.

'Where's Gianni Campanelli?' Monahan barked.

'*Who?*' Jameson responded, taking a step back. He and Lawrence had already moved back to within three yards of the back exit, and hopefully this would be seen as a natural reaction to the four men confronting them. As if an extra guarding reaction, Jameson held his cane up in front of him. 'Don't believe I know the man.'

'We know he was here,' Monahan said flatly. 'Our runner saw him come in here only minutes ago.'

'Ah, *that* Gianni,' Jameson said after a moment; spinning time as much as possible. 'You just missed him.'

'We didn't see him leave as we approached.'

Jameson smiled dryly. 'Yes, I do believe that's what 'missed him' means.'

Jameson shuffled back another half-foot as he became more aware of the guns trained on him. Two men at Monahan's side had handguns levelled at him, and Monahan's gun, until that moment held limply at in one hand, raised now as well to point directly at him.

'*Again* — where is he?' Monahan pressed, cocking his gun.

'And as I say again — I don't know.' Jameson met Monahan's icy gaze above the gun aimed steadily at him, worrying that he might have pushed the bluff too far.

With Monahan's hesitation, one of the other men said, 'Let's just shoot the fuckers.'

That frozen moment stretched out, Jameson finally easing out his breath. 'If you must know — they left because a lookout runner saw you on your way half a mile away. So now they're hotfooting it to Mulberry Street to call reinforcements.' Jameson smiled tightly. 'So I don't think shooting us is a particularly good idea. Your guns would still be smoking when the cavalry arrived — would simply ensure you're all strung up on the gallows next to each other.'

A few anxious looks exchanged, two of the men looking expectantly at Monahan for their next instruction. But Monahan in that moment appeared to shift his attention to the door behind them.

'What's through there?'

Jameson glanced behind for a second, nonplussed, as if he'd only then noticed the door. More time eaten up. 'I've no idea.'

'Out of the way!' Monahan ordered, waving his gun.

'We're not armed,' Jameson answered, holding up his hands. Lawrence followed suit a second after. But they stayed in the same position two paces in front of the door.

'Throw your cane down and step aside!' Monahan said, a sharper more insistent tone. Perhaps the comment of 'not armed' had reminded him that Jameson's cane was a swordstick.

Jameson threw his cane down, but stayed in the same position, and as Monahan's gun levelled more pointedly at him, he commented. '*What*? You're going to shoot me? I thought we'd decided that wasn't such a good idea.'

Jameson's nerves were racing with the bluff, Monahan's eyes steely, as if he was seriously contemplating it. Then, obviously decided that with his bulk and the team behind him, he didn't need a gun to shift two men aside:

'I don't have time for this,' Monahan said brusquely, barging into Jameson and shoving him two feet aside. But as he went to do the same with Lawrence, it was already too late: Lawrence had got behind him as he pushed against Jameson, grappling Monahan from behind and taking his gun out of his own jacket all in one motion. The action was so swift, that by the time Monahan's team had realized what was happening, Lawrence had Monahan gripped from behind around the neck, gun barrel an inch from Monahan's head and the trigger cocked.

'Drop your gun!' Lawrence ordered Monahan, whose gun had been held loosely at his side as he'd pushed Jameson. Lawrence could see Monahan's team four paces away trying to bead a shot at him, but he held Monahan's bulk solidly in front of him; a clear shot would be near impossible. Jameson had also shifted behind their grappling tableau, so that he was also guarded. Monahan's gun reluctantly dropped after a second, and Lawrence nodded towards his team. 'Yours as well!'

More anxious glances exchanged between themselves and Monahan, as if awaiting his signal. Monahan just stared back impassively, and Lawrence added, 'You might have heard I'm somewhat mentally unstable — so I simply don't have the same compunction about shooting a man as most. Don't in fact realize there's anything wrong in it.'

Monahan closed his eyes and sighed. 'Do as he says.'

Two of the men dropped their guns, but the third held his firm, aiming and pointing more insistently. 'I think I can get him,' he said.

'Well, this is an interesting stand-off,' Jameson commented, noticing the man's hand trembling on his gun. He smiled dryly. 'Lawrence, perhaps you should shoot this man first, then Monahan — if he hasn't already been shot in the crossfire.'

CHAPTER THIRTY-SEVEN

Argenti was flustered when the entourage of Nico and two fellow runners arrived breathlessly at his door. He was halfway through changing, so Sophia went to get the door.

'This isn't a good time,' he started to explain as he came up the hallway behind Sophia, doing up his tie. 'Myself and my wife are getting ready for an evening function and...'

'We just got away from Monahan and his men!' Nico cut in. 'Jameson and Lawrence are still holding them off now.'

But it wasn't so much Nico's words that made Joseph stop short mid-sentence, it was seeing Gianni Campanelli emerge from the shadows behind the furthest boy.

'You'd better come in.' Argenti nodded hastily and halfway back down the hallway, Mrs Mendoza — the middle-aged local nanny who took care of Marco and Pascal when they had to go out together — looked out from the kitchen with the disturbance. Argenti gave Mrs Mendoza a strained smile and showed the men into the dining room.

They sat around the dining table, Gianni choosing to stay standing, hands wringing together at points as he related what he'd heard in the warehouse that night with Tierney and Sombra. As Gianni came to the part where it appeared that his daughter, Ariana, was the next target, Argenti's face flushed heavily, a tingle rising up his spine. But then his next reaction was to push the suggestion away. He shook his head vehemently.

'Surely not. Tierney might be mad at times — but he knows the rules! We don't involve each other's families.'

'I know what I heard,' Gianni said flatly. He looked down in penance, as if he was partly to blame for bringing this news. 'I'm sorry.'

Argenti looked down as well for a moment, getting fully to grips with the fearful news. 'And you say he hopes to identify her by her diary. Her red diary.' Joseph recalled seeing Ariana with the diary by her piano one day.

'Yes. That's what was mentioned. Her blood red diary.'

'But Ariana usually only carries that with her to her music academy.' He looked blankly into space for a moment before shaking his head again. 'I still don't understand why Tierney would take such a risk by stepping over the line like this.'

'Because I don't think he expected it to trace back to him. Most people still think he works for Corcoran and Maccione. He's kept the few jobs he's given Sombra quiet.' Gianni held a hand out, shrugged. 'And of course he didn't expect me to overhear him that night.'

'Yes, of course.' Argenti nodded slowly. Then another thought quickly hit him, made his body go rigid. That cry from Maccione when he'd been arrested, '*You betrayed me*!' No doubt Bill Griffin would have passed that news to Tierney, and so this now would look like the perfect payback from Maccione for that betrayal. The only thin thread tying Tierney to Sombra and this action now was what Gianni Campanelli had overheard. He cradled his head in one hand for a moment, sighing as he looked back at Gianni Campanelli. 'The only saving grace is that Ariana hasn't been at the music academy for the last couple of days. They had the last of the rehearsals three days ago, and the last few days she's been practicing at home ready for the big event tonight. That's what myself and my wife are getting ready for now.'

Gianni looked suddenly concerned, his face paling. 'Monahan mentioned something about a music event coming up... but I didn't hear all of it.'

Argenti looked at Gianni sharply. 'The Olympia Music hall — did they mention that?'

'As... as I say, I didn't fully hear.' Gianni was suddenly more uncertain, flustered under Argenti's intense stare. 'They were mumbling then, just before Monahan passed Sombra a slip of paper.'

'On one hand, it makes no sense: this is very much a one-off occasion, Ariana would go a different route to normal. And she was meeting her friend James just up the road before they took a Hansom together to the concert hall...' Argenti broke off as a chilling thought suddenly gripped him. *It was almost 600 yards to James's house, surely Sombra couldn't have struck in that short distance?* Then he reminded himself that Ariana had left almost an hour ago to prepare, and most of the neighbours knew her; if that had happened, he'd have no doubt already had a knock on the door of another kind. His eyes darted. 'But we need to check. *Sophia*! We've got to leave early!' He braced his hands on his thighs as he stood and called out.

Sophia appeared in the hall as he was already halfway out the door. 'What's wrong?'

'Too involved to explain now — and I might be wrong.' He sighed. ' But we need to get to the concert hall early.' He turned to Nico, taking a five-dollar note from his wallet. 'You grab a Hansom and go with one of your boys to the Olympia

Music Hall on Broadway. If you see Sombra there, point him out to the nearest theatre guard or copper — we'll be right behind you in a few minutes.' He looked towards Gianni. 'It wouldn't be safe for you to come with us. So meanwhile, you and Nico's other boy stay here with Mrs Mendoza. I'll give her strict instructions not to open the door to anyone but Jameson and Lawrence.'

* * *

Sombra saw the girl as she left the Argenti household and, sure enough, she had the red diary clutched in one hand. That had been a good identifying marker, but it had earlier struck him: *what if there were other girls with red diaries*? Unlikely, but rather than take the risk he thought it best if he actually viewed her leaving the Argenti home, so that there was no possible doubt.

Also, unless she jumped in a Hansom cab straight outside, there might be the opportunity of striking close to her home. And as she started to walk steadily away from it with no Hansom in sight, that hope began to grow. He crossed the road and shadowed her discreetly from forty yards behind. She hadn't appeared to notice him, and his natural gait was faster than hers anyway, that gap closing to thirty yards, *twenty*... she half turned then, but didn't seem to pay him too much attention. *Ten*. His hand reached into his jacket for his stiletto. *Five*...

But just two yards away, ready to pull out and strike, a couple came out from a house to one side, the woman nodding at Ariana Argenti and the man tipping his Derby. Ariana smiled back — Sombra ambling past them as they paused to exchange a few '*Fine evening*'... '*Yes, most certainly* is' greetings.

Sombra was about eight paces ahead of Ariana as she

continued on — but ahead he could now see a young man smiling and waving her way. Sombra crossed the street and was thirty yards past them as they embraced and the young man raised one hand to hail a passing Hansom cab.

CHAPTER THIRTY-EIGHT

'It's too risky now,' Monahan said. 'We've got to somehow stop Sombra going ahead.'

Tierney nodded slowly. 'Looks like a lotta things are too risky fer your blood now.' He couldn't resist the swipe back, despite the obvious sense in Monahan's advice now. Argenti would now have heard Gianni's account, would know that they were behind it rather than Maccione or it simply being some unguided, disconnected revenge from Sombra. 'Maybe yer should have just taken Callum's advice and shot the fuckers.'

'Yeah, *sure*. Good advice,' Monahan sneered. 'While I wouldn't have told who sent us there — I'm not sure the others could be trusted to do the same. One way of ensuring you were alongside us on the gallows platform, as the toff warned.'

Another slow nod from Tierney. The sober warning related from Jameson that had no doubt stopped a hasty shot being fired, had steered Monahan towards just barging them aside. Still, the account of Monahan and his crew being taken advantage of by the toff and his half-mad sidekick wouldn't spin well at the street level. Not a slight that Tierney was likely to forgive and forget easily.

'An' what do you reckon made Jameson suddenly give up on waitin' for the police cavalry he mentioned to arrive?'

'Don't know. That might have just been a bluff.' Monahan shrugged. 'Or maybe he was keen to get to Argenti and warn him... and with us already subdued and no threat, there was little point in waiting any longer.'

'Maybe.' Tierney sighed. Monahan had related how, after a tense stand-off, Callum had finally dropped his gun. Having collected all their guns and picked up his cane, Jameson then went outside, drew his blade from it and cut the reins from their two wagon horses and shooed them away. His sidekick Lawrence, still holding them at bay at gunpoint, then retreated and joined Jameson and they'd headed off in their Hansom. Monahan and his team had to grab a separate Hansom to return to the Pearl Street brewery.

'You see the problem now,' Monahan pressed.

'I most certainly do.' Tierney's face carried the weight of it. While Jameson not being shot might be the first bit of gallows-dodging, Argenti's daughter being killed under their orders would certainly ensure they faced a noose. Gianni's account on its own, coming from a criminal on the run, might be discounted as 'unreliable'. But a confirming first-hand account from Sombra would be a different matter. The two together would surely seal their fate. Sombra would have to be taken care of. If not before he'd killed Argenti's daughter — *if they were already too late on that front* — then certainly straight after.

But as Tierney's mind turned to how best to deal with the problem, he was suddenly struck with another thought, a leer slowly rising. 'Just remembered. Sombra wasn't the only one we had to hide away after that fateful night when he stabbed a copper...'

* * *

The Olympia was a monstrous edifice commissioned by impresario and musician Oscar Hammerstein on Broadway, containing a theatre, music hall, concert hall and roof gardens. It's construction only completed two months ago, New Yorkers were still getting used to its size and grandeur.

The De Schuymer music academy had combined with two other New York music academies and a local orchestra to put on a recital in the concert hall, with Ariana Argenti to give a rendition of Debussy's *Arabesques, No 1*, scheduled seventh Sombra noted when he checked the printed programme. *He'd have a little time to prepare*.

He'd quickly discovered that the Olympia was a maze of corridors inside, which suited his purpose. *Now it was a matter of choosing the right corridor and time*.

Sombra had watched Ariana Argenti get out with the young man accompanying her and proceed towards the entrance of the Olympia as he got out of his own Hansom and paid. A doorman pointed Ariana towards a side entrance, then held a hand out for James towards the ticket office. The young couple spent a moment more talking together before the young man nodded and Ariana made her way around the side of the building — obviously the musician's and performer's entrance.

For a moment, Sombra wondered whether he could attack her there — but she was ten paces ahead and swiftly in sight of others at the side. A small queue of eight or nine musicians being led in through side door and being checked off by a man at the door on his clipboard. Further along, Sombra got brief sight of another door opening and closing to let in stage hands, workers and cleaners — though these seemed to be let in with a prompter nod from the doorman there. Their names more easily checked on his clipboard.

He'd toyed with the idea of accosting a musician further along the road, getting his name and then coshing him, dragging him out of sight to then use his identity getting in. But if he came around quickly or his body was found, that could raise an early alarm that would spoil everything. But the 'behind the scenes' workers and cleaners had given him an idea.

Sombra went in the front entrance and made his way to the theatre ticket desk. He'd purposely avoided the concert hall ticket desk, in case questions were asked there. Then, once inside and approaching the theatre hall, he headed to the washrooms. Sure enough, to one side was a door marked '*staff only*.' He dived into it. A short corridor, voices behind one door — sounded like some sort of staff canteen. He went past and knocked on the next door along. No answer. Opening it was a small office; he as quickly closed it again and next along found what he was looking for: a small storeroom with buckets, mops and brooms and a few beige coat overalls — the uniform of many stage-hands and cleaners. He took one off its hook, slipped it on over his jacket and made his way out.

Sombra headed deeper along the corridor from the way he'd come, and a door at the end led him into a plusher corridor. The door shutting behind was also marked '*staff* only'. He was obviously back in a public area, but he had no idea *where* — and he was just checking the signs and a theatre lay-out at the end of the corridor when a man's voice came from behind.

'Looking for somewhere in particular?'

Sombra turned. The man was dressed in a dark grey suit — perhaps theatre management or one of the regular performers. 'I... I was looking for the concert hall musician's area?'

'Don't you know where it is already?'

The man's brow was raised quizzically; obviously thinking that a stage-hand or cleaner should know where it is. Sombra smiled meekly. 'Sorry. Quite new. Only my second day here.'

'Yes, well... took me a little to find my way around, given the size of this place.' The man sighed, pointing. 'But you're quite a way from it. You need to make yourself up to the second floor at the next stairway on your right — then the full length of that corridor, then next left.'

'Thank you.' Sombra gave a small bow — the expected courtesy from workers to management or anyone above their position in life — and made his way swiftly along.

A melee of musicians back and forth as he finally came to the area. While there were a number of corridors and dressing rooms leading off which could mask his intended action, they seemed equally as busy. He was unsure there'd be a moment where he'd be unseen. Though maybe equally he could use that frenetic activity as a shield.

He'd shuffle quickly by her, plunge the stiletto through her heart, and as quickly away. It could appear as any of the other stage hands, fellow musicians or others near her at that moment. *He recalled the killer Argenti had been tracking a couple of years ago killing in such a swift, opportune way — often with others passing close by*. The knife wound so swift and clean that even the blood might not appear until moments afterwards. By which time he'd be completely clear of the scene.

The remaining problem now was he hadn't yet seen her. Already the first four musical performances had played and still no sign of Ariana Argenti. He had no idea which dressing room she was in or the direction from which she'd approach.

Sombra busied himself between the wings and rear of the stage, between sets of ropes that presumably shifted curtains or scenery, checking them but without any adjustment — and finally as the main approach corridor half-emptied, a group of almost a dozen musicians moving into the wings ready to go on stage for the sixth performance, Sombra finally saw her.

No red diary now, her hands clasping together at points with nerves, smiling and a few words exchanged with her colleagues as they moved onto the stage. A ripple of applause from the auditorium as they appeared, and a group of three emerged into the wings from the stage. One of them spoke briefly with Ariana for a second, then they headed back along the corridor to their dressing room.

Sombra tensed. *In that moment, she was practically alone in that dark portion of the wings, nobody else immediately in sight.* He moved swiftly towards her, preparing to strike, reaching for the blade in his jacket as he was only two yards from her.

His hand froze on the blade halfway through pulling it out. Voices approaching, a young couple suddenly in view by the curtain. He slipped the blade back in and walked past her towards another set of curtain ropes.

He needed a time when she was either all alone or people bustling all around, where he could merge with them and go unnoticed.

* * *

Joseph Argenti found himself almost drifting off to sleep as Ariana played. The auditorium had fallen to a muted hush, and Argenti found the gentle rhythms and merging cadences soothing, soporific.

He'd heard the tunes many times before Ariana had started playing them, but hadn't immediately associated them with Debussy. He'd been quite surprised when Ariana had informed him that Debussy was a modern contemporary composer — his music seemed to belong to a bygone, gentler and more romantic era — a world apart from the more strident, jerky rhythms of Scott Joplin — Ariana's other favourite modern composer.

Of course, the other reason he'd found himself so restful and soporific was that he'd heard this tune a hundred times before, particularly over the past few weeks. Perhaps also a winding-down from the dramas with Maccione and Griffin, then on top this final terrifying worry with Ariana — except that now she was finally in front of him. Nothing had happened, nor was likely to happen in such a crowded auditorium.

So suddenly all of that winding down had washed over him, washed away his tightly-coiled fears, and he'd found himself close to drifting off.

Sophia was sat to his side, enrapt with the music, her face alight with glowing pride, young James sat just beyond her.

Sophia had asked him again on the way in the Hansom, '*What's wrong?*' and he'd told her only a half-truth. 'Something about one of the suspects in these recent knifings.' Hadn't wanted to tell her directly that Ariana might be in danger.

Holding back secrets from Sophia all these years, and still now he was holding back from telling her the full truth. Was he doing it simply because of a woman's sensitivities, protecting her from the harsh realities of the streets and what he faced daily. Or was he doing it as much for himself — because he lacked the guts to tell Sophia the full, unguarded truth.

Sophia reached across and clasped his hand, and he clasped back, returning her smile. Shared joy in Ariana's accomplishment.

Oh, God, how could he keep deceiving her? But tonight at least Ariana was safe. He'd checked briefly with Nico upon arriving, no sign of Sombra. And now that they knew Tierney's and Sombra's plans, they could keep a close watch on Ariana. So she'd be safe too from hereon in, no need to worry Sophia unnecessarily...

Joseph experienced a sudden jolt, a cramping in his stomach. Something suddenly sprang to mind from the investigation of that fateful night when Sombra had knifed a copper. The policeman himself hadn't identified Sombra — Sombra had approached him from the shadows behind and stabbed him, completely unseen. It was a policeman on the ground, heavily coshed and just coming around, that had witnessed it. '*Sombra didn't expect that to happen*,' one of the other robbers they'd arrested informed them, co-operating in hope of a lesser sentence. '*Sombra used to boast about takin' people out with his knife while there were loads of people around without being seen. Felt more than anythin' it showed off his skills as a killer. Sombra didn't expect that copper to come around at that moment and see what he'd done*.'

Argenti's eyes suddenly fixed on the wings. He couldn't see anybody directly, only vague shadows. No doubt other musicians and stage-hands — *but who else might be among them?*

'Something I've got to check,' he said, squeezing Sophia's hand reassuringly. 'I won't be a minute.'

CHAPTER THIRTY-NINE

Argenti did the same as Sombra had earlier — dived through the first '*Staff or Performers* Only' door he saw.

But he must have taken a wrong turn along one of the corridors, because the background sound of music seemed to become more distant, muted. He stopped a young man in a chequered waistcoat carrying a folder midway along.

'Can you tell me — which way to the wings of the concert hall?'

The young man gave him a quick appraisal. 'I'm afraid members of the public aren't allowed there. Unless you're a musician or perf...'

'*Policeman*!' Argenti cut in sharply, flashing his badge. 'I fear there might have been an incident there.'

'Yes, yes... of course.' The young man pointed hastily. 'End of this corridor, first sharp left, then left again at the end.'

'Thanks.' Argenti was quickly into a half-run, then a full-run by the time he turned left — fearing he might have lost vital seconds. Already he could hear the music stopping, the applause rising. *Ariana was no doubt leaving the stage, walking into those shadowy wings...*

As Argenti burst into the last stretch and came to a corridor junction, he tried to make sense of the melee of people drifting back and forth.

He quickly realized that the wings and back-of-stage curtains were twelve yards to his left. He took a quick scan — couldn't see Ariana there, she must have already passed that point, unless she was still on stage. The dressing rooms and longer stretch of corridor were to his right, and finally beyond a heavier group of people — at least a dozen milling back and forth between them — he saw Ariana.

He called out, '*Ariana*!'

Her face registering surprise at hearing his voice, she half-turned towards him.

But another figure shadowing her in a beige overall — looked initially like a stage-hand — also half-turned at that moment, and as he caught the profile, he realized he might already be *too* late.

'*Sombra*!' he called out, hoping to jolt him from his intended action, a quick flash of blade visible as Argenti draw his gun.

But it seemed to have a reverse reaction — Sombra clutched hold of Ariana as if his life depended on it, swinging her quickly around so that she was facing Argenti, Sombra's stiletto blade pressed hard against her neck.

* * *

Argenti was such a fool, Sombra thought. He'd resolved seconds ago to just walk past the girl — try his luck another day. The people on her far side were a clear yard away, would have no doubt seen him knife her.

But then with Argenti's voice booming out, he'd been forced to take action straightaway. If he hadn't grabbed her for protection and quickly spun her around, without question

Argenti would have downed him with a couple of bullets there and then.

Now he had the satisfaction of forcing Argenti to drop his gun so that he could run away. Or if Argenti wanted to play hardball, he'd see his own daughter die in front of him — with a well-timed push of her bloodied body towards Argenti and a quick dart into the melee of people on the corridor, Sombra reckoned he'd have a fair chance of getting away. Maybe having killed Ariana, he'd simply grab another musician or showgirl as a shield as he backed away. *Would Argenti primarily be concerned with tending to his dying daughter, or following him?*

'Drop the gun, Inspector!' Sombra glared. 'That is — if you want her to remain alive.'

'You might kill her anyway,' Argenti said, appearing to try and eye-up a clear shot.

'I might do,' Sombra conceded, smiling tightly. 'But it's a question of whether you might wish to be wholly responsible for her death, or just leave it as a fifty-fifty possibility.'

* * *

Lawrence raced the Hansom along the last stretch of Broadway towards the Olympia.

'They left just fifteen minutes ago,' Mrs Mendoza informed them when they'd got to Argenti's door. 'Told me to tell you where they'd gone and join them as soon as you could.'

'Sounds as if Joseph has some underlying concerns,' Jameson commented to Lawrence as they got back in the cab.

'So why not mention them directly?'

'I'm not sure.' Jameson hadn't wanted to get into the intricacies of Joseph sharing with him that he'd held back from Sophia his deeper concerns about Maccione. *Would he wish to alarm Sophia that their daughter might be in danger?* 'Just best that we get there as swiftly as we can.'

They made fairly good time, but then in the last stretch were held up by a tram crossing the early part of Broadway.

They ran frantically into the Olympia concert hall, Jameson noticing from halfway down the aisle that the seat next to Sophia Argenti was empty. He calmed himself the last few paces, not wishing to alarm her with an agitated demeanour. He tipped his hat.

'Sophia. I wondered where Joseph might be?'

'He said he'd just gone to check on something.'

'Oh, I see.' Jameson joined her in looking towards the stage, where Ariana was just finishing the last segment of *Arabesque*. 'A fine performance by the sound of it.'

Applause rose from the audience as Ariana finished, Jameson joining in with it as she bowed twice and left the stage.

'Yes, it was delightful.' Sophia beamed, applauding enthusiastically. 'Marvellous.'

Jameson smiled his appreciation. 'And I do hope Joseph caught at least most of it?'

'Yes, he did. He left only left a moment ago.' Sophia paused briefly in her clapping, as if only then addressing something which had struck her as out of place. 'He was watching Ariana's performance throughout — but then in the last moment, his gaze seemed to drift to the wings to one side.'

Jameson nodded, his eyes too fixing on the shadows and vague shapes in the curtain wings that Ariana had just walked towards. He tipped his hat again. 'I suppose I'd better go and check what he's up to.'

* * *

'Eddie... Eddie Conley,' Eddie said to the man at the Olympia staff entrance door.

The man, thick set with a ruddy complexion and bristling moustache, consulted his clipboard. 'I have you down as coming in over an hour ago.'

'Yeah, well.' Eddie shrugged. 'I left a short while back to get something, and now I'm coming in again.'

The man consulted his clipboard briefly again, as if that might give him some extra guidance, then waved Eddie in. 'Okay.'

Eddie made his way swiftly towards the back-stage area of the concert hall. His real name was Eddie Mulvane, and Tierney had simply picked out an 'Eddie' from the list of 'dues paying' union members he had down for the Olympia. All he'd needed then was a brown overall tunic, the uniform of many stage-hands.

Eddie felt the reassuring bulge of the Remington .38 in his inside jacket pocket. Tierney had personally given him the revolver, along with his instructions, so he knew it was important not to let Tierney down. 'You wouldn'a believe what that madman Sombra has planned now. If it wasn't enough that he stabbed a copper in the neck and put a fifteen-year sentence hangin' over y'all — now he plans to kill a copper's daughter.'

As Tierney had filled in the details, Eddie had asked meekly, 'Why on earth would he do that?'

'Some sort of sworn revenge against this fella Argenti from year's back. But he's gotta be stopped. Tha's one line we don't cross.'

Eddie felt the blood boiling in his head as he paced along the last corridor towards the concert hall wings. If Sombra went ahead with this, it might not just be the fifteen years they were facing, but maybe another five on top. Purely by association of being in the same gang as Sombra. *But if he was the man that stopped it, surely that would count in his favour?* As

Tierney had rightly pointed out, 'You'd be seen as some kinda hero.' That might be worth five years off his sentence, maybe even ten? And he owed Tierney in any case. If Tierney hadn't kept him low and hidden out of sight for the past long months, no doubt the coppers would have arrested him long ago.

Activity and movement ahead in the last twenty yards leading up to the wings. Eddie didn't know what the girl looked like, so his eyes scanned purely for Sombra.

* * *

As the point of Sombra's blade pressed harder against Ariana's neck, drawing a small trickle of blood, Argenti's jaw set tight. He held one hand up.

'Okay... *okay*.' He slowly crouched down and put his gun on the floor.

His head pounded, desperately afraid that Sombra would still kill Ariana, but seeing little other choice. The only satisfaction he'd get was pumping Sombra full of bullets as he tried to escape, *but his daughter would already be dead*. A chill gripped him, his body starting to tremble.

'Father — *help me*!' Ariana pleaded, her eyes full of dread.

'I will... *I will*.' Argenti held a hand up again. Empty words, not knowing how he might possibly help her in that moment. He could see the trickle of blood now heavier on her neck, the stiletto point digging into her more as she'd spoken. 'Just don't make any sudden moves, that's all.'

'It's nice to see you so powerless.' Sombra gloated. 'Now you know what it was like for me stuck in prison and unable to help when my little sister died.'

'I didn't push that case as strong as you think. It was mainly the prosecutor who didn't accept your alibi.' Not entirely true, but he needed something to try and diffuse the situation. He knew that the feelings of many fellow officers, not just himself, was that Sombra had been guilty of many other crimes, *so what did it matter that the only one he could be nailed for he wasn't guilty of?* But now that questionable rationale might cost his daughter's life. Though he could see at least that his comment had the desired effect: Sombra's eyes drifted uncertainly for a moment.

'Make no mind,' he said, resolve firming-up again. 'All as bad as each other. You're equally as guilty as the prosecutor that I wasn't there to help my sister when she needed me.'

Argenti nodded sombrely. Unbidden images of Mariella assaulted him... *not there to help my sister when she needed me*. He shook them away. That was the last thing he wanted to feel at this moment: any sort of understanding or affinity with Sombra.

Uncertainty again in Sombra's eyes, as if he was trying to fathom Argenti's thoughts in that moment.

The corridor had half-emptied out as Sombra had grabbed Ariana and Argenti pulled his gun — gasps of alarm and people scampering away or pinning themselves tight into the corridor walls each side. So it was easy to pick out anyone appearing more proudly in that space — Argenti's breath catching in his throat as he saw Jameson and Lawrence appear beyond the half-dozen people each side.

Sombra appeared to pick up on that tell-tale shift in his gaze, half-turning towards it.

But at that same moment, Argenti watched in horror as Lawrence started to pull the gun from his jacket. All pretence gone, Argenti held his hand up: a clear 'stop!' signal.

'No... *no*!' Knowing that while Lawrence might get a clear shot at Sombra, Sombra would still have every chance of stabbing Ariana before or during his fall.

Lawrence's gun hand wavered uncertainly, his gun half-out but not pointing anywhere directly.

So when two gunshots still came, it caught everyone by surprise, including Sombra.

Argenti focused then on the man who'd fired the shots. Along with many others, he'd shifted to one side — but it had been more with the purpose of not drawing undue attention to himself rather than keeping out of the way of the altercation.

Something was familiar about the man's face, but Argenti couldn't place from where — although the recognition appeared stronger in Sombra's eyes in that moment as he slumped to the ground. The man immediately dropped his gun and raised his hands.

But as Sombra fell, Argenti saw the tip of his stiletto blade, already pressed hard into Ariana's neck, rake savagely downward, drawing even more blood — their two intertwined bodies a mass of blood as they hit the floor, with it almost impossible to tell where the blood of one ended and the other's started.

Screams and cries of alarm now from the corridor, Argenti's cry of 'Ariana... *Ariana*!' almost lost among it as he leant over his daughter's broken body.

CHAPTER FORTY

'So, tell us again — what made you suddenly try and intervene and end up shooting Salvatore Gallo, otherwise known as Sombra?'

'Because I heard he planned to kill Detective Argenti's daughter, an' the thought of that horrified me. Bad enough that he'd stabbed a copper before — but this was going too far.'

'And who informed you of all of this?'

Eddie Mulvane paused, as if — second time now it had been asked — it might be a trick question. 'Like I said, Liam Monahan.'

'And Mr Monahan is an associate of Michael Tierney's?"

'Yes. He's his right-hand man.'

'So, it stands to reason that Mr Tierney would have also been aware of all of this?'

'Yes, I daresay he would'a been. But I can't say for sure.'

Jameson sat to one side of John Whelan, had said little so far in the interview aside from an initial introduction. He'd smiled tightly towards the large mirror to their side at the outset of the interview, acknowledgement that he wasn't the only one there mainly as an observer. He knew that Joseph Argenti sat behind the one-way glass keenly watching the interview unfold. Argenti was still on leave until Roosevelt had made his final deliberations on the case — of which this interview now would play a crucial part — but on compassionate grounds Roosevelt had allowed him to be present purely as an observer.

They'd in fact had to wait an extra hour to commence the interview for Joseph to return from Bellevue from seeing Ariana. Still no firm news on her progress. Jameson and Lawrence had tended to her as best they could at the scene, and stemmed the main blood-flow — but an added complication had been Ariana's head colliding first with the floor beneath with Sombra's weight on top. She'd suffered a hairline fracture and there were concerns too about internal cranial pressure and bleeding. Thirty-six hours now she'd been unconscious, and as Jameson knew well, if it reached the three-day mark she'd be listed officially as in a 'coma'. Sophia had spent much of that thirty-six hours praying by Ariana's bedside.

'And Liam Monahan also informed you where Sombra might be at the time?'

Eddie shrugged, a crooked smile rising, as if Whelan was stating the obvious. 'Of course.'

Jameson picked up. 'And how do you think Monahan, and likely Tierney too, might have known about Sombra's whereabouts at that moment?'

Another crooked-smile-shrug. 'I don't know. You'd have to ask them.'

'Don't you think the most likely scenario would be because they'd sent Sombra there in the first place to attack Ariana Argenti?' Jameson rolled on.

'Whoa... *whoa*.' Edie held a hand up defensively. 'I know nothin' about that. All I know is what Monahan told me —

that they'd heard on the street that Sombra was plannin' an attack on her.'

'If that was the case, it's doubtful they would know where such an attack was taking place — because it's unlikely that Sombra would announce it in advance.' Jameson smiled uneasily. 'As I say, a bit too convenient that they knew *exactly* where to send you.'

'Like I said. I can only repeat what I was told.' Eddie's eyes shifted uncomfortably for a second. 'Besides, why on earth would they send him to do that, then suddenly send me to stop him?'

Jameson hit him with it then. 'Because they discovered that their dastardly plan had been overheard — the game was up! So they desperately needed another plan put in place. Because if Ariana Argenti had been killed, it would lead directly back to them. That's why you were then brought in.'

'I can't say.' Eddie's eyes darted more anxiously. 'I can only tell yer what I was told at the time.'

'So you claim.' Jameson exhaled tiredly, sat back as Whelan picked up again with some more straightforward, mundane clarifying of details — when Monahan initially informed him, time he left, where he got the gun from?

Jameson didn't think anything useful would come out, but perhaps they might have sufficient already to create doubt in Roosevelt's mind. As the interview wound down, Eddie Mulvane looked at them anxiously.

'Whatever the circumstances — in the end I saved the girl's life.' He held out one hand, as if in plea. 'Surely that must count for somethin'?'

'Yes, I daresay it might.' Jameson sighed, his quick glance towards the side mirror more pained, as if in apology that the subject had been broached. 'If indeed Ariana Argenti survives and you have saved her life.'

* * *

Four days later.

Theodore Roosevelt stood by his office window looking out. Unlike his predecessor, who he heard kept the curtains drawn for much of the time, Roosevelt liked them wide open and the light streaming in. He'd also instructed that the nets there be removed: he wanted a clear view of the street and activity outside. *Clarity*. What he also liked from the internal dealings within his police department, although often — and this case now was a prime example — that appeared elusive.

He heard the men ushered in by his secretary behind him, but simply muttered, 'Thank you' without turning around. Two days he'd spent reading the various reports and still his thoughts weren't totally clear on the matter. But enough time had passed; the wheels of justice, or perhaps in this case *lack* of it, needed to keep rolling.

'Thank you for joining me, gentlemen,' he said, turning to face Jameson and Argenti sat the far side of his desk. Taking his own seat his side in a broad leather chair, he gave a weighted, taut smile. 'Especially yourself, Detective Argenti, because I fully appreciate you have other matters to attend to now.'

'Yes, sir.' An equally strained smile in return from Argenti.

Roosevelt patted some folders on his desk, took a fresh breath. 'I've now finally had a chance to review everything in this case. Some conclusions I've already arrived at, but others I might still need some help with.'

Jameson exchanged a quick look with Argenti. 'Yes, of course. In any way we can help.'

'You claim here that the chain of killers involved — Frank Campbell, Erik Larsen and finally Salvatore Gallo, known as *Sombra* — all lead back to Michael Tierney, with instructions for their actions given directly either from Tierney or his right-hand man, Liam Monahan?'

'Yes, sir.' Argenti nodded numbly. 'The first targets were girls at the Beth Jacobs refuge, then finally it shifted to my own daughter. And each time one killer became exposed or close to being unmasked, Tierney would ensure they were removed by a fresh killer to shield his involvement. He became fearful they would speak out.'

Roosevelt opened his hands out above the folders. 'And to what purpose? Purely revenge against both yourself and Mr Jameson?'

Argenti sensed the doubt in Roosevelt's tone. 'Yes, sir. Our conflict with Michael Tierney has some history to it. You'll in fact see on file that he did much the same with trying to frame Mr Jameson here for a past Ripper murder, and he largely blames us for the demise of his past henchman, Tom Brogan.'

'I see.'

Jameson interjected. 'Also much of this was engineered as a diversionary tactic from the current focus on police corruption. To dilute as much of the police department's attention as possible with a fresh Ripper investigation.'

'Certainly, it did have that effect.' Roosevelt smiled grimly. 'And while on one hand, I should feel flattered that my new initiative here is worthy of such attention, it pains me to think that I was somehow responsible for these girls' deaths, however tenuously. Although perhaps that was part of the intention too.'

'Blame laying is decidedly one of Tierney's tactics,' Argenti commented, sensing Roosevelt swaying. 'Because we shouldn't forget that part of this action now was aimed at Enzio Maccione, his arch rival — trying to frame him for Campbell's and Larsen's murder.'

'Yes. I'm glad you brought up the subject of Mr Maccione

rather than me.' Roosevelt slipped out the lower folder before him, put them side by side. 'Because of course we have the contrary account that Mr Maccione was very much involved, and Michael Tierney had nothing to do with any of this.'

Jameson eased a sardonic smile as he glanced towards the folder. 'No doubt much of it from Detective Griffin, whose view can hardly be seen as reliable since he's in Michael Tierney's pocket.'

Argenti was glad that Jameson had said it rather than he, especially given Roosevelt's red-faced reaction at that moment.

'No more or less than it has been suggested that Detective Argenti is in Mr Maccione's pocket.' Roosevelt eased his fluster after a second. 'But as a result, gentlemen, I think you can see the dilemma I'm faced with.'

Dilemma. With Roosevelt's softening tone and the fact that he was now sharing it with them, it struck Argenti that Roosevelt was inclined to believe their account over Griffin's. But for whatever reason Roosevelt felt hampered to openly admit it. His own tone in turn softened.

'We might not have believed it ourselves,' Argenti said, 'if it wasn't for the testimony of Gianni Campanelli, Frank's brother, with the conversation he overheard between Tierney, Monahan and Sombra.'

'I know. I too have read that testimony and have no reason to doubt it.' Roosevelt contemplated Argenti steadily. 'But Mr Jameson here mentions 'unreliable' in relation to Detective Griffin — and unfortunately that too would be very much the problem in a Court's eyes in accepting Gianni Campanelli's testimony.'

'Are you suggesting there's not sufficient here to push Tierney to trial?' Argenti held one hand out. *It seemed unthinkable that after the scourge they'd suffered at Tierney's hand, he'd still be allowed to slip free.*

'Unfortunately, yes, that's the case.' Roosevelt's pained expression reflected his frustration. 'But that 'unreliability' of evidence also applies to Eddie Mulvane's testimony in that Tierney's and Monahan's motives certainly weren't as benevolent as made out — though their real reasons were never shared with him.' Roosevelt took a fresh breath. 'Yet despite all of this not being sufficient to guide trial cases one way or the other, it doesn't preclude me making my own decisions. First of all regarding Enzio Maccione. As with Tierney, there's not sufficient against him here to support prosecution — but certainly enough pointing towards Larsen and Sombra being responsible for the murders he was previously suspected of. So, earlier this morning, I ordered Mr Maccione's release.'

'Solomon's Justice,' Jameson muttered.

'Yes, of sorts.' Roosevelt smiled and nodded. Whether pleased to be compared to King Solomon, or in recognition of Jameson's knowledge, it wasn't clear. 'But in this case, that's all that's been left to me.' Roosevelt's gaze shifted to Argenti. 'By the same token, I was probably somewhat hasty in sending you on leave — because it was little more than a suspicion. No more or less than has been pointed at Detective Griffin. So that matter will be set right too: as of today, he'll go on the same three-day leave, at the same time as you are reinstated, Detective Argenti. Everything therefore impartial and even-handed on that front too. Remind me again — why did you go to see Maccione that day when he was apprehended?'

With the question thrown in as if an afterthought, Argenti paused for a second to get his thoughts clear. 'Uh... because I simply didn't believe he could have been responsible for Erik Larsen's death. I wanted to hear his account first-hand before he was arrested.'

Roosevelt leafed back a few pages in the first report, holding his finger at one point as he read. 'Yes, well... it does appear as if he couldn't have been responsible for that murder — so I can't really recriminate you for that, can I? Will that be all gentlemen?'

Caught off-guard by the abruptness as Roosevelt looked at them directly, Argenti stammered, 'Just wondered what might happen with Gianni Campanelli and Eddie Mulvane?'

'Your concern for such seasoned criminals is touching — though I suppose both did play a part in trying to save your daughter from Sombra's clutches. So while I'm still on my Solomon's Justice rostrum' — a brief strained smile towards Jameson — 'I'll be recommending to prosecutors and the Courts that be taken into account. Hopefully it will carry some weight.'

Jameson nodded. 'That is — if we accept Mulvane's altruistic reasons for intervening.'

'Of course. I don't think Tierney would have exposed his real reasoning to Mulvane in any case, do you?'

'No, I don't. I do believe he recounted accurately what he was told.'

'In which case we are duty bound to accept that — however much he might have been misled. The actions he took that day were in good faith. Now, gentlemen. I suggest you leave my office before I change my mind.' Roosevelt fully opened the folder, leafing back through some pages. A clear indication the meeting was finished.

'Thank you, sir,' Argenti said meekly.

Roosevelt looked up as they were by the door. 'Because I understand you have a daughter who needs you by her side right now rather than wasting your time listening to me prattling on.' A faint smile broke his stern countenance. A clear signal his bark was worse than his bite. 'Please give her my best wishes, will you?'

CHAPTER FORTY-ONE

It seemed that Argenti had spent more time at Bellevue Hospital these past days than at home; and for Sophia that bedside vigil watching over Ariana had been even more intense. Whenever he'd returned to the hospital, he brought Sophia fresh tea or coffee from the canteen, and on a couple of occasions a hot pie or plate of food, knowing that Sophia was so consumed with not leaving Ariana's side that often she'd forget to eat. Clinging desperately to any faint signs of hope.

'I thought I saw her move a bit,' Sophia would comment as he handed her a fresh hot coffee, or '*Her eyes were flickering heavily a short while back*.'

'Yes, could be a sign of fresh brain activity,' Ariana's main consultant had commented when Sophia had shared that with him, and Jameson on one of his visits had concurred. 'Yes, REM — rapid eye movement — is something often experienced when people are dreaming. So it shows that certainly some functions are very much active.'

Ellie Cullen had come with Jameson on that occasion, offering her heartfelt condolences. 'Bad enough that these knifemen were attacking my own girls at the Beth Jacobs — but I never thought for a minute they'd turn to attack one of your own, Joseph.'

Some shared empathy, Argenti reminded himself, because those girls attacked had indeed been among Ellie's favourites. *Perhaps they should have read more into the fact that these attacks were personal in nature, and so an attack on someone close to himself wouldn't be out of the question.*

And then the day before Roosevelt had hauled himself and Jameson into his office, Ariana had finally awoken.

Joseph had in fact worried that they might still be red-eyed and groggy at the meeting with Roosevelt, because after the hugs and tears of gratitude between Sophia, Ariana and himself, with Ariana taking her first drink and food in days — Jameson had returned with Ellie, and, along with a bouquet of flowers, he'd brought a bottle of champagne to celebrate.

A ward matron had clucked her disapproval as she'd seen them raising champagne glasses and cheering, 'Alcohol's not allowed on the ward, need I remind you? I'm going to tell the doctor.'

'Alcohol is very much present on the wards to clean wounds,' Jameson reminded her. 'And I swear this temperance attitude is going to get this country into trouble.' He shooed her away. 'So do what you wish. Meanwhile, we've got someone's life and well-being to celebrate.'

Joseph had smiled. What would he do without Jameson's upper-class gung-ho spirit, often defying all conventions. The matron hadn't returned, so he could only surmise that the doctor had shared Jameson's spirit on the issue, or had simply chosen to turn a blind eye.

That had been two days ago, and now with Ariana more lucid and eating regularly, he was feeling more settled as he headed along Bellevue's corridors away from Ariana's room. Sophia said that she was staying for another hour, then would partake later of whatever Mrs Mendoza left in the pot from cooking for Marco and Pascal.

Somebody clutching Joseph's arm from behind suddenly jolted him. That stretch of corridor was dimmer, one of the side gas-lamps recently blown. He craned his neck in the semi-dark: *Enzio Maccione*!

'Let's go this way, shall we, Joseph?'

'I can explain,' Argenti said, suddenly fearing that Maccione still suspected he'd betrayed him.

'*Can* you?' Maccione's voice flat, doubting.

'I didn't know that Griffin was going to turn up at that moment,' he spluttered. 'But it was all part of a test to see if he was in Tierney's pocket or not...' *He'd be steered into a side-storeroom along this dim corridor, his throat cut, and nobody would ever know*. Argenti closed his eyes for a second. It seemed cruel, ironic punishment straight after the joy and relief of seeing Ariana awaken. 'Because how else would Griffin have known we were there at the time? Certainly, I hadn't told him...'

'I know.'

'You *know*?' His own voice cracking, incredulous, reality taking another sideways slip.

And then Argenti saw that Maccione was leading him towards the hospital canteen.

'Gianni Campanelli told me everything when he arrived at the Tombs the other day, just twenty-four hours before I was released myself.' Maccione smiled tautly as he took a seat opposite Argenti in the canteen. 'And Nico filled in any gaps I was missing.'

Argenti nodded slowly, his breath easing out along with his pent-up tension. Maccione asked if he wanted a coffee, and he just nodded numbly, still trying to get his thoughts clear. But when Maccione returned from the serving counter a minute later, he had two small glasses along with their cups on a tray. Maccione reached into his side-pocket as Argenti took his first sip of coffee.

'You still look partly in shock from it all,' Maccione said, taking a bottle from his side pocket and pouring two inches of dark-brown fluid in each glass. 'So thought you might need this. Best *grappa*. Also to celebrate now that your Ariana's awake... *Saluti*!'

'Saluti!' Argenti smiled wanly. *What was it with those around him thinking he desperately needed alcohol at this time?* But at least on this occasion the woman at the serving counter didn't complain, merely smiled knowingly and continued tea-towel drying some cups.

'I left some flowers earlier for Ariana,' Maccione said.

'Oh, I didn't know.' Many bouquets had arrived, though he hadn't checked the cards on a number of them. *Still too numb*.

'I just left them with the desk, didn't want to intrude.' You and Sophia needed your own private time with your daughter then.' Pained, indulgent grimace, then after another slug of grappa, Maccione asked, 'And what's going to happen with Tierney now?'

Now they were getting to the nub of it, Argenti thought; equally why Maccione had been keen to meet with him now. Hear what might befall Tierney. But as he explained what had transpired in his last meeting with Roosevelt, that there simply wasn't sufficient to build a trial case against Tierney — 'The evidence is mainly circumstantial and hearsay, and the only direct witness of any substance, Gianni Campanelli, as a fellow criminal is seen as unreliable' — Maccione shook his head in disbelief.

'After all he's done.' Maccione took another hasty slug of grappa. No doubt glad for another reason that he'd brought the bottle. Something to temper the hard-to-swallow news. He leaned forward with burning intent; eyes as fiery as the grappa that had just trickled down his throat. 'You realize that now Tierney has got away with all of this, he'll no doubt try again.'

Argenti nodded sombrely. 'I know.'

'He'll feel now that he's invincible.' Maccione let out a sneer on a burst of air. '*Hah*! Probably feels he can walk on water now.'

Another slow, defeated nod. 'With what's happened with Ariana, I feel robbed of justice as much as anyone.' He held one hand out helplessly. 'But what can I do?'

Maccione in turn nodded in acceptance, *shared defeat*. But then after a moment, another light seemed to shine behind his eyes. One that Argenti had seen before, but had never felt comfortable with. 'If normal justice can't be served, then maybe there are *other* ways of dealing with this.'

As Argenti saw the import beneath Maccione's look, he shook his head. 'You know I could never condone any action like that.'

'I know, Joseph, and you wouldn't need to. Nor would I expect you to.' A stronger gleam edged into Maccione's eyes. 'And just think. Tierney now has given the signals of just how such an action could be masked. Oh, the irony of it.'

All those young girls at the Beth Jacobs killed. The past nightmare days and nights he and Sophia had been by Ariana's bedside, clutching her hand as they feared she might join them. It would be so easy just to nod and say, '*Yes, go ahead, he deserves this retribution and more*.' But instead he found himself shaking his head again, though perhaps less certainly than before.

And perhaps, sensing that uncertainty, Maccione said, 'I fully appreciate that you couldn't condone such an action, Joseph. That could make you complicit in it. But as long as you didn't vehemently say no, *no*, you mustn't go ahead with any such action — I would know in your heart what you really wanted. You wouldn't need to say any more...'

Argenti felt himself trembling faintly, the long vigil hours by Ariana's bedside catching up with him. His long association with Maccione boiled down to little more than this moment now. *A clearly defined line, a precipice beyond.* Cross it and he risked falling and betraying everything he stood for, and *against*, as a policeman. Stay this side and he was showing cowardice, leaving the city he loved — *and God knows how many more young girls and innocents* — to the scourge of Michael Tierney. And turning his back too on any final hope of the justice owed to those young Beth Jacobs girls and Ariana.

'Silence would be enough,' Maccione said, sensing that Argenti was teetering on that precipice edge and only a gentle final push would be needed.

Joseph Argenti said nothing.

* * *

JAMESON & ARGENTI THRILLER SERIES:

If you enjoyed ***Diary of the Dead*** and haven't read the other books in the Jameson & Argenti series, you can purchase them from Amazon. They are all available on Amazon—just type "John Matthews Jameson & Argenti" into the search box at the top of the Amazon sales page.

THE JAMESON AND ARGENTI THRILLER SERIES:

BOOK ONE: Murder in Manhattan

BOOK TWO: Diary of the Dead

BOOK THREE: A Blood Red Diary

* * *

CAN WE KEEP IN TOUCH? A FREE BOOK OFFER . . .

More books from **John Matthews** will be available soon from The Write Direction Publishing, so if you enjoyed this one, we would like to keep in touch. This is not always easy, as there are many authors and books out there. So the best way is for you to be on our Readers Group email list. We can then send you updates on the next book, plus occasional special offers. There's no spam and you can unsubscribe at any time.

Write Direction Publishing is also the publisher for another thriller author, **Andrew Turpin**.

If you would like to join our Readers Group and receive the email updates, we will send you, **FREE**, the ebook version of a spy conspiracy thriller, ***The Afghan***, written by **Andrew Turpin** and which is a prequel to his Joe Johnson thriller series. It normally sells at $2.99/£2.99 (paperback $9.99/£9.99).

The Afghan is set in 1988 and features CIA officer Joe Johnson. Most of the action takes place in Afghanistan, then occupied by the Soviet Union, and in Washington, DC. We think you will enjoy it!

The Afghan can be downloaded **FREE** from the following link:

https://BookHip.com/QVACXP

The other thrillers by Andrew Turpin in the Joe Johnson series are as follows:

Prequel: *The Afghan*
1. *The Last Nazi*
2. *The Old Bridge*
3. *Bandit Country*

4. ***Stalin's Final Sting***
5. ***The Nazi's Son***
6. ***The Black Sea***

To find the books, just type "Andrew Turpin Joe Johnson thriller series" in the search box at the top of the Amazon page.

IF YOU ENJOYED THIS BOOK PLEASE WRITE A REVIEW

I find that honest reviews of my books are the most powerful way for me to bring them to the attention of other potential readers.

I am committed to producing books of the best quality I can in order to attract a loyal group of readers who are happy to recommend my work to others.

Therefore, if you enjoyed reading this novel, then I would very much appreciate it if you would spend five minutes and leave a review—which can be as short as you like—preferably on the page or website where you bought it.

You can find the book on the Amazon website by going to the Amazon website and typing "John Matthews A Blood Red Diary" in the search box.

Once you have clicked on the page, scroll down to "Customer Reviews," then click on "Leave a Review."

Reviews are also a great encouragement to me to write more!

Many thanks.

John

AUTHOR'S NOTE

Dear Reader,

I hope you enjoyed reading *A Blood Red Diary*.

Something of a landmark for me, because among several standalone books, this marked the first time I'd written a series with the same characters, in this case a trilogy. I think that alone stands as testament to how taken I'd become with its main characters, and felt there were more meaningful (and exciting!) investigations for Jameson & Argenti to pursue. And, of course, Lawrence, Tierney, Ellie and Maccione.

One other factor struck me during the writing of this trilogy: it allowed character development that the constraints of a single, standalone, book might not allow. Not only shades filled in which might not have been known before, but also 'evolvement'. Characters changing or modifying their core ethos, thoughts and principals due to changing events and pressures. Sometimes too this creates an intriguing conflict within characters, perhaps even self-examining and self-doubting those changes, *'Am I moving too far from my core ethos? Abandoning principles I've always sworn by?'* This is particularly true of Joseph Argenti in *A Blood Red Diary*, as he finds himself caught even more in the power struggle between Michael Tierney and Enzio Maccione.

Jameson and Ellie have also transformed through this period. Jameson far more pragmatic and accepting of the ills of New York's mean streets – far removed from his own privileged background. With Ellie undergoing the largest transformation: from a street-girl to now using her past expertise to part-manage a refuge saving girls with similar backgrounds.

The times too were fast changing in New York in this period – more trams, telephones and trains, automobiles starting to take over from horse-drawn carriages, 30-floor buildings one year, 40- and 50-floor the next – all of which adds an extra zest. New York went through one of its most dynamic and exciting transformations through this period.

With one particular change which I felt was significant to this series: Theodore Roosevelt – who later went on to become one of the more notable US Presidents in history – became New York Police Commissioner in 1895. Particularly pertinent, because Roosevelt's main drive was to clean up the corruption endemic within the New York police force. An added, poignant pressure for Joseph Argenti, one of the force's main past 'untouchables', but now finding himself walking a tightrope with the power struggle between Tierney and Maccione. Roosevelt has featured in novels before, but not with the same significance: in this case, focusing heavily on Roosevelt's anti-corruption drive, and the counter-balances and fraught allegiances this might bring to bear on the Detectives at Mulberry Street in the pocket of the City's leading gangsters.

If you liked *A Blood Red Diary* sufficiently to write a review on either **Amazon** or **Goodreads**, I would be enormously grateful. Or if you wished to have direct contact and would like to know more about my other books, I can be reached through my Facebook page: https://www.facebook.com/johnmatthewsauthor or my website: http://booksand-ebooks.com.

I look forward to hearing from you!

John Matthews

ABOUT THE AUTHOR

John Matthews is a leading British writer. His books span genres of crime, action, mystery and legal-thriller and include: Basikasingo, The Crescent Wars, Past Imperfect, The Last Witness, The Second Amendment, Ascension Day, The Shadow Chaser, Blindsided, The Prophecy, and his current book series set in 1890s New York with the first days of criminal forensics: *Murder in Manhattan*, *Diary of the Dead* and *A Blood Red Diary*.

They have been translated into 14 languages with total sales of 1.6 million. In 2007, Past Imperfect was included in a top ten all-time best legal thrillers list in *The Times*. He was one of only two British authors in the list.

John is also an accomplished screenwriter, including a film adaptation for Past Imperfect and original screenplays, with two recent projects in collaboration with Nigel McCrery, creator of TV's Silent Witness and New Tricks.

As a journalist, he has covered a wide range of issues, but with a predominance on Middle East Affairs. He has worked for Reuters and was an early pioneer of electronic media, developing one of the first online magazines. And after running his own design and architectural magazine, went on to become editor of European Brief for three years, the main magazine for the European Parliament.

ALSO BY JOHN MATTHEWS

The Jameson & Argenti Thriller Series

Murder in Manhattan
Diary of the Dead

Manufactured by Amazon.ca
Bolton, ON

15024393R00189